FORT BENNING BLUES

FORT BENNING BLUES

A NOVEL BY MARK BUSBY

Texas Christian University Press / Fort Worth

Library of Congress Cataloging-in-Publication Data

Busby, Mark.
    Fort Benning Blues : a novel / by Mark Busby.
        p. cm.
    ISBN 0-87565-238-7 (alk. paper)
    1. Fort Benning (Ga.)—Fiction. 2. Soldiers—Fiction. I. Title.

PS3552.U792 F67 2001
813'.54—dc21

                                                              00-049747

*"I Feel Like I'm Fixin' to Die Rag," words and music by Joe McDonald ©
1965, renewed 1993 by Alkatraz Corner Music Co., BMI, used by permission.*

*"Hair," by James Rado, Gerome Ragni & Galt MacDermot © 1966,
1967, 1968, James Rado, Gerome Ragni, Galt MacDermot, Nat Shapiro,
United Artists Music Co., Inc, Used by permission Warner Bros.
Publications, Miami, FL 33014.*

Design: Shadetree Studio

To Vietnam veterans everywhere,
to those who went
and those who didn't.

At the End of Our Time: A Prologue

All of this happened a long time ago, long enough that it should be as dim as a fading taillight on the horizon. But it takes so little for it to spring on me unbidden. One day walking through the zoo, I came upon an old black bear at the back of its cage looking over its shoulder at me and standing in a position that suddenly jolted me. I stood looking at it with tears rolling down my cheeks, the other zoo goers walking softly past me like I was a sidewalk loony.

Or maybe I'll catch snatches from an old song like "Bridge over Troubled Water," "Let It Be," or "Rainy Night in Georgia," and I'm arrested and cast back into the world of memory. The sound of a helicopter or the sight of a fading peace symbol will do it, a bed of pine needles, the heft of an old knife, even a woman in a dark blue evening dress, if she's got dark hair and white shoulders. I'll go for awhile without sliding back into the past, and I'll think it's disappeared finally, slipped into the crevices of memory, and then I'll see someone riding a horse or maybe hear the sound of a train, and there it'll be. The faces and names—Budwell, Trailer, Rancek, Shrode, Garrett, Thompson, Hays, O'Hara— spring to the mind's eye, and I see them as in an old newsreel.

I thought that this was just my story, something I'd carry silently around with me, but now I've decided that yes, it's my story, and I guess that it might be others' too, those who were there and who lived through it, those who traveled in the wake of it, and maybe even a story for those who came after.

One

Arrival

Sitting quietly looking out the window, I vaguely heard the pilot announce that we would be arriving in Columbus in fifteen minutes. It was a beautiful morning for flying—the sky was clear at our altitude; below I could see the clouds looking like cotton neatly arranged in a surgeon's tray. Occasionally there was a break, and the tops of the green pine trees and red, sandy roads showed clearly.

The GI beside me woke and stretched.

"You headed for Benning, kid?" the NCO asked.

"Yes," I replied.

I looked at the sergeant and noticed that he was young, probably not much over twenty, small and slim with a wispy, premature mustache. On his chest were two rows of ribbons, but the only one I recognized was the Purple Heart. He was probably two or three years younger than me, but since he was a buck sergeant and had been to Nam, he could call me "kid."

"What are you going to do at Benning?" the sergeant asked.

"I'm supposed to go to Officer Candidate School. You?"

"I just got back from Nam, and I'm going to check in with my new unit before I go on leave."

"Your new unit?"

"I'm going to be an instructor in Jump School. You goin' airborne?"

"No, I don't think so. I've got to get through OCS first."

"Yeah and that's a bitch I've heard, but so's jump school."

At that moment the pilot announced that it was time to fasten seat belts, so we both did and became quiet. Again I looked out the circular window and watched the plane descend through the cloud cover. As we came through the mist, I felt as though I were passing through some kind of mystical barrier in a science-fiction movie, and for some reason I had the urge to bend down in my seat, draw my knees up, and put my head between them. I felt the plane's wheels touch down, causing a momentary rush of fear and excitement until the reassuring sound of the wheels rolling solidly on the asphalt caused me to sigh and relax.

I had been drafted in January '69, right after I'd graduated from college and just as Nixon was inaugurated, and although I didn't have much faith in Nixon's campaign promise of a secret plan to end the war in Vietnam, I thought the country's mood would change within a year or revolution would thunder in the streets. So after I was drafted, I learned that I could volunteer for Officer Candidate School and delay my entry into the Army for four months. Given the four months for Basic and Advanced Individual Training and the six months of OCS, I could bide my time for months. Long before my time was up, I expected the fighting would be over.

I had decided not to go to Canada, not so much because I was afraid of losing my country but mainly because of my grandfather, the first Jefferson Bowie Adams, the man for whom I had been named. Granddad was a veteran of World War I and worked on the railroad before he settled down on his ranch in Mariposa, Texas, to raise a few Herefords and a lot of hell with his neighbors. He was a curious combination of southwestern independence and patriotism, spoke with pride about his military days. He had joined the cavalry before the war broke out, and he would bring out his pictures of himself in uniform riding his favorite mount, Chief Bowles, named for the leader of the Cherokees in East Texas. Then he would tell war stories about the Argonne Forest and Belleau Wood. They still called them cavalry units then, even though horses weren't effective in war by then and were mainly ceremonial. So it was for Granddad that I, Jefferson Bowie Adams, II, had decided to go to OCS, knowing that if Granddad's namesake hightailed it for Canada, his disgrace would be too great a burden for him to carry and for me to live with.

I also wasn't sure what to think about the war in Vietnam. I had been raised to believe in my country and its leaders. I had read about military heroes and had seen Audie Murphy, a slight orphan boy from Texas, in *To Hell and Back* at least five times as a kid in the 1950s. There was something of a fascination with the belief that each generation had a war in which the boys became men. I had been brought up to believe that Americans had a God-given right to lead the world and that American leaders sought truth and justice against the forces of darkness, in this case the Communists working through the Vietnamese. And I had also learned to believe as I grew up that the little peoples of the world needed our help in learning to walk the straight and narrow.

Now in November 1969 I was on my way to Infantry OCS while the war continued like a bad movie. The end of the runway approached, and the plane taxied toward the terminal. When we were stopped, the sergeant stood up, got his gear from above the seat, turned to me, and remarked: "Good luck, kid. If you make it through, I'll salute you and call you 'sir' one of these days."

"Thanks, if I make it through."

In the terminal I learned I had an hour to kill before the taxis could take me out to the base, so I began to look around for coffee. I moved out through the passenger waiting area and saw a small room where several servicemen sat. I took a cup of coffee from a pretty, round-faced, dark-haired girl wearing a striped outfit and tried to hand her a dime.

"Oh, no," she protested, "compliments of the USO. We still take care of the boys."

"Thanks," I replied and walked to a corner table, careful not to spill my coffee. I took a drink and let the liquid flow slowly into my stomach, warming me and pricking my mind alert as I thought about six months of OCS. I had heard many rumors about jumping off the truck and being forced to low-crawl across the cement dragging my duffel bag, but I knew that an army travels on its rumors, so I wasn't worried. Nor was I really anxious about the physical requirements. But I was concerned about my decision to carry out an act that required me to do something I wasn't sure about.

The Columbus, Georgia, airport looked like the kind of airport you would expect in an army town. It was small, with telephones lining the walls. Wherever there wasn't a telephone, there was a pinball machine, one of the many money-takers aimed at getting a quarter from a guy who wants to forget where he is. GIs were everywhere—hunched over the machines, talking passionately into the phones, sprawled wherever there was enough room for a man to get. It was another big day at the airport.

At an information booth I found a Columbus Chamber of Commerce brochure that told me a little about the region. Columbus stands at the central western border of Georgia on the Chattahoochee River between Georgia and Alabama. It's in the lower Piedmont region, higher than the Coastal Plains. Fort Benning is six miles southeast, with 182,000 acres of river valley terraces and rolling terrain.

I found my duffel bag, slung it over my shoulder, and walked out to a row of old taxis. I stopped at an old, dark Plymouth squatting like a scarab under a tree and looked in at the driver, an old man smoking a cigarette and reading the paper.

"Can you give me a ride to Fort Benning?" I asked.

"Sure, for two bucks," the old man responded.

"All right."

"Get in. Put your bag there in the back."

I put my bag in and got in beside it. The old man turned the starter and the old Plymouth protested but finally started. As we turned out onto a road named Victory Drive, I looked at the driver. He had lost an ear. A dirty white patch covered the side of his head where his ear should have been.

"What part of the fort you goin' to?" the driver asked.

"I don't know. My orders say to report to 58th Officer Candidate Company. You know where that is?"

"Yeah, I know where it is. I've taken pleny a you suckers out there. Taken pleny back too. You in for a rough time, boy. 'Specially this time a year. It's gonna git cold out there this winter, and it's gonna be damned hot after it gits cold. The weather mixed with the bullshit is hard for a man to take."

"I've heard about it," I replied, "but I guess I can make it. There are lots of things in this world that folks learn to take."

"You damned right there are. Look at this goddamned ear or look at what ain't this goddamned ear."

"I noticed. You lose that in the war?"

"Hell no. That's what so bad about it. It woulda been a lot more honorable if I had. Cancer got my ear. Creeped up on me without me really being aware of it. But I learned to live with it. I just put me a clean patch on it every day or so. I can hear all right, too.

"Yeah, I wisht I had lost it in the war. I was in the war. Dubya Dubya Two. We fought, and we had some grand times. Not like now. You punks got a hard time. I don't envy you none. This Vetnam thing is shit, I tell you."

We arrived at the MP's stand that signaled the entrance to the post. After the old man slowed to a stop, a young MP walked over.

"Hiya doin' today, Mr. Phillips? Everything OK?"

"Everything's fine. Got another live one for OCS."

"Good. They're always looking for fresh meat."

"Much obliged. Take care now, you hear."

The one-eared old man ground the Plymouth into low gear, and the car lurched forward.

"They used to not stop us," he explained, "but there's been a lot of racket around the country about radicals bombing army posts in protest over the war. Now they check us pretty careful."

We drove past a group of soldiers with their faces covered with camouflage paint.

"That's a group headed for one of them make-believe war games," he said. "Goop themselves up, and go out in the forests shootin' blanks, makin' noise, and blowin' smoke."

We passed a neatly landscaped parade ground, and I saw several tanks and artillery pieces. Beyond the idle machines rows of men walked on line like automatons bending and picking up debris and cigarette butts, the continual mindless activity of military training.

"Up here I'm going to show you where you'll spend a lot of time. That big cream-colored building there is Infantry Hall, and it's one of the nicest teaching buildings in the country."

We slowed and rounded one corner of the immense building.

"Out there in front you can see that statue. It's supposed to be the spirit of the infantryman."

I looked at the statue of a huge soldier standing with his rifle raised high into the air as if he were gesturing "follow me," his mouth open in what was supposed to be a yell. It looked more like a grimace.

The old man stopped his taxi near the statue.

"Why don't you go up there and take a look? That's what they say you're here for."

I got out and walked up to the statue where in large letters was carved, "I am the Infantry. Follow Me." On the other side were the words of a song or a poem:

"I Am The Infantry"

I am the Infantry—Queen of Battle! For two centuries I have kept our Nation safe, Purchasing freedom with my blood. To tyrants, I am the day of reckoning; to the suppressed, the hope for the future. Where the fighting is thick, there am I ... I am the Infantry! FOLLOW ME!

I was there from the beginning, meeting the enemy face to face, will to will. My bleeding feet stained the snow at Valley Forge; my frozen hands pulled Washington across the Delaware. At Yorktown, the sunlight glinted from the sword and I, begrimed ... Saw a Nation born.

Hardship ... And glory I have known. At New Orleans, I fought beyond the hostile hour, showed the fury of my long rifle ... and came of age. I am the Infantry! FOLLOW ME!

Westward I pushed with wagon trains ... moved an empire across the plains ... extended freedom's borders and tamed the wild frontier. I am the Infantry! FOLLOW ME!

I was with Scott at Vera Cruz ... hunted the guerrilla in the mountain passes ... and scaled the high plateau. The fighting was done when I ended my march many miles from the old

Alamo. From Bull Run to Appomattox, I fought and bled. Both Blue and Gray were my colors then. Two masters I served and united them strong ... proved that this nation could right a wrong ... and long endure. I am the Infantry! FOLLOW ME!

I led the charge up San Juan Hill ... scaled the walls of old Tientsin ... and stalked the Moro in the steaming jungle still ... always the vanguard, I am the Infantry!

At Chateau-Thierry, first over the top, then I stood like a rock on the Marne. It was I who cracked the Hindenburg Line ... ... in the Argonne, I broke the Kaiser's spine ... and didn't come back 'till it was "over, over there." I am the Infantry! FOLLOW ME!

A generation older at Bataan, I briefly bowed, but then I vowed to return. Assaulted the African shore ... learned my lesson the hard way in the desert sands ... pressed my buttons into the beach at Anzio ... and bounced into Rome with determination and resolve. I am the Infantry!

The English channel, stout beach defenses and the hedgerows could not hold me ... I broke out at St. Lo, unbent the Bulge ... vaulted the Rhine ... and swarmed the Heartland. Hitler's dream and the Third Reich were dead.

In the Pacific, from island to island ... hit the beaches and chopped through swamp and jungle ... I set the Rising Sun. I am the Infantry!

In Korea, I gathered my strength around Pusan ... swept across the frozen Han ... outflanked the Reds at Inchon ... and marched to the Yalu. FOLLOW ME!

In Vietnam, while others turned aside, I fought from the

*Central Highlands to the South China Sea. I patrolled the
jungle, the paddies and the sky in the bitter test that belongs to
the Infantry. FOLLOW ME!*

*My bayonet ... on the wings of power ... keeps the peace
worldwide. And despots, falsely garbed in freedom's mantle,
falter...hide. My ally in the paddies and the forest ... I teach,
I aid, I lead. FOLLOW ME!*

*Where brave men fight ... there fight I. In freedom's cause ...
I live, I die. From Concord Bridge to Heartbreak Ridge, from
the Arctic to the Mekong, to the Caribbean ... the Queen of
Battle! Always ready ... then, now, and forever.*

I am the Infantry! FOLLOW ME!

I walked back to the taxi.

"They seem to put a great deal of money into all of the trappings here."

"You bet, "the old man responded. "They got to let you know how
much they think of themselves. There's a lot of showmanship in the Army.
But I don't care. If it wasn't for the Army this town would die like a flower
with no roots. We're glad to have 'em."

I got back in and we drove on, past the other end of the enormous
building, where I saw a large field with three towers.

"What's that over there?" I asked.

"That's something else you'll get used to here. Those three towers are
for paratrooper training, but you won't use them unless you go airborne.
That track there that circles those towers, though, you'll get to know real
good. You'll be runnin' around it 'bout every morning."

I looked at the asphalt track and guessed it to be a mile and a half to
two miles long. That wouldn't be too bad, I thought. But I was still afraid
of the running.

"Well here we are," the old man said.

There were rows of buildings that looked like college dormitories, all in
the same cream-colored brick as Infantry Hall. Each building was neatly

landscaped with straight rows of rocks lining the sidewalks. Despite the general similarity, each building was distinguished by some decoration with the company's number on it. In front of the building with 58th Company was a line of men standing beside their duffel bags.

When Phillips got my bag out of the car, I handed him two dollars and thanked him for the ride and the information.

"Good luck, son. You'll need it."

Shouldering my duffel bag, I walked up to the line of men where a slight soldier with a skinhead haircut stood about as if he were in charge.

"You here for OCS?" the soldier asked.

"That's right. Where do I go from here?"

"Stand over there in line with the others, keep your mouth shut, and no smoking. We'll call you when we want you."

I wondered who the little guy was since there was no name tag on his fatigues, and he also had brass on his collar that said "OCS."

I moved over to the line, watching the others who looked much like me and who stood quietly examining me as I did them. In the building across from 58th Company men were coming and going. They all wore sharply starched fatigues with OCS brass on their collars. At their necks were light blue scarves with an OCS patch. Whenever they left their building, they ran wherever they went. Walking casually along the sidewalk were other soldiers who wore white scarves, and the ones with blue would slow to a walk and yell, "Good morning, sir," when they passed them.

All of us new recruits stood anxiously in line for some time before it began to move. The word was that we were to process in.

* * * *

I got through the bureaucratic jumble easily enough and was assigned a room. As yet I had seen no officers or anyone else who seemed to be in charge. Everyone working the desks had been other "candidates," as we learned to call ourselves.

My two new roommates and I walked to our room. I looked them over and wondered how we would get along. One of the two was small. He already had a skinhead haircut, and I noticed also that he had at least ten sets of fatigues starched with the regulation blue and white OCS patch on the left shoulder, showing a soldier like the statue in front of Infantry Hall yelling, "Follow Me!"

"I see you came prepared," I said.

"Yes," the small soldier replied, "I heard that it was a good idea to be ready. I went to OCS preparatory training after AIT, and they told us to have our fatigues ready when we got here. I think it's going to help."

"By the way, my name's Tommy Trailer." He extended his hand.

"Jeff Adams."

The other roommate now turned from his locker and introduced himself, "Hugh Budwell." Budwell was a large, bear-like man. He made slow, deliberate movements, but his eyes were quick and penetrating.

The introductions were now over, and we returned to our unpacking. The room was a small rectangle with a regulation double Army bunk on one side and a single one on the other. Since I had been the first in the room, I took the single bunk. At the head of each bed were large wall lockers. Under the single bed was one wooden footlocker; two were beneath the lower bunk. In the middle of the room three small student desks were pushed together.

We now worked quickly and quietly getting our things put away. First we hung our fatigues, dress green uniforms, khakis, raincoats, and overcoats in the wall lockers. In the footlockers went our underwear, T-shirts, green cotton boot socks and black nylon dress socks, ties, shaving and toilet gear, and personal items.

As I put the three paperbacks I had brought discreetly underneath my underwear—a collection of Hemingway's short stories, Camus' *The Stranger*, and Heller's *Catch-22*—I suddenly remembered a scene from the movie *The Young Lions* where Monty Clift had a copy of Joyce's *Ulysses* taken away from him by a fat sergeant, and I wondered if my books would be removed. The books were left over from my college days when I double-majored in business and English, because Granddad insisted on the business courses. Next I stashed Granddad's Case knife. Just before I left, Granddad had called me into the barn.

"Jeff, this here knife has been with me a long time. I cain't right remember when I first got it, but it's good and sharp enough to cut a saplin'. I want you to take it with you. I don't right know how it might ever hep you, but I just want you to have it. Mebbe it'll come in handy some time."

Just as I finished putting my things away, I heard loud, sneering voices interrupt the silence of the hallway.

"Why doesn't somebody call this platoon to attention?" a voice demanded. "There are senior candidates here. You there, dummy, call this platoon to attention."

"AttinHUT!" another voice yelled.

"Not 'a tin hut,' you shithead. A tin hut is your wall locker. Say it like this—'ATTINSHUN!'" The voice throatily emphasized the last syllable. "You punks got a long way to go."

I was glad that my room was at the end of the hallway. That would give me a few seconds to get ready for whatever happened. Now the hall was quiet as everyone stood at the awkward position of attention. I heard combat boots move down the hall.

"All right, all right, as you were," someone directed, "but if we come into a room, you come to attention, and from now on as soon as the first person sees a senior candidate enter this platoon, they better call this bunch of pansies together, pronto. You understand?"

"Yes, sir!" a few voices responded feebly.

"Do you understand?" the senior candidate again called. "I want to hear it from you!" he demanded angrily.

"Yes, sir!" the platoon called out strongly.

"That's better. Now get back to work."

I heard the scuffling sound of feet as everyone returned to what he had been doing. Budwell looked at me, winked, and whispered, "We might as well get used to this; we've got six more months of it."

I nodded and heard the senior candidates moving down the hallways, stopping in rooms and talking quietly with other new arrivals. Finally, they stopped outside our room and Trailer announced, "Attention!"

"Not yet, dummy," one senior candidate responded, "wait until we're physically inside your room."

So the three of us continued to act as if we were doing what we had been doing, but Trailer anxiously watched the door. Finally, the two senior candidates stepped inside the doorway, and when they did, Trailer gleefully snapped, "ATTENTION!"

"As you were," the shorter one said. I recognized the voice as the one who had done all the talking in the hall. "We're not here to harass you; you'll get enough of that later. We're here just to answer some of your questions about the program. We graduate next week, so if there's anything you want to know, shoot."

"Have you got your orders after graduation?" Trailer wanted to know.

"Yeah, I'm going to Fort Polk as a training officer in a basic training company before I go to Nam," answered the tall one. "Smitty here is going to Ranger School."

The short one acknowledged this bit of information by growling, "Yowww, snake eaters, yeah!"

"Does everyone who completes Infantry OCS go to Vietnam?" I asked.

"You bet," answered the short one. "We're going to kill some gooks for Christ. What's the matter; don't you want to go?"

"I don't know; I was just wondering."

"Well, you better get ready, fella, 'cause if you finish here, you're Nam bound. Hell, nobody finishes here unless he's crazy to be heading for that two-way rice field shootin' range. If you got any ideas different, you better sign your drop letter now."

"What about transferring to another branch, like the Adjutant General Corps or Military Intelligence?"

"So, that's what you want, huh? Well, you can toss that idea, too. The only branch transfers out of Infantry OCS are for the top three graduates, but by that time the only ones left love the Infantry."

"What happens to the people who drop out of the program along the way?" asked Budwell.

"Three weeks in Casual Company across the street waiting for orders and then straight to Nam as an Infantry PFC. You're goin' over there any way it goes. Ol' Unca Sam's got you boys by the balls," laughed the short one.

"You see," he explained, "nobody can leave here for six weeks, and since you take Infantry training for those six weeks, that satisfies the legal requirement for time trained before combat. So even if you had been classified a clerk before you started OCS, you will be a grunt carrying a rifle when you drop out of the program. It costs the Army big bucks for each person who signs in here, and one way to recoup some of the investment is to have this way of classifying bodies."

Budwell smiled and replied, "I don't remember my recruiting officer explaining these technicalities. But it doesn't matter. I don't expect to end up in Casual Company."

"That's the attitude," said the short one. "But a lot of people don't make the choice on their own. The TAC officers bounce a lot of people out in the eighth, twelfth, and eighteenth week boards. Some guys have even been dropped as late as the twenty-second week board, so don't get too cocky about it."

We stayed quiet for a minute, thinking about the senior candidates' answers. There was an anxious aura in the room. Finally, I asked, "What's the hardest thing here?"

"Everything," snapped the bellicose one.

But the tall one, the quiet one, said, "The longevity, the length. It's a long time and what matters is how you feel when you reach the end of your time here."

Yes, that's it, I thought, how we feel at the end of our time here; that's what's important. Even if you're not here long, that's still the important thing—how you feel about yourself for the time you're here.

Just at that moment, voices in the hall began yelling, "Formation! Formation! Out in front! Now!" We hustled out and were told to gather by platoons. We were then marched one-by-one into the mess hall where we stood quietly until a tall, slim, bookish captain with close-cropped, dark hair and glasses, wearing the distinctive Green Beret uniform walked crisply to the front of the room.

"At ease, men. I'm Captain Lederer, the commanding officer of 58th Company," he said with a gentle Southern drawl. "I'm here to welcome you to the best training outfit in the country. You men are embarking upon a great adventure, an experience that will make you the most important fighting men in the world. At the end of six months you will be Infantry combat platoon leaders, the most important element in the American fighting machine."

Captain Lederer spoke very softly, almost inaudibly. As we stood at parade rest, we leaned forward to catch every word. I later learned that he was a history graduate of the University of Virginia before he joined the Army and that he had served with distinction in Vietnam before he came back to command 58th Company.

"We are engaged in a war of monumental proportions," he continued. "This battle is comparable to the other great wars in our history—the fight against the British for independence; the great Indian wars against Crazy Horse, Sitting Bull, and Cochise; World Wars I and II to make the world safe for democracy and to stop fascism; and the engagement in Korea. It is American right versus the Communist wrong. We are obligated to make the world safe for democracy, to ensure that American values of freedom and self-reliance go forward. Without us Vietnam goes, then Laos, Cambodia, and the world follows. We must make a stand here, and that's what we're doing. We've drawn a line in the sand, and it is our responsibility to bring the might to protect the right.

"More importantly, this war symbolizes the turning point for modern America. We have become complacent. We've lost the frontier spirit of industry, determination, and self-reliance. Our schools have become factories for incompetence; our factories foster mediocrity. This war is a God-given opportunity for America to turn around; it is our chance to rededicate ourselves to purpose and vision, to move toward the image we have always had of an America as the place of high moral courage and right.

"Consequently, it is our job at 58th Company to ensure that the men who graduate from this company know the consequences. You must be committed to this great enterprise, or you will not become U.S. Army officers. We will challenge you, we will drill you, we will harass you, we will find your weaknesses, and we will know your strengths. The strong ones will survive to become the next generation of heroes abroad. The weak ones will break and go on to become the fodder for the enemy. If you can't make it here, you can't make it in life. But there are plenty who can't make it in life. We will know who you are.

"Now, men, look to your left and look to your right. One of the two men beside you will not be here in six months. It's as simple as that. We usually graduate fifty percent of the men who begin this course. Look around now; we'll see later who remains." We all turned and looked carefully at the men next to us. Budwell was on my right and Trailer on my left.

"That's it, men. March out quietly and return to your rooms and square away your gear. And remember, if we do not win in Vietnam, it will be the end of American life as we know it."

Two

Welcome

It was night. Outside a light mist floated over everything and because we had to keep all three windows open (at exactly the same spot), that same mist crept softly inside every room. It covered the desks, the wall lockers, and settled into the blankets of our beds. It smelled of sulfur, dust, and exhaust fumes, and it wormed its way into our joints and our minds.

No one slept comfortably, so we all heard the boots coming up the stairs even though he was being quiet. And then we all heard him when he walked into the first room and rolled somebody out. And we all heard him when he quietly asked the first man what the fuck he was doing here. And we all heard the first man reply that he was here because he wanted to be a soldier. And we all heard him laugh and say that his first victim was too much of a pussy to ever be an Infantry platoon leader, so he better go back to sleep and get his beauty rest.

I heard it all too as I lay in my bed feeling and seeing the mist in the shadow of the hallway light. And I heard the boots walk out of the first room into the next and the next and on down the hall. They followed the same pattern.

I felt a strange sensation in my crotch as if the mist were affecting me there. I wondered if I were allergic to something in the air, but before I got a chance to think more about it, the boots were in my room and the light exploded the darkness and the mist. Budwell, Trailer, and I jumped out of our bunks into a clumsy position of attention. Budwell, I was surprised to see, was nude.

The owner of the boots noticed, too, and he smiled as he looked up and down. While he looked at Budwell and Trailer, I looked at him closely. He was a thin, wiry man of medium height. His heavily starched fatigues clung to him, and I wondered how anyone could get army issue clothes to be anything but baggy. He was a first lieutenant, and he no doubt was not old except that he was completely bald, his head shining under the bright lights in the room. On his name tag sewn above the pocket and beneath an Airborne patch, I read the name: Rancek.

Rancek seemed to slither toward us, his arms tight against his side, fists clenched and tucked against his buttocks. He moved up close to Trailer, looking him over without comment. His baldness in the light made his face look like a gray globe, blighted and pasty. His eyes in shadows were the color of tarnished brass. As he stood silently looking at us, he rocked up on the toes of his spit-shined combat boots. This sudden movement made him appear taller—elongated. But when he moved closer, it was clear that he was probably no taller than five-eight.

He continued to walk around the room looking at our gear and then returning to each one of us, the rocking-up-on-toes motion continuing as well. Finally, he stopped before Trailer. Silent for a moment, he rocked up on his toes and looked closely at Trailer, who looked pleased with the attention.

"What's your name, dud?" sneered Rancek.

"Sir, Candidate Trailer!"

"Whatthefuckareyoudoinghere, Trailer?"

"Sir, Candidate Trailer, I'm here," Trailer answered gleefully, "to become an Infantry combat platoon leader and go to Nam and kill gooks, sir!"

"Y'are, huh? So you're gung ho."

"Yes sir, gung ho!"

"Shut up, dud, I'll tell you when to speak, you piece of shit. And I'll tell you this now—you won't make it here. Do you hear me? You won't make it here, because you're the kind of dumbfuck who'll get his ass and his men's asses blown off the first step you take out of Saigon. And I'm going to make it my personal task to see that no asshole is leading the platoon on my right. You understand that?"

Trailer stood rigidly at attention, his curled fingers burrowed into his bare white, almost hairless legs. Sweat had begun to bead on his forehead and his upper lip. Rancek rocked within inches of Trailer's face, waiting for a reply.

"Well, answer me, shithead."

"Sir, Candidate Trailer. Do I have permission to speak?"

"Don't play with me, turkey. I asked you a direct question; give me a direct answer!"

"But, sir, you told me not to speak until I was given permission."

"When I ask a question," snarled Rancek, "you answer me. Now, do you understand what I said?"

"Sir, Candidate Trailer, yes sir!"

Rancek now moved around the room looking at items on the desks and peering into the wall lockers. When he got to Trailer's locker, he looked at the starched fatigues hanging there, examining the name tags and the OCS "Follow Me" patches on the shoulder. "Come here, Trailer," ordered Rancek. "You're real prepared, aren't you?"

"Sir, Candidate Trailer, yes sir!"

"Well, this is an example of what we call the 4Ps. Do you know what the 4Ps are?"

"Sir, Candidate Trailer, no sir!"

"The 4Ps are Piss Poor Prior Planning. Here you got all these fuckin' fatigues with blue 'Follow Me' patches on them. How many?"

"Ten, sir."

"Ten sets of fatigues with blue patches costing fifty cents apiece plus forty cents each to sew them on. That's $9.00, right?"

"You were makin' about $90 last month as a PFC, so that's ten percent of your salary that you pissed away."

"Sir?"

"In this outfit, boy scout, you are required to wear OD patches. Do you know what OD means?"

"Sir, OD means 'olive drab.'"

"That's right, olive drab, the color of pussy and the color of heaven. So, the next time I see you, you'd better not be wearing any blue patches. Do you read me, shithead?"

"Sir, Candidate Trailer, yes sir!"

I noticed that Budwell seemed wryly amused at the confrontation. And Rancek also recognized Budwell's amusement and went at him.

"What's so funny, you piece of shit?"

"Sir, Candidate Budwell, nothing, sir."

"Don't try to be coy with me, fat lips. I've got a sixth sense that tells me when a pisshead is trying to pull some wiseass with me. Knock out twenty."

Budwell dropped quietly to the floor and counted out his pushups in the same calm, amused voice as usual. I noticed that Budwell's penis hung straight down toward the floor and smashed under his huge body as he completed each exercise. I waited for Rancek to rip into Budwell for being nude, but Rancek seemed to lose interest. He merely glanced at me and then was out of the room and down the hall, and 58th Company went back to an uneasy sleep.

Three

Learning

And, it's 1, 2, 3 whatta we fightin' for?
Don't ask me 'cause I don't give a damn.
Next stop is Viet Nam.
—"I Feel Like I'm Fixin' to Die Rag"
—Country Joe and the Fish

The major purpose of the first few weeks of OCS, I decided, was to harass us as much as possible so the breakable ones would be gone soon. The most stressful and the simplest way to torment 256 men was to place more demands on our time than we could possibly accomplish.

We had to be in bed by 2230 and no one was allowed to get up except to go to the latrine, a rule that kept us from writing letters, polishing boots, straightening gear, etc. during the only time left. Of course, we often were up during the nights. Rancek's nightly blitzes became regular.

The next morning at 0500 the lights would come on, and people would start yelling, "Out of your bunk and onto your feet, off your ass and into the street!" By 5:15 we had to have our clothes on, have our bunks made, and be outside in formation ready to take the morning run around the Airborne track. Back at 6, we would clean our rooms from 6 to 6:15, eat from 6:15 to 7:30 (most of that time spent moving through the chow line), and be in formation ready to move out for the day's instruction at 7:30.

We would then run the mile over to Infantry Hall where we had such classes as "Character Guidance" and "Rules of War" or to one of the ranges where classes on mines, grenades, .45 caliber pistols, M-16s and other weapons were held. At night we had a mandatory study hall from 7:30 to 9:00. Then from 9:00 to 10:30 we had to spit-shine our boots, polish our brass, clean the platoon area, and get our rooms ready for the next day's routine. But there was never enough time to accomplish everything, and so everyone took to letting something slide. Some cut corners on boots, others on brass, still others tried to take care of their personal equipment and slack off on duties as platoon members (cleaning the toilets, for example). It was the TACs' duty to find out where the corners were cut, and when they did, they reveled in their discoveries.

"Grunson, what's this green shit growin' on yore brass, boy? You mus' like layin' in that mossy crap on the groun', so whyn't you jus' drop down there an' knock out twenty-five."

So, Grunson or whoever was unlucky enough to get caught would dutifully begin the increasingly difficult task of pushing up and longing for sleep and a little peace.

I found that at first I had been able to blend into the mass of bodies without calling attention to myself. Listening to some unlucky soul strain at pushups during the first week, I had been able to look over the company area carefully as I stood in formation at attention. I looked cautiously, for we were supposed to stand rigidly, eyes forward at all times.

My company, like all of them, had a small open space in front of it that was known as the "pride of 58th Company." Landscaped with rocks, grass, and a few flowers, 58th Company had a small wooden arch erected in front of it. Painted in careful letters on the arch, which was supposed to resemble an Eastern pagoda, was a quotation that must have been taken from a Hemingway sound-alike:

> For Those Who Have Fought for It
> Life Has a Flavor the Protected Never Know.

The company next door had a similar area, a similar pagoda, but its motto was more mundane:

> Our Training is Designed to Let Charlie
> Give His Life for His Country.

"Charlie" was the universal reference to the Viet Cong, though there were more derogatory terms like "gook" and "slope."

When the unlucky candidate with the green brass got through with his pushups, the company was ready to start out for its first class of the day, which was supposed to be about leadership and one later that morning about Claymore mines. Before we left, though, one of the TACs, a short, stubby second lieutenant named Satmonelli, had something to tell us.

"Men, you're about to begin your classes here at Fort Benning, and one of the important parts of working together as a unit is the way you look and sound when you enter the building and when you take your seats. If you don't move into the classroom briskly and if you seem uninterested, it reflects on the company and if anything looks bad for the company, it makes us very angry.

"So when you move into any classroom during your six months here, we want you to be yelling in unison, your company's motto, which was selected to get you in the right frame of mind to be platoon leaders in Vietnam. You will yell as you move in, the following: 'We're going to rape, kill, pillage, and burn; we're going to rape, kill, pillage, and burn, yeah, yeah, yeah.' You will repeat it in that sequence until the last man is standing, and then you will continue until the instructor of the class appears before you and signals for you to be quiet. At that time the student company commander for that day will instruct you by saying, 'Take seats!' to which you will respond, '58th Company, the best damn outfit in Fort Benning!' Is that clear?"

After a rousing "Yes, sir," 58th OC Company was ready for its first full day of military instruction.

We were, of course, required to run everywhere we went, even as a company. When we double-timed it, we always ran to the lyrics of a marching song. The lyrics would first be sung out by either a TAC or by a company member who had been discovered to have talent. This morning Spenser from my platoon was singled out to count cadence and lead the songs. Spenser, who had been a pre-ministry student in Minneapolis before he had been drafted, had supported himself in college by playing at a piano bar at night. He had a beautiful tenor voice, and he also had a good memory for the numerous songs, most of which were about some phenomenal satyr named Jody who took everyone's girl: "Jody's got your girl and gone."

For a change we sang one that went "I wanna go to Vietnam. I wanna kill ol' Charlie Cong," all in perfect cadence to the stamp of our left boot. Later we sang, "I don't know but I've been told, Vietnamese pussy is mighty cold." Or "Hey soldier, have you heard? RMN has passed the word. Hey, soldier, have you heard? We're gonna kill in Vietnam." Under their breath, some rephrased the last sentence to "We're gonna die in Vietnam."

Most of the classes were held in the large building I had passed with the taxi driver, Infantry Hall. It was a multi-million dollar building that was a marvel of advanced technology for 1969. The classrooms, each large enough to hold 260 students, were graduated so that the instructor stood in a pit below, and everyone had a clear view of the teacher. Each classroom was equipped with a complete sound system, a stage, a movie screen, and observation rooms with two-way mirrors; and on each student's desk was a test box, a small box connected to a computer. Tests could be taken and graded almost simultaneously. The instructor would pass out the tests, the student would use the test box to record his answers, and the computer would grade immediately.

I fidgeted in my desk as I listened without interest to the lecture on leadership. The instructor had classified leaders as being authoritarian, like Patton, or persuasive, like McArthur, and was now in the middle of a discussion of the traits of each one. Meanwhile, sitting in the very last row of desks at the top of the classroom, I had a view of my entire company beneath me. I couldn't turn my head in an obvious manner because the TACs were standing behind me in the observation room, but I could scan the room and found myself wondering about this group of people with whom I was about to spend several important months of my life. The sameness of the uniforms and the skinhead haircuts (which we had gotten as a unit, marched to the barber shops and sheared like little lambs in less than thirty minutes shortly after we had processed in) was belied by the variety of those skinned heads.

Some of them were black, but not many compared to the number of black draftees being sent to Vietnam. One of the skinned black heads belonged to a member of my platoon, Garrett. I recalled hearing Rancek enter Garrett's room:

"Sir, Candidate Garrett."

"What's your first name, Garrett."

"Sir, Candidate Garrett, Patrick, Sir."

"Well, Patrick Garrett, no shit, Pat Garrett, you shot Billy the Kid in the back, didn't you? As you were, Sheriff."

And so it seemed destined that Garrett would be called "Sheriff" by all of us. There was something about Garrett's self-assured bearing that made the nickname ironically appropriate.

Besides the black company members, a few Hispanic and oriental heads bobbed before me like prickly corks. And to my surprise, I noticed a few grizzled heads among them. I would later learn that there were several enlisted men, some with a couple of tours overseas already, who had decided to take their chances against younger men as they sought commissions through OCS.

My reveries were suddenly halted by the end of the fifty-minute period. Our next class was to be at a nearby range so we had to hustle out, gather our clipboards, pistol belts, and ponchos and get in formation. As a ritual, we wore pistol belts with a canteen attached so that it hung on the right hip and a poncho rolled up into a nine-inch square attached to the back of the belt with a boot string. Before we entered classes in Infantry Hall, we had to remove our pistol belts, lay them on the asphalt in a line, and place our clipboards neatly on top of the belts so that the back side of the clipboard faced up. On the clipboards we had stenciled and centered our last names on a piece of white tape. For the first eighteen weeks, the clipboards were black, but when we became senior candidates after week eighteen, the ones that were left painted their clipboards the baby blue color of the infantry.

It was now mid-morning; the sun had risen brightly into the Georgia sky. I could tell that this next run over to the range for the Claymore mine class would be the end of the starch in our fatigues. Even though it was November, it was still quite warm once the sun was up, and it was especially warm after running for a mile and a half in starched fatigues and combat boots. Spenser was again designated to lead the run, and, as he sang out about Jody, we twisted our way across the post toward one of the many outdoor areas designed for teaching today's assigned weapon.

The Claymore mine was an important weapon in Vietnam. An oblong piece of plastic filled with explosive and metal shot, it was not the kind of underground mine that most of us had images of. We all recalled those World War II films where GIs were supposed to step perfectly into preexisting footprints so that they could wend their way across a field filled with underground mines that would be set off with just a little bit of weight. In those movies, they would always make it all the way across and then some dolt would throw down his pack in relief and blow them all up.

But the Claymores were supposed to be placed at the perimeter of a firebase, wired up, and used as a first line against enemy sappers. We learned all this from Sgt. Rooker T. Jones, the instructor in charge of Range 101. Sgt. Jones was a huge black man, about six-four, weighing at least 285 pounds. Jones looked like he could have played defensive end for the Dallas Cowboys, but instead he was an instructor at Fort Benning, a job he took seriously. From the time we first arrived, it was clear that he enjoyed his job. Usually the instructor would take over the class after the student officer of the day had instructed the company to be seated, but Jones was in charge from the time we began to march in. He raised his huge arms and encouraged us with our march-in chant: "We're going to rape, kill, pillage, and burn, yeah, yeah; we're going to rape, kill, pillage, and burn!" Jones hunched his body to the rhythm of the chant and raised his arms higher: "WE'RE GOING TO RAPE, KILL, PILLAGE, AND BURN, YEAH, YEAH; WE'RE GOING TO RAPE, KILL, PILLAGE, AND BURN, YEAH; WE'RE GOING TO RAPE, KILL, PILLAGE, AND BURN!"

And it was Jones who gave the order, "Seats" instead of the student company commander, and when he did, the rafters in the bleachers where we sat vibrated with the sound of his voice.

"Mens," he began, "you certainly do remind me of the good ol' days I had across the water. I shore have had some times in the two-way rifle range."

Jones was to become for me the archetypal enlisted instructor. Most of the officers who taught at Fort Benning were young ones who had not yet been overseas. The regular pattern for officers was to complete Officer Candidate School or Officer Basic if they had attended R.O.T.C. and then to spend a year either as a training officer at a basic training unit, as a TAC with an OCS company, or as a teacher of something like tactics or weapons. Then they were shipped overseas to Vietnam where they completed their military duty, if they lived. If they were lifers, they would be promoted to captain when they returned and become commanding officers of training companies, or they would go to an advanced course somewhere and then take an overseas tour in Germany or Korea.

But enlisted instructors like Jones were almost always veterans of Vietnam, and just as there was a disproportionate number of draftees who were black, so was the number of black enlisted instructors in various military training posts much greater than average. But Jones, because of his size and his voice and because he was one of the first enlisted instructors that I saw in OCS, was much more memorable than the others. Beyond his physical presence though, it was his "war story" that impressed itself into my memory.

The instructors who were veterans almost always spiced their classes with stories of their war experiences, and Jones told one story about how effective the mine was during a sapper attack that his platoon had known about beforehand. After Jones finished his required instruction about the Claymore, one of the guys asked him how he knew beforehand about the attack.

"Well, now, mens," he responded, "we gots ways of gittin' information outta Charlie Cong, and I swear that the chopper is one of the bes' ways I knows of doin' it.

"We had captured three gooks a few days before, an' we wanted to git 'em to talk. But they was hard, an' as much as we tried, we couldn't git no info outta them three.

"So we took 'em up in a chopper and doncha know they ain't got no doors on 'em. So oncet we was up we started askin' questions through our 'terpreter, and those dudes still wouldn't tell us nothin'. So first, the lieutenant tol' me to push out one of 'em. Out he goes, and we watch him splash into the rice paddy below.

"Then we asked 'em again, and doncha know they's beginnin' to be a bit more cooperative, but they ain't answerin' fas' enough, so the lieutenant motions for me to drop the nex' one, and out he go.

"Now, doncha know, the las' one was singin'. And thas when he tol' us about the sapper attack."

"Well, what did you do with him?"

"Whatcha mean?"

"What did you do with the one who finally cooperated with you? Did you have him impounded in the brigade prisoner camp?"

At that, Jones let out a laugh that again shook the rafters; he slapped his huge thighs and broke out in a sweat laughing.

"Impoun' him! Hell, no, we didn't impoun' him. We push him out too. We ain't got no time for that bullshit, man.

"Awright, mens, on yore feet; class dismissed."

Four

Garrett

If you've got them by the balls,
their hearts and minds will follow.
—Army saying

The mist crept in on tiny rubber-tire sandals. It slipped soundlessly around the room and snaked into the corners, under the bunks, into the wall lockers, through the military tucks in the blankets, into our bones and minds, and into our dreams.

I dreamed that I was riding my grandfather's favorite horse, Chief Bowles (actually Chief Bowles number five) out on Goodnight Ridge near the ranch. It was early morning before sunrise and the ducks were flying southwest. I could not see them because of the mist, a heavy fog that seemed to lift from the grass and swirl into the sky in folds, but since I could hear the whir of their wings, I knew they must be low. Their soft sounds beckoned me to follow, but the harder I looked for them, the more difficult it was to see them. I urged Chief Bowles forward, first at a trot, then at a gallop. At the outset, the mist clung to him and seemed to slow him as if it were a net, but then Chief Bowles seemed to break free and was just about to burst into the clear starlit Texas morning when up loomed a barbed wire fence, forcing him to turn sharply—too sharply—and I felt myself tumbling over the stallion's mane, and I saw the ground, covered with mist rising up to meet me. ...

Light exploded into the room, causing a montage of fireworks across the back of my eyelids, and I knew that Rancek was on the prowl again.

"On your feet, numbnuts!"

I opened my eyes to the bright dots of the fresh light and blinked in defense, struggling for consciousness and attempting to toss off the covers at the same time. I could tell that Trailer and Budwell were already out of their bunks and on their feet. Entangled in my dream, I had been late in getting out of my bunk, so Rancek concentrated on me. "C'mon, sleeping beauty, let's see some quick reaction time from you. Hustle! Hustle!"

I made it to the floor and quickly assumed the position of attention. Lucky so far, I hadn't yet called any focus upon myself, but it looked like my luck had run out.

"What's your name, Rip Van Winkle?"

"Sir, Candidate Jefferson Bowie Adams."

"Well, that's a hell of a moniker. Jefferson and Adams. Your poppa think you're presidential stock, huh? But, I don't think I remember President Bowie. Did Poppa get his history mixed up?"

"Sir, Candidate Adams. No sir. Jim Bowie was one of the heroes of the Alamo in the war for Texas independence; my grandfather was named for him, and I was named for my grandfather."

"Another friggin' Texan. Well, Adams I'm from New Jersey, and I've just about heard enough bullshit about the great state of Texas, and I've seen enough Texans bounce their asses out of here to know that Texas macho is crap. Got it?"

"Sir, Candidate Adams, I understand."

"Damnit, you pussy, don't you have any self-respect? You mean you're just going to let me heap shit on your home state and you're just goin' to take it? I don't want no pussies here, Adams. I'm goin' to bounce your ass too."

Rancek walked around the room, looked into the wall lockers and under the bunks while we stood at attention. Budwell, I noticed, was now wearing olive drab jockey underwear. Rancek also seemed to notice by glancing at us, but he said nothing, took another turn around the room, and said to me:

"I'm goin' to keep my eye on you, Adams, you hear me, dud?"

"Sir, Candidate Adams, yes sir."

"As you were," he commented as he flipped the light switch, and as we stood in darkness, he added, "and pleasant dreams."

* * * *

And so it came to pass in the mess hall the next day that Rancek was good to his word. As everything in OCS, the mess hall had its rules—rules of entry, rules of eating, rules of exit. To enter the mess hall, every candidate waited in line at the parade rest position with legs in a V and arms behind the back until the person in front moved forward. At that moment the next person in line was to snap to attention with the hands rolled into a fist and held tightly against the leg. He was then to step smartly forward (stepping off on the left leg first) until he came to within an arm's length of the man in front, at which time he stopped and resumed the parade rest position only to begin again and go through this same routine until each man had passed into the mess hall.

The line moved in fits and starts because just outside the mess-hall door was a chinning bar, and before anyone could enter the mess hall, he had to complete ten chinups. As a result, the line would only move one man at a time. Even then, it moved according to the speed with which each man could perform his chinups. The able ones cruised through and the line moved quickly. But there were a few men who always had trouble with the last few and those were the ones the TACs worked on.

Once inside the mess hall, I moved steadily, observing the ones who were already eating as well as I could out of the corner of my eyes. We had all learned the eating rules well: you had to sit up straight in your chair without your back touching, and you had to eat a square meal, meaning that after you took a spoonful of peas, for example, you had to lift the spoon straight up from the plate, stop even with your mouth, head remaining perfectly level and eyes looking forward, and make a perfect right angle move to your mouth, thus squaring the corner of your motion. You then had to replace the spoon beside the plate and chew purposefully until you had completed that bite. Then you could begin the routine again until you were through with everything on your plate.

It was supposed to be another way to learn how to pay attention to details, but it seemed to have arisen from some cretin's sense of humor, and it provided the TACs with numerous opportunities to make corrections and generally raise hell with anyone they wanted to.

"What are you doin', dud? Where'd you learn how to make that move?"

"Sir, Candidate Baker. ..."

"Don't you speak with your mouth full, you turkey; finish that bite before you speak to me."

And so Baker sat chewing until he was through and then the TAC would let him continue after some meaningless interchange. When I finally sat down, I tried to get a seat in the middle of the mess hall where it was more difficult for the TACs to get, but just as I headed for an open seat someone else took it, and I was forced to sit on the end, one of the most vulnerable places because it was so visible.

Army mess halls in the states were almost all alike: we had long tables arranged in a file seating sixteen to twenty men. The tables were covered in a turquoise vinyl tablecloth with a glass vase containing plastic flowers flanked with glass salt and pepper shakers at each end of the table.

I began my square meal with exaggerated movements up to the first position, full stop, then a pronounced move to the mouth, with the return following the same pattern. My problem, as usual, was that I wanted to look around and see what my messmates were doing, and one of the cardinal rules was the eyes forward one. I had finished my pancakes and was working on my eggs when my wandering eyes suddenly landed on the scowling face of Rancek, who stood halfway across the mess hall, looking directly at me. Transfixed at first, I stared back for what seemed like a full second, my gaze locked in a forty-five-degree angle.

At first I expected Rancek to yell at me, as I had often heard him do at others he found with wandering eyes. But as I braced for the attack, Rancek quietly meandered across the mess hall, seemingly purposeless, until he finally got directly behind my seat, where he stopped and stood silently for what seemed like several minutes. I continued eating with a heightened awareness. I thought I could hear Rancek's breathing behind me, and suddenly I was right. Rancek's face loomed up on my right so close that he was breathing directly into my ear. Saying nothing at first, he stood waiting until I had taken my next bite. Then he whispered intensely into my ear:

"I see you lookin' at me, dud; well, I want you to know that I'm lookin' at you, too, and I'm goin' to keep lookin' at you. But. ..."

At that point, Rancek stopped whispering and yelled directly into my ear: "KEEP YOUR FUCKIN' EYES FORWARD, CANDIDATE ADAMS!"

I was so stunned by the yell that I turned abruptly toward Rancek, bumping into Rancek's forehead with my own, the way Curly used to do to Moe. Rancek, in turn, was so startled by my jolt to the forehead that he stepped quickly back.

It just so happened that as Rancek stepped backward, Garrett, the black candidate, was walking by toward a table, his tray carrying a large bowl of the hot gruel that passed for oatmeal, and Rancek stepped directly into him, knocking his tray out of his hands, sending it flying. Garrett stood calmly watching the warm liquid spread slowly across the mess hall floor, but Rancek, suddenly finding himself out of control seemed to go berserk. His wrath, however, was not directed toward me; rather, he lashed out at Garrett.

"You shithead," he thundered, "don't you know to watch out where you're going. Clean it up. NOW!"

Garrett stood looking at the floor. Then he slowly looked toward Rancek before moving. I expected Rancek to jump him again immediately, but there was something about Garrett that seemed to defuse Rancek's immediate wrath, or at least, kept him from continuing his attack. Garrett stooped over, picked up the bowl and headed toward the back of the mess hall. Rancek still seemed stunned, turning around once and then taking a step to leave. But before he did, he seemed to remember something, turned back to me, leaned over, and whispered, "I won't forget this, Adams; I won't forget."

Five

Training

And it's 5, 6, 7 open up the pearly gates
Well there ain't no time to wonder why
Whooppee we're all gonna die.
—"I Feel Like I'm Fixin' to Die Rag"
—Country Joe and the Fish

And so I wasn't surprised to hear Rancek in the platoon area that night. After hitting us late every night for the first few days, he had slacked off, and it appeared that perhaps his late night raids were only part of our initial welcome. Because of the mess-hall debacle, I had expected that Rancek would be there to harass me again. I was surprised, though, when Rancek walked into another room before he got to mine.

Puzzled, I lay in the dark listening to the other candidates jump out of their bunks when Rancek turned on the light. I listened as Rancek pulled his usual routine of asking questions about our purpose and dedication. It wasn't until Rancek got to the third man in the room that I understood what was happening.

"So it's you again, Sheriff," I heard Rancek say, and I knew why Rancek had not entered my room first.

"Sir, Candidate Garrett, yes sir."

"You know why I'm here to see you, don't you, Sheriff?"

"Sir, Candidate Garrett, no sir."

"Don't play the innocent with me, Garrett. You can't get away with sloshing that greasy gruel at my feet the way you did at the mess hall."

"Sir? That was an accident. You bumped into me as I was walking to sit down."

"Don't play the fool with me, Garrett. You walk around here with your head in the air like you're untouchable, like you're so handsome or something that you'll just breeze through here with no skin off your black ass. Well, I'm on to you, Garrett."

"Sir, Candidate Garrett. I'm sorry, sir, but I don't know what you're talking about. I didn't spill that bowl on purpose."

"Don't talk back to me, Garrett. Tomorrow night, 1800 hours, I'll see you at the Airborne track, and we'll see what you're made of."

And with that remark, Rancek flipped off the light in Garrett's room, and I lay quietly in my bunk, wondering how Rancek could have deflected his anger to Garrett so easily. I thought fleetingly that perhaps Rancek had forgotten me, but just as I was caught between the conflicting emotions of guilt for Garrett's involvement and relief for being left alone, the structure of the moment changed abruptly when Rancek stepped into my room and the lights boomed on.

I hit the floor first, my roommates having been deeply asleep. Standing beneath the lights, Rancek looked like one of those lizards that stay out of the sun. His bald head had a skull-like whiteness about it, and I thought briefly that except for the pulsing blood vessel at his temple, he could in fact be dead.

My reverie ended quickly, for it was clear that Rancek was there for me. "Adams!" he barked.

"Sir, Candidate Adams," I replied and stepped forward just as Trailer and Budwell were making their way out of their bunks and onto their feet.

"You didn't really think that I had forgotten you, did you, Adams?"

"Sir, Candidate Adams. Forgotten, sir?"

"Oh, so you're going to play the ignorant ass, too, huh, Adams?"

"Sir, Candidate Adams. I don't know what you're talking about, sir."

"Stifle it, asshole! I want you and your buddy Garrett to meet me out front in the company area tomorrow at 1800 hours pronto. We're going to go over and inspect the Airborne track and the low-crawl area at close range. Nobody makes a fool of me!" And with that remark, Rancek rocked up on his toes, and, with the blood vessel in his temple pounding, he stomped out into the night.

The next day promised the sameness of all the others with a full schedule of classes and exercise. In the morning we were to have a PT class; that afternoon we were scheduled to begin studying the M-60 machine gun. Just as it was with all our weapons study, the first session was indoors where we would learn the operation of the weapon on paper.

I was distracted. I thought first about what Rancek had in mind for me that evening, but when I forgot my personal anxiety, I felt guilty for getting Garrett involved in my private affair with Rancek. Garrett was innocent of any wrongdoing; he had just been walking by with his cereal bowl at the wrong time. I hoped to get a chance to talk to Garrett during the day.

Sleep the rest of the night before had not been restful, so I was out of bed as soon as the last watch called reveille. Expecting too that my room would get extra scrutiny, I worked hard to insure that all the things were in order; I even measured the distance that my display toothbrush was from the end of the drawer. The regulations called for three-quarters of an inch, and I was surprised to discover that I had been at least a quarter of an inch off for the past several days.

Budwell and Trailer worked intensely on their gear as well. They, too, expected that Rancek would come through and inspect our room carefully during the day since he was not the officer of the day. Trailer seemed upset.

"I just don't understand why you did that, Adams. You ought to watch out more carefully. When he gets on your case, we all suffer, you know."

"Look, Tommy, I sure as hell didn't do it on purpose. My god, all I did was cut my eyes around the room at the mess hall. I bet you've done that a thousand times."

"Not with Rancek standing there, I haven't. You know as well as I do that he's got this thing about not keeping your eyes forward. You shoulda been more careful."

"Forget it, Trailer," Budwell inserted. "There's no use blaming Adams for anything. It could have been me or you just as easily as it was him. Besides, it makes all of this more interesting. If I wanted to go through it without any trouble, I'd be wondering some about myself."

I paused for a moment to think about Budwell's comment before asking, "Are you saying that you don't really care what happens to you as long as it's not boring?"

Budwell smiled and replied, "Well, I wouldn't generalize quite that far, but I'm in the Army mainly because I got bored doing what I was doing. I remember reading a story once titled 'The Beast in the Jungle,' and it was about this guy who spent his life thinking that something remarkable was going to happen to him, like a beast leaping on him from the shadows. He ended up being the one man to whom nothing happened and that was the bad thing he'd been waiting for. Life is short, and I don't see any reason to let some of its most interesting features pass me by."

"And you think Vietnam is one of its more interesting features?"

"Ancient oriental philosophers used to say that it was a curse to live in uninteresting times, Adams. And I think if we make it through, we'll look back and say that we damn sure weren't cursed."

"Just a minute, Budwell. I thought you said that you too had been drafted and then signed up for OCS the same way I did."

"That's right."

"Well, what did you mean a few minutes ago when you said that you're in the Army because you got bored with what you were doing? If you got drafted, then you didn't have any choice."

Budwell continued to work on his gear, straightening his drawer and placing his display items in order before answering. Finally, he responded, "Adams, I happen to believe that you control your destiny, sometimes subconsciously.

"For me, it was this way. I got my law degree and went to work for a small firm in California where my job was doing wills. It was dreadful work after fighting my way through law school and graduating with images of significant investigative research and last-second, case-breaking discoveries.

"But these old farts would come in to have their wills drawn up, guys who had some of the most interesting lives. One old guy, for example, came in, and as I started going over the details of his will, he began telling me his life story. He'd signed on with Teddy Roosevelt at the bar in the Menger Hotel in San Antonio. Then, during World War I he'd served on the *U.S.S. Delaware*. And during World War II he'd been in the foreign service in Asia.

"As I listened to him, I began to believe that my life in California was dwindling away, and I secretly envied the people who were in the Army."

Trailer, who had been shining his brass while Budwell talked, suddenly broke in, "Me, too. I really wanted to be in the Army, so as soon as I finished junior college, I joined. Man, I want to go to Vietnam."

"Hold it, Trailer," said Budwell, "I'm not gung-ho for Vietnam; I have some real reservations about this war."

"Well, then, you shouldn't be here," responded Trailer earnestly.

"Let Budwell finish, Trailer," I broke in. "I still don't understand how being bored with your job got you drafted."

"Jesus, man," replied an exasperated Budwell, "sometimes you've just got to stop looking for all the rational answers to things. You know, some things in the world arise from deep mysteries."

"Come on, now, Budwell," I scoffed, "are you giving me some bullshit about fate?"

Budwell paused and looked at me, "No. I'm talking about the human condition."

From down below, we heard the whistle calling us to the moveout formation.

"Omigod," responded Trailer, "I shouldn't have been listening to you guys. My stuff's not together."

"Let's get a move on," commanded Budwell. "You can do it, Tommy. Here, give me your brass; I'll finish it while you get your shoes in order."

The three of us now worked quickly. Trailer finished spit shining the toes of his dress shoes that were left displayed under the foot of the bed. As Budwell finished shining a piece of collar brass, he handed it to me, and I leaned over Trailer's shoulder and pinned it on his shirt, eyeballing the proper placement.

"O.K. That's it. Let's go."

* * * *

The day moved slowly for me; even the physical-training class slowed to a dull thud. Every time I tried to get close enough to Garrett to speak with him, something happened to get in the way. We went back to the company areas for lunch, but I still couldn't get a word in with Garrett.

For the afternoon class we were to be in a classroom at Infantry Hall studying the workings of the M-60 machine gun, and I hoped to be able get near Garrett at a break.

In the classroom I continued to be distracted. The day had brightened into a beautiful fall afternoon; the sun shone brightly and the clear sky reminded me of spring. Yet the instructor droned on, naming the parts.

"And here we have the upper sling swivel. ..."

Finally, I got a chance to see Garrett at the break. Lt. Satmonelli, the TAC on duty that day, had given us coffee privileges, which meant that instead of standing at parade rest in the hall during the break, we could buy coffee from the concessionaires along the hallway.

I saw Garrett behind me in the line, so I bought an extra cup, and as I walked back, I motioned to Garrett to join me. Even though we had coffee privileges, we still had to be careful about our conversation, so we walked down toward the entryway to the latrine where we would be out of sight of the main hallway.

"Say, Garrett, I'm Jeff Adams; I bunk down the hall from you. We haven't met before, but I was the guy Rancek was getting on in the mess hall when you walked by yesterday. I wanted you to know that I'm sorry for what happened. I sure as hell didn't mean to get him down on you like that."

Garrett seemed to be as calm and self-assured as usual. Standing there in sharply pressed fatigues, he almost could have been a statue of one of those African gods. He shook his head and replied, "Don't worry about it, man. I've got no fear of Rancek."

"Thanks, Garrett. I feel guilty about getting you involved. He had started on me the night before, so I should have been expecting him in the mess hall. I let down and deserve what he might do to me. But he had no reason to jump on you like that."

"Look, Adams, forget it. He was going to get to me sooner or later. The bowl incident just gave him a chance to get to me now. I don't care if it's now or later, so don't let it worry you."

"I'm glad you feel that way, Garrett. But you know I expect there are some people who might make it without Rancek's special attention. If it hadn't been for me, you may have been one of them."

Garrett finished his coffee, looked at his watch, crushed and threw away the Styrofoam cup before he replied. Then he looked me directly in the eye and said, "Adams, if you'll look around, you'll see how many black officer candidates there are here, and you'll know as well as I do that I wouldn't make it through without some special attention.

"I'm not bitchin'," he went on, "but I've come to expect it. You'll hear no gripin' about racism from me, although I see racists at work all the time. It's just that it simplifies my life to expect to be treated special because I'm black. You, for example, have to sit and wonder if you're going to be singled out, thinking you might be able to slip by without being forced to prove yourself. But I don't have to wonder, and I also expect that I can take whatever Rancek gives. So I'll see you in the company area at six and we'll give him a run for his money. C'mon, break's over. Thanks for the coffee."

Six

Low Crawl

Our goal is peace with honor.
—Richard Nixon

I ate lightly at evening chow, expecting that if I ate too much, I would see it again. I also ate quickly and, when I was through, went to my room where I first greased up my underarms and crotch with Vaseline, carefully applied one Band-Aid and two layers of tape to each heel, and changed into a pair of old fatigues. I expected Rancek to run us around the track a few times, but a few laps would probably not be enough for him. The low-crawl pit that I had heard about but never seen would probably be in store for us, and I didn't want to ruin a newly starched and altered set of fatigues. I then put on my oldest and most comfortable pair of combat boots.

Just as I was getting through, Budwell walked into the room, pulled out his desk chair, and sat down heavily.

"I don't suppose there's much that I can say of any help, Roomie," he began. "But I want you to know that I'll be pulling for you while you're out there."

"Thanks, that's all I could ask for. I don't really know what to expect, but I don't think it's going to be something that I will want to do again any time soon."

"Yeah, well, that's probably true, but you know what I said about boredom, and this sure as hell won't be boring. I do, though, have a little theory about how you can get through things that you don't like."

I finished tucking in the laces of my combat boots, began taking the things out of my pockets that I wouldn't need—cigarette lighter and Granddad's Case knife—and replied, "Well, you might as well go ahead and tell me. I expect you will whether I ask you to or not."

Budwell laughed, "All right, here it is. When I was in law school, I had one particularly hard brief that I had to get through with. I only had about a week and a half to get through, and I had to read through a stack of papers on more complicated cases than I had ever tried to assimilate before. So after about three days and nights, I began to panic. I first told myself that there wasn't any way that I could read all I had to and make enough sense out of it to write a decent brief.

"But for some reason, suddenly a phrase came into my head. It must have been the Latin phrases that I had been reading in the law books I had been poring over that called it forth, but whatever the reason, the phrase *tempus fugit*, like the melody of a song, began to play through my head."

I held up my hand to stop Budwell's reverie and asked, "Just a minute, now. What does that phrase mean in the law?"

"Nothing," Budwell responded. "It has nothing to do with the law as far as I know. It's a Latin phrase that means 'time passes' or 'time flies.' The phrase was a release for me, like letting out the bears at the zoo or getting a last minute pardon. Suddenly the weight of time was lifted."

I shook my head, "I'm sorry, Budwell, but I don't see how such a simple phrase could really make any difference. You still were responsible for the brief. It sounds too much to me like some of those silly, born-again fundamentalists I knew in college who would throw up their hands, raise their eyes to the sky, and say that their fate on the next pre-calc test was in God's hands. Then they'd flunk their way back to Snook or Bug Tussle and never take any of the credit for their failures."

"C'mon, Adams," Budwell angrily retorted, "I'm not talking about the same thing, and you know it. Don't belittle my point." Softening, he went on, "Hey, friend, I'm just trying to tell you something that helped me."

I clapped my friend on the back, "Thanks, Roomie, I know you are. I guess I'm just a bit uptight. I only have a few more minutes before I have to be out there."

"You'll be okay, friend. Just remember, man, *tempus fugit*. Time passes. As long as you're alive, time will pass. You can just do what you can while you're doing what you're doing, and eventually it'll be over. Somebody I read once said, 'In the life of a man, his time is but a moment, his being an incessant flux, his sense a dim rushlight, his body a prey of worms' or words something like that. So I just try to hold on and stay afloat in these rushing waters as best as I can. That's all I've been trying to say. Just hold your head up and you won't drown, and eventually *tempus* will *fugit*."

I checked my brass one last time, grabbed my helmet liner, and stepped to the door, "Thanks. If I can keeps my wits, I'll try to remember."

Down in the courtyard Garrett, waiting at parade rest, didn't acknowledge my arrival, so I took my proper interval to Garrett's left and assumed the same position. It was a cool November evening; the sun had begun to disappear, and the Georgia breeze was beginning to blow through the opening between the buildings. Senior cadets from 56th Company would occasionally walk by, and we would have to come to attention, salute, and call out, "Good evening, sir!"

The sky's pinks turned to gray, and the evening breezes brought the yellowish, bitter taste of sulfur, the by-product of the base's heating plant. Both of us stood at parade rest, quietly wondering if Rancek could have forgotten, when we heard boots ringing on the cement walk behind us.

We both stood rigidly waiting for a command, but the boots' owner stood still and quiet for several minutes. Then we heard him quietly walk up behind us and hiss, "Now, babies, are you ready?"

We both came quickly to attention and sang out our names and our affirmative answer, to which Rancek said, "All right, then, let's go. Leave your helmet liners here, and untuck your shirts; we're going for a little run."

As we followed Rancek out of the courtyard and toward the Airborne track, I noticed that he was wearing gray sweatpants and an olive drab T-shirt. He'd come prepared for a little run, and I wondered how far we would go. It was the uncertainty, I knew, that added to the difficulty. If I knew that we were to go two miles, then I could pace myself effectively, but if we were to go six or eight miles instead, then the pace for two miles would be much too fast. I had learned that the only realistic way was to act as though we were going to run for twenty miles; then I could be sure to make whatever we ended up doing.

With Rancek running with us I felt somewhat relieved. The hardest runs were those when the TACs stood around the track and simply yelled out at us. When the TACs ran with us, they got tired and headed back to the company area. Of course, what might happen was that Rancek might run until he got tired; then he would know that the more he pushed us, the more difficult it would be.

Rancek's pace was brisk but not difficult. We rounded the mile-and-a-half track once and then again. Rancek kept up his pace without looking back at us; he seemed to sense that we were both with him. On the third lap, he picked up his pace at the halfway mark. Garrett seemed to feel little pain and speeded up easily. I kept up too for the first hundred yards or so but then began to tire and drop back a few paces.

At first Garrett stayed up with Rancek and allowed the gap to widen between him and me, but when he saw over his shoulder that I was dropping back farther, he slowed down. Rancek continued to pull away, so Garrett circled back to me.

"C'mon, man," he urged. "You can do it. Look, this speed means that he's got us on the last lap. Hell, you can finish off this last half mile. Let's go."

With that comment Garrett grabbed me by the arm and helped me pick up the pace. By that time Rancek had broadened the gap between us to about fifty yards. It required almost a sprint for us to catch up to him, but with Garrett's pulling and cajoling along the way, we got up within twenty yards of him before he finished the lap.

Rancek then pulled off the track, and we followed him, but he pointed to the track and shook his head, "No, take another one, and don't forget that I can see you. Keep up your pace."

So we started on another lap, but as soon as we got to the first curve, we slowed the pace to a jog. Night had now fallen, but the track was lit by two high phosphorus street lights that threw an eerie gray glow over the runners.

I ran with my arms dropped to my sides, my lungs gasping for breath. My head lolled from side to side; I tried to walk, but Garrett was firm, "No, don't stop now; he'll just make it harder on us if he sees us walking. C'mon, now. We'll take it easy to the light, and then when he can see us clearly, we'll pick up the pace."

Gasping, I tried to answer, "No, go on. I can't make it. You go on or he'll get down on you more, too. Just let me catch my breath here."

But Garrett wouldn't let me stop. Grabbing me again by the arm, he kept me jogging, and when we reached the curve with the light, we picked up the pace. I began to catch my breath, and by the time we reached Rancek, I was breathing steadily.

Standing with arms crossed, Rancek watched us approach. When we reached him, he motioned for us to stop and said, "Well, I'm pleased to see that you boys are sufficiently warmed up. Let's get down to some exercise now. Move over there to the grass; we'll do it by the numbers. Get arm's length apart, and we'll begin with the side-straddle-hop."

My breath coming in ragged heaves, I desperately wanted to bend over at the waist, but seeing Garrett take his exercise position encouraged me to do the same. Rancek then directed us to begin exercising, and he took us through several of the army standards: toe touches, squat thrusts, pushups, leg lifts.

"Now, I want to see you do one of my favorites; let's have a few minutes of butterflies."

The exercise fondly called "butterflies" is deceptively simple. All you do is hold your arms out cruciform and wiggle your fingers. It takes little real energy to do, but the difficulty comes from having to hold the arms out for a long time, and that, of course, was just what Rancek had in mind.

So Garrett and I stood doing butterflies, and the time passed. For variety occasionally Rancek would call out, "Now, tickle your titties," which mean that we would draw our arms in with our fingers almost touching our chests, elbows out. The same muscles were being used, so there was no relief. Soon he would call out for us to return to the butterfly position.

I had great difficulty holding my arms out straight. Rancek walked around us, but as soon as he seemed to be looking at Garrett, I dropped my arms a little trying to give my aching muscles some rest. But when Rancek looked at me, he recognized what I was doing and shouted, "Get your arms up, you pussy. Do it right."

Soon the exercise became excruciating in its simplicity. The sweat beaded on our foreheads; our arm muscles began to burn, but Rancek continued to walk around us, smiling at our agony.

"I love seeing you boys squirm; it gladdens my heart because I know that you can't take it, and if you can't take it, you're going to quit. We don't want people who can't take the heat here. I don't want anybody leading the platoon on my right who doesn't have courage. And I don't want people in this company who try to make me look bad in front of the others the way you two did in the mess hall."

Rancek's monologue continued as he circled us. Occasionally he would stop and address one of us: "You're hurting aren't you, Garrett. You ready to quit?"

To which Garrett would respond, "Sir, Candidate Garrett, no, sir!"

Finally, Rancek formally gave us the order to cease exercising, but as soon as we dropped our arms, he told us of his next plan.

"Now, let's see how you two can do in the low-crawl pit. On the double!"

We double-timed around the track to the low-crawl pit, delighted with the opportunity to swing the aching muscles of our arms but apprehensive about what Rancek was going to do next. Even though the long exercise had been difficult, it had at least given me time to catch my breath.

And the low-crawl pit was much less frightening to me than to many of the other cadets. Low-crawling was considered important to traditional military training, having grown out of trench warfare of WWI and the archetypal assaults against machine-gun nests in WWII. It had little real application to the kind of jungle warfare required in Vietnam because the thick jungle foliage offered little opportunity for quick, straight crawling. It, nonetheless, was one of the major military exercises. I, who had approached military training with apprehension about long-distance runs, had been surprised to discover that I was one of the best low-crawlers in my company. To get the full 100 points on physical training tests, you had to crawl forty yards in twenty-three seconds or less; I consistently finished under nineteen, but many of my friends who ran well and were otherwise good athletes had trouble with the event.

As we headed to the low-crawl area, I began unbuttoning my fatigue jersey; I had learned that I could get more protection and have less friction by turning my shirt around backwards. That way the buttons would be to the back and only the slick fabric of the shirt without buttons to slow me down would touch the earth. I advised Garrett to do the same, but he shook me off.

"I'm sorry, man, but nothing helps me here."

"What do you mean? You're a good athlete; you'll do fine."

"I'd like to think you're right," Garrett responded, "but I have trouble with the low-crawl pit. That's all right. Don't worry about me."

At the pit we lay down on our stomachs and waited for Rancek to tell us what to do. For me being close to the ground gave me a feeling of security. The dead winter grass smelled like hay and recalled days at home breaking out bales for Granddad's cattle. The pleasant smell along with the relief from lying down bolstered me, but I could see that Garrett seemed to react just the opposite. Where Garret had made the run without much effort, he now seemed to be sweating a great deal. Beads of sweat formed on his forehead and lip; even his breathing seemed more labored. I realized that Garrett must feel the same anxiety that I had felt about the run.

"All right, girls," sang out Rancek gleefully. "It's time to see you hump mother earth. I'm expecting big things out of you here, Garrett. I keep hearing that you black folks are great lovers, so you ought to be able to mogate down there in this fuckin' position. Now hit it."

The low-crawl pit here was unlike most of the ones used for physical training tests. They were usually grassy and clearly marked at start and finish. This pit was obviously selected for its present purpose: extreme physical hardship. It was rocky, not grassy, so the fatigue jacket didn't slide smoothly along the earth. Still, I took off swiftly the way I always low-crawled. I always kept the image of an alligator in my mind as I moved along; even the rocks didn't bother me.

But I saw that Garrett was having trouble. His athletic form was obviously not built for the low-crawl position. His arms akimbo appeared out of joint, and he moved with a jerkiness that he never showed while he walked, ran, went through the obstacle course or whizzed along the monkey bars. By the time I reached the end of the forty-yard pit and made my turn to head back, I had outdistanced Garrett by twenty feet. I slowed my pace and urged Garrett along as I passed him.

"C'mon, brother! You're an alligator; you can do it. Watch the way I move and follow me."

Garrett made his turn and picked up some of the space between us and had closed the gap to fifteen feet when we finished the first lap back at the start where Rancek stood with folded arms.

"That's not a good start, boys," he said. "I didn't time you that time, but it sure seemed like a long time. Let's do it again."

Breathing heavily, we got in the ready position.

"I think I'll go along with you this time. For encouragement. Ready, go!"

I tried to slow my pace to keep from getting too far ahead of Garrett. Rancek jogged along between, telling us to pick up the pace. As we neared the turnaround, Rancek suddenly put his foot on Garrett's rear and pushed his hips to the ground.

"Get your ass down, Garrett. With your butt up in the air like that you make a good target. You'd be riddled with .50 caliber holes crawling along like that. Keep it down!"

I made the turn and started back, but Garrett labored, particularly after losing his momentum with Rancek's kick. Rancek seemed to glory in Garrett's difficulty.

"So, now we know, Mr. Garrett. You ain't shit after all. I've seen you walking around with that flat nigger nose up in the air, like your shit don't stink. Well, you ain't shit; you're scum, and I'm going to have you out of here. Are you ready to quit?"

With great difficulty, Garrett crawled along and managed to gasp, "Sir, Candidate Garrett, no sir!"

I had reached the end and was able to catch my breath before Rancek and Garrett made it back. Rancek, intent on intimidating Garrett, seemed to forget about me.

"C'mon, Garrett. You might as well hang 'em up. You're not going to make it here, man. Let's send you over to rack out company. We need boys like you in Nam. PFC Garrett—it has a nice ring. Just give me the word that you're ready to quit, and I'll let you stop."

"Sir, Candidate Garrett, no sir!"

"Well, let's do it again, then."

For three more trips through the low-crawl pit Rancek continued his assault on Garrett and almost ignored me. I tried to encourage Garrett as much as I could, but I could see from the determination in Garrett's eyes that nothing would make him quit. At the end of the fifth time in the pit, the steam seemed to disappear from Rancek, and he told us to get up and double-time back to the company area.

When we stood up, we noticed that our fatigue jackets were shredding as well as our T-shirts underneath. Our hands were bloodied from the rocks, but we started back at an even pace. Rancek followed without saying anything.

Back at the company area, we came to a stop, took the position of attention, and waited for Rancek. He came up behind us as before and walked around quietly, before finally saying, "I'll get you two yet. Now fall out."

Seven

Birthday Boy

Yeah, C'mon Generals let's move fast
Your big chance has come at last.
Gotta go out and get those Reds
Cause the only good Commie is one that's dead.
—"I Feel Like I'm Fixin' to Die Rag"
—Country Joe and the Fish

We discovered that the days passed almost unnoticeably, since we weren't allowed radios or other connections to the outside world. No newspapers made their way into the company area, so it was almost as if we were out of time. But I had found a newspaper rack outside the battalion office just across from the rear of the chow hall. Full-time staff members could buy papers there, and senior cadets received news privileges too. The best that I could do was to drift by the machine on the way after chow. I had to move cautiously, though, for if a TAC or a senior cadet from another company caught me looking at the newspaper without news privileges, I would be in big trouble, and I knew that Rancek needed little more pushing to be on me again.

I had learned in the first two weeks that if I ate late and was one of the last to leave the mess hall, I had a better chance of being able to see the headlines. The next morning I was necessarily one of the last ones in the chow hall. My whole body ached from the workout of the night before, and so I had moved slowly getting my things together for the day.

As I left the mess hall, I angled toward the newspaper racks. One rack held the *Atlanta Constitution*, the other *The New York Times*. The Atlanta paper would be current, since Atlanta was only about a hundred miles from Fort Benning, but the *Times* was usually a day or so behind. That meant that I could get two different days' headlines whenever I found it possible to go by the racks.

As I neared, I saw *The New York Times* headline: "Nixon Not to Reveal Plan," it read, and I knew that the story had something to do with Nixon's campaign pledge that he had a secret plan to end the war in Vietnam. He had now been in office almost eleven full months, but the war seemed to be escalating rather than scaling down. Nixon's advisor, Henry Kissinger, who reminded me of Peter Sellers as Dr. Strangelove, seemed convinced that more bombing of Hanoi and North Vietnam would lead the North Vietnamese to make concessions for peace. I thought it ironic that Alabama Governor George Wallace's running mate, General Curtis LeMay, had declared that the U.S. ought to bomb the Vietnamese back into the stone age, and Nixon seemed to have adopted it as his secret plan.

The more current headline in the *Constitution* seemed more sensational: "Massacre Alleged at Vietnamese Village." I squatted down to read the text and discovered that there had been charges of a massacre of civilians, including women and children, at a small Vietnamese village complex called My Lai.

So what else is new, I thought. I had already heard enough war stories about how young girls of nine or ten would walk into American camps, saunter up to headquarters nonchalantly, and pull a grenade from under their skirt or out of the fold of their black pajamas and toss it into a group of unsuspecting GIs. I could recall Sgt. Jones' booming voice, saying, "You trust 'em, and you're dead meat. Blow 'em away first, ask questions later, increase the body count."

The war dominated all the news, but I thought Americans were numbed to the fighting by now. Students still protested on college campuses around the country, and there had been some large voices of protest against the war—Eugene McCarthy, Robert Kennedy, and Martin Luther King, among them. McCarthy hadn't gotten the nomination, and Kennedy and King had been assassinated. So stories of massacres and other atrocities in Vietnam seemed commonplace to me. I had long since decided that my earlier hope that public outrage and protest would force Nixon to end the war quickly was a pipe dream.

Only a headline such as "War Over, Troops to Come Home" would have affected me then. I stood and returned to my platoon area to get my gear together for the day. As I walked in, I noticed Ferona, a big Italian kid from New York, beaming.

"What are you so happy about, Ferona?" I asked.

"Hey, man, I just discovered today's date. It's my frigging birthday! I had lost track of the dates."

"Well, congratulations, buddy. How old are you?"

"Nineteen."

"Nineteen? How'd you get in OCS at eighteen. I thought you had to have some college to get in here?"

"I got college. CCNY for a year. General Studies. I graduated from high school at seventeen. All you got to show is some college. So I flunked out. Big deal. You don't need big brains to get your ass shot off."

"Well, happy birthday, Ferona. Take that and a nickel and you can get a cup of coffee at our break today at Infantry Hall," I laughed.

"This is my day, Adams. You watch. I'm going to take it easy on myself today. My family has a tradition; every person is a king or queen on birthdays, and I'm going to take my holiday."

I shrugged and replied, "Well, you better remember that Uncle Sam's Army doesn't live by your family's rules. You better be careful about laying off around here."

The time had come to form up outside in the company area. We were scheduled to have an early physical training class and then go to Infantry Hall for another class on the M-16.

The PT class went as usual, with the standard drills and exercises, ending with a run around the exercise area. Normally the run after PT was easy—no more than a mile—because the PT instructors had classes to teach all day and they wanted to conserve their energy.

On this particular day, after the PT instructors led the class around for a mile run, the TAC officers took over and directed the company to keep running. On the north side of the field was a brushy area where occasionally candidates would withdraw during runs, supposedly to take a piss but usually to avoid a few laps, and then reenter the group on a later lap.

I saw Ferona disappear into the bushes as we began the next lap. Ferona stayed in the bushes during the next two laps, and on the fourth and final lap he came back into the group just in time to finish the run. None of the TACs said anything to him as we returned to our gear we had left lined up near the platform, so I thought Ferona was safe.

The rest of the day passed with ferocious boredom as we listened to military lecturers describe the parts of the M-16 rifle. We spent most of the day taking apart and putting back together the practice models.

At evening chow, I was sitting in the mess hall, circumspectly eating and watching what was happening. When Ferona came into the mess hall, I saw the TACs at the head table begin to talk among themselves. It should have been a clue that something was up. But it wasn't until Ferona sat down that I connected the two events. After Ferona took his seat, three of the TAC officers got up and nonchalantly began making their way toward him. Satmonelli, the short, pugnacious Italian, took the lead while Swanson, a tall, blond Nordic type, who was unusually quiet for a TAC officer, moved to one side, and Martin, a big, boisterous former football player at Northwestern, took the other.

Satmonelli walked to where Ferona was sitting and bent over so he could yell in his ear. Swanson fronted the prey, and Martin stood to the side and sported an amused smile.

"Say, Ferona," began Satmonelli, "didn't I see you take to the bushes at this morning's PT run? I think you're a quitter, you dud."

Almost simultaneously the other two TACs moved in and yelled at Ferona, too, battering him with the word "quitter." Ferona hurried to his feet, locked his heels at attention, hands straight by his sides. He presented an impressive figure. His dark Italian face was rigid and the position of attention accentuated the broadness of his shoulders. He was much larger than any of the three TACs, even Martin, the ex-football player. The scene suddenly reminded me of a time I'd seen a huge bear treed by yelping dogs.

Ferona tried to respond, "Sir, no sir! I am not a quitter. I had to heed the call of nature, sir, and went into the bush to urinate."

"Bullshit! You went to the latrine right before class. You better get your kidneys examined; they must be pea-sized, like your brain. Besides it doesn't take three laps to take a piss. If it does, then you better go on sick call and get your whanger squeezed for you.

"We know your type, Ferona. You're a goddamn quitter, and we're going to have your ass out of here. You missed the run this morning, but you'll get one tonight. Now finish your meal; it'll probably be your last one as a regular candidate."

Ferona took his seat, the TACs returned to theirs, and I knew what Ferona faced. It would be harder for him than it had been for me and Garrett, because Ferona was facing a run on a full stomach. Mess hall rules were "take all you want, but eat all you take," and Ferona, perhaps to celebrate his birthday, had stacked his plate full of meatloaf.

I finished and spent much of the rest of the evening wondering about Ferona. Tonight was a study night, since we had a long class on the M-16. But I found it hard to concentrate on the manual. Snatches of songs played through my head, songs such as "Scarborough Fair" and "Leaving on a Jet Plane." Before long, the sound of boots echoed in the hall. At first I could see nothing from my position at my desk, and I knew better than moving from the required seat there.

Soon, though, I heard Ferona and the three TACs moving slowly down the hall. Then Ferona braced himself against the wall and requested permission to speak. Satmonelli silenced him.

"Shut up, you quitter. I don't want to hear anything from you. Get your things together in twenty minutes; I want your signature on the drop letter now."

The three TACs disappeared, but Ferona stood pasted against the wall. I could just make out his profile and heard him bang his fists against the wall and sob quietly.

I risked getting out of my seat, knowing the TACs were gone. I stepped to his door and tried to comfort Ferona. "It's all right, Ferona. They went for you, and it's damn near impossible to stay if they decide they want you to go."

Tears began to roll down Ferona's face, cutting through the sweat and grime from his ordeal. Ferona looked at me and sobbed, "It's my fucking nineteenth birthday, and I'm crying like a baby."

Ferona moved down the hall, head down in defeat. I returned to my desk and tried to remember one of the tunes floating through my head earlier, but all I could call up were the simple strains of "Happy Birthday to You."

Eight

Thanksgiving

Kill a Commie for Christ.
—latrine graffiti

With Ferona's drop the floodgates opened, and several others rushed quickly through. I knew the ones who dropped out traded some momentary relief for future problems. But they had to stay at Benning for six weeks while they qualified for the Infantry. They could be—and most were—sent straight to Vietnam as PFCs. Several who had come to OCS from other training programs such as communications or clerk school, thought that they would be able to go back to their old assignments. As badly as the Army wanted Infantry first lieutenants, it also needed grunts. For many, it was a real shock to hit Casual Company and then, within thirty days, get orders to Vietnam. The powers that be moved them out of the assigned platoons into a few rooms at the back of sixth platoon until after Christmas, when they would move to Casual Company and wait for orders.

The TACs continued to try to pinpoint people they thought wouldn't make it, and they kept on harassing us. One day they only gave us twenty minutes for lunch. I was in the line early and got to eat, but half the guys were standing in the chow line holding trays when the call to fall in came. The only break in the third week was Thanksgiving. We weren't very aware of it until dinner that day, two days after the twenty-minute lunch. We marched back from a day of training at Infantry Hall on "Character Guidance" and were told to put on our dress uniforms and fall out in the company area in a half hour.

As usual we had no idea what was happening; we just followed orders. We hustled to put on our dress green uniforms and go outside to the company area. We marched over to the battalion mess hall and discovered it decorated for Thanksgiving so that it looked like a grade-school library with paper turkeys and silhouette Pilgrims hanging on the walls. Another company was ahead of us in the line, so it took almost forty minutes to move through to get served. We did the usual, standing at parade rest until the line moved, when we would snap to attention, step up, parade rest again, over and over until we got to the front of the line. But as the members of the company ahead of us first began to take their seats, it was clear that the usual requirements of the "square meal" were relaxed. There was no talking and everyone sat with their eyes ahead. But we could eat fairly normally without putting down the fork or knife after every bite.

It was a traditional Thanksgiving dinner, turkey and dressing, sweet potatoes and cranberry sauce, pumpkin pie. I was so hungry after a long hard week that I don't think I really tasted the food, but the pleasure lay in eating fairly normally. Before the meal was over, Rancek stood up.

"As soon as the meal is over, you men will go to the chapel where you will give proper thanks for being in this Army on this glorious last Thanksgiving of the 1960s. You will pay respect, and you will think seriously about what the future holds for you. And while you're there, look at the man on your right and then the man on your left. When we're done here twenty-one weeks from now, one of them won't be there. Now on your feet and into the street."

Each battalion area had a small chapel, but we were headed to the main Fort Benning chapel and we were going in trucks. It felt good to have the dress green tunic, for the night air was cold, especially in the back of the truck.

We marched into the chapel and sat quietly in the darkened pews until the chaplain arrived. The first three weeks had been so frantic and stressed that an opportunity for quiet contemplation was a gift. I had long ago left my mother's church and the trappings of formal religion, but the chapel held an atmosphere that spoke, especially in the silence. On the outside, even in church, people whisper and break the silence, but in here, no one moved.

Just as I began to get fully into the spirit of the moment, the chaplain took the podium. He was a short, pot-bellied man, almost completely bald except for a few short blond hairs that showed when he stood smiling under the light. He looked out at us and then stepped to the microphone.

"Yes, men, it is a time to give thanks. You must give thanks to the Lord for what you got. Think of all that God has given you that is good. Think of the opportunity you have to serve your country in this time of war. You aren't like those long-haired hippies protesting in the streets. You know that God has told you to fight for your country. You has taken the Lord's purpose, and some of you will soon be able to lead men in firefights against the enemies of God in Vetnam. You should give thanks for that opportunity on this day. You should thank your TAC officers for working to git your stuff together. Damn right you should. And you should thank your forefathers for fighting and dying to give you the right to fight and die. It is a glorious calling, the calling to arms."

Whatever contemplative feelings I had soon disappeared listening to the little hypocrite. He mouthed all the usual clichés, throwing in a few "damns" and "hells" to make us see he was a regular guy, I guess. But his ignorance made me pull back inside myself. I continued to listen, but the sense of openness that the chapel had initially created disappeared like blown smoke.

"Just days ago in our wonderful nation's capital, Washington, D.C., 250,000 aided and abetted our enemies by marching against our government and our military. Those traitorous left-wing, godless people are the scum of the earth. They believe in free love and smoking dope. Hepped up on that damn psychedelic music, they stomp and disrespect the flag. Those hippie, dippy, yippie dregs do not know duty, honor, and country the way you do. They will be the lost of the earth, while you will glory in the grace you will receive for your dedication.

"And so now, men, I invite you to join me as we bow our heads to pray. 'Dear Lord, we are gathered here in the shadows of the great Infantry Hall on this Thanksgiving day nineteen hundred and sixty-nine, and we asks thee to bless these young men who are on a mission of learning, a mission to be leaders in the rice paddies of Vetnam as they will do your work against the heathens and the communists, the non-believers. You will be with these men as they take their training, as they learn the spirit of the bayonet. For this great chance, we give thanks oh Lord, and in the name of your great and sacrificed Son, I say to thee oh Lord, in Jesus' name, oh Lord. Amen.'"

It hadn't taken him long to break the quiet of the chapel and send whatever essence that was there scurrying into the dark. I was back in OCS and all those troubled thoughts I was trying to forget rushed back like storm troopers. The only good thing about the crazy pace was that I didn't have much time to ponder what I was doing. It was easier to run from detail to detail, worrying about avoiding demerits and bad ORs than it was to think about the war, about Granddad or Nixon. I didn't want to think.

Marching out to the truck, I began to hum Arlo Guthrie's "Alice's Restaurant." Ever since he'd been at Woodstock last summer, singing "Comin' into Los Angeles, bringin' in a couple of keys," Guthrie had been popular. Guthrie's ballad tells about his draft physical and how his conviction for littering on Thanksgiving placed him with the "mother rapers" and the "father rapers" and kept him out of the draft. Sitting in the cold truck, I remembered my draft physical story about the redneck who stripped down to his socks and, ordered to "bend over and grab your cheeks," dutifully leaned down with his fingers clasped tightly to each side of his nose.

* * * *

Vietnam continued at its deadly pace, despite Nixon's announced withdrawal of 25,000 men. I learned too that the media had reacted strongly to the story of the massacre at My Lai I had seen mentioned in the newspaper earlier. I had seen several references to the small village as I walked by the newspaper racks. By reading a few lines over the days, I had discovered that the attack had taken place at least a year earlier and was just now coming to light. I still found it unusual that there seemed to be such a reaction. At Fort Benning everybody took those actions as a matter of course.

It was a surprise, then, to get a letter from Granddad, a man who cared about as little for the news as any man I knew. Granddad had a cowboy's love of succinctness, so his letters were always only about a page. He only knew about commas, and he disdained paragraphs. After morning mail call on a day we went to the rifle range to practice with the M-16, I held onto the letter until I could get into a latrine, where I opened it and read:

Fall '69

Dear Jeff,

*All goes about the same here, got the cotton in on time, and
the cows are still fat.*

*Winnie that old cow you used to help me with is about to calf,
I wish you was here to help me with her again. I'm getting too
old to take care of them cows.*

*Lost that big old Bodark tree out front. Hate to see that old
thing go. Bugs I guess.*

*Been pretty wet fall here. Lots of rain slows me down, I feel it
in my elbow, I have a hard time turning left in that old pickup with my elbow, I'd get me a knob except it'd look like a
niggers truck.*

*That old dog got screw worms, I havent seen any in a long
time, they almost ate his guts out before I found they was
there. He'll be alright, maybe.*

*Well, that's about all. Take care of yourself. I dont like to hear
about people killing women and children. I remember seeing a
John Wayne picture once where that happend to the Indians.
You tell them majors and captains that aint right.*

Love, Granddad

*Ps That old horse needs you to ride him when you get home
over xmas, hes ornery.*

Granddad's reference to the Indians puzzled me at first. I'd grown up
watching western movies with Granddad. Randolph Scott had always

been Granddad's favorite actor, and throughout the fifties Scott made a number of good movies we went to together. Granddad especially liked to go to drive-ins on summer nights. He'd fix up a big bag of popcorn beforehand, put some beer and Cokes (for me) in the cooler, and we'd back into our spot at the drive-in. Later we would take folding lounge chairs and sit on them to watch the movies (almost always double features), but in the fifties we sat on the lowered tailgate of the pickup (until I got tired and rolled up in a moth-eaten, olive-drab, wool blanket left from Granddad's WWI days).

In those early days of the fifties, the Indians were always the bad guys. They were blood-thirsty savages that sneaked in on cat's paws and slit the throats of unsuspecting frontiersmen and carried off their screaming women and children into the evil night. Many a night, I would pull the blanket up to my eyes and watch with trembling limbs as made-up white actors portrayed the ultimate embodiments of evil.

So it seemed odd that Granddad would seem sympathetic to the Indians until I recalled seeing a John Wayne double feature once. The first show was *Stagecoach*, and the second was *The Searchers*. It was in *The Searchers* that John Wayne played an ex-Civil War officer who returned home just before his brother's family was killed by Comanches and his niece kidnapped. The Duke spent years searching for her, and during that time he became as ruthless and savage as the Indians had ever been. He adopted their own techniques, such as shooting out the eyes of corpses so they couldn't go to the happy hunting ground and scalping the dead. In one of the scenes the whites stormed into an Indian camp and mowed down the women and children. Granddad had gotten real upset with that scene, and that must have been what his letter referred to.

In fact, John Wayne references flowered around OCS. A good many of the Vietnam returnees talked about being in Indian Territory and seemed to think of the Vietnamese as the Indians had been portrayed in old westerns and themselves being the heroes in movies. It seemed to have been a way to distance themselves from their experiences. They could look upon what they were doing as happening to someone else, to a character in a movie.

Granddad's reference to Christmas in his letter reminded me of another of the many unknowns about OCS. When I was at Fort Polk at an OCS orientation, I asked if we would get any Christmas break, and the officer there, a recent OCS graduate, said he had heard that there was a break for the classes that lasted over Christmas. He wasn't sure because he hadn't been there during the holidays. When I tried to find out after I got to Benning, I got the usual "yours is not to question" response. So we were in the dark until after Thanksgiving. I'm sure they wanted to heighten the tension and uncertainty as long as possible, but with Christmas three weeks away, I think they decided we had to be making arrangements. So the word began to spread that we'd get off for Christmas, but how long, beginning-when details floated on rumors. Finally, at an early morning company formation before breakfast, the first sergeant came out and casually announced that we'd get to leave on 19 December, classes would resume as usual on the morning of 5 January 1970, and we would each get five minutes at the phones that night to call someone to pick us up or to get someone to make flight arrangements.

The reality of a two-week Christmas break began to sink in during the classes on tactics that day. I would have to call my mother in Mariposa so she could get my bother Jim to make my arrangements. Mother had worked hard in Messer's Drug Store ever since my father died, but she had no experience making plane reservations. Jim hadn't flown much either, but he'd had to travel for the National Guard and knew what to do. The sudden reality of a break in three weeks instead of having to go straight through for twenty-one more weeks felt like winning the lottery.

Calling home that night, like almost everything in OCS, was a long game of waiting. The TACs had assigned the designated platoon leaders to be in charge of supervising the phone calls. Tempers were always short anyway, but the emphasis on giving orders and being leaders led to quick confrontations. The guys designated to be in charge of something often leapt to telling people what to do with heavy-handed gusto. We lined up by platoon at the row of pay phones in the battalion area. Ruzinski, a round-headed, round-shouldered, round-bodied Nebraskan, was our platoon sergeant for that week. Usually quiet, he transformed into a martinet once he put the silver sergeant's insignia on his collar.

"All right, Deuce Platoon, make it snappy. I'm timing you. You get five minutes at the phone so you better make it good," he bellowed.

"Ease off, Ruzinski," someone said. "If the line's busy or something, you may have to cut us some slack."

"Shut the lip," Ruzinski said, even though he knew without any TAC officers around, he didn't have much real authority. Still, he stood at the phones looking at his watch while everyone called. Some of the guys were calling their wives, and they wanted some privacy while they called, but Ruzinski would have none of it. We'd gotten to phone home briefly soon after we arrived, but we hadn't had phone privileges since.

I was lucky and got Mother on the first try. She was surprised to hear from me and even more surprised to learn that I'd get to come home for Christmas. She had to find something to write on, and Ruzinski yelled at me when he saw me standing and not talking.

"Tell Granddad I want to go fishing when I'm there."

"Oh, he'll be glad to take you fishing. You better get ready to ride that old horse. He keeps saying he needs to get rid of him since he can't ride Chief Bowles now."

"I can't think of anything else I'd rather do."

"Well, we keep thinking of you and praying that you will be safe. I sure wish this war would end, and I think President Nixon will do what's right."

I didn't want to talk with her about the war; besides, my time was up. My head was spinning with thoughts of going home, fishing with Granddad, and riding Chief Bowles.

Nine

Candy Raid

So put down your books and pick up a gun,
We're gonna have a whole lot of fun.
—"I Feel Like I'm Fixin' to Die Rag"
—Country Joe and the Fish

After the top sergeant's announcement and the night of calling home and being focused on the Christmas break, when the reality sank in that we still had three weeks to go before leave, the whole company sagged like a punctured blimp. I began thinking that I could take anything for three weeks to make it to that recess, but for some of the guys, thinking about going home pushed them over the edge.

The next week was something called the Leadership Reaction Course. We were split up into groups and assigned to do various difficult and often ridiculous tasks with one person assigned as the leader for that task. We did things like moving a barrel filled with water from the ground to a platform twelve feet up or taking a table apart and reconstructing it in a different shape. All of the tasks required some clear planning and group work, with nothing particularly a military objective. Each goal could be accomplished if you had the time to think it through, but in each case you had just less than enough time. The point was to see how people reacted under stress, and it took almost all week for everyone in the company to have a turn as leader. The TACs roamed the course, scouring the place looking for weak leaders. They knew this assignment would weed out those who floundered under pressure.

I was on the first day, before anyone knew much about what was going on, and my group caught the task of moving the water barrel. I listened to suggestions from my people, and we got the thing hoisted about halfway up before the time ran out. It wasn't particularly stressful or successful, but I made it through. As each day wore on, the guys who hadn't yet been tapped as a leader had time to chafe, fret, and get completely psyched out.

Thursday night the anxiety level rose and produced a casualty. I was on guard duty from midnight to 0200, which meant simply that I had to get up, get dressed, sign in at the guard station, check to make sure everyone was accounted for, do a couple of fire watches, and wake up the guy who was on duty next. Guard duty was routine, disruptive, but usually insignificant. Depending on how the duty roster went, I caught it for a couple of hours about every third night.

It wasn't unusual to find guys out of bed. The latrine was almost always busy all night, but I usually kept a count of the empty bunks and matched the number with the guys in the latrine. On my first run-through I found six guys out of their bunks, but when I got to the latrine, I only found five men. I looked under the stalls but still could only account for five.

I didn't think much about it, figuring I'd simply made a mistake in my count. On the second pass, Sugarman had gone back to his bunk, so I had only five empty bunks. When I got to the latrine, I counted four men. This time I was getting worried. I didn't want to be on duty when someone sneaked off, so I decided to go back through and find out who was missing. In the latrine were Trotter, Garcia, Livingston, and Shrode. The fifth bunk was Donaldson's, three doors down and across the hall from my room.

"Where's Donaldson?" I asked the latrine crowd, but no one had seen him.

I began to worry and wondered what to do. No one was supposed to leave the platoon area after lights out, but the guy on guard duty could check with the guards on duty at another platoon, or he could check in with the candidate who was on "CQ" for the night in the first sergeant's office. CQ (charge of quarters) duty meant that someone was in charge at night to call the company to quarters in case of fire or attack. The assignment was done by roster for four hour shifts.

I went down the long hallway that separated the first from the second platoon. Some guy I didn't know was sitting at the guard table. The name on the front of his T-shirt was so faint in the darkness that I couldn't make it out. I got up close and whispered.

"Hi. I'm Jeff Adams from second platoon, and I'm on guard duty this shift. I can't account for one man. Have you seen anything unusual in the last hour?"

"Klein," he said and reached out his hand. I could see his name stenciled across the front of his T-shirt now. "You know, I thought I saw someone go down the stairs right after I came on duty, but I thought it was the CQ making rounds."

The CQ had to check in with the guards at midnight, so it made sense that Klein might have seen the guy coming around. I hadn't seen the CQ when I took over, though. I thanked Klein and decided to go downstairs to check in with CQ. I even thought that maybe I'd looked at the duty roster wrong; maybe Donaldson had caught CQ duty for that night instead of Silva from the sixth platoon, whose name I remembered seeing.

But when I got downstairs, there was Silva sitting at top's desk, wearing the CQ armband.

"Hi, Silva. I'm on guard duty in the second platoon this shift, and I can't account for one of my guys and wondered if you knew anything about Donaldson. Is he signed out for some reason? Or maybe on sick call and in the infirmary for the night?"

"Not that I know of. Let's look at the book." Silva pulled out the sign-out book. Almost nobody had gotten permission to sign out yet. One guy had to go home for a funeral during the second week, and his name appeared in the book, but other than that, the book for "Class 10-70" was clear. The sick-call list was always long for the morning, but very few guys ever got to stay overnight, as much as they might want to malinger for a while.

Silva looked over the list for sick call for the morning, tracing each name with his finger.

"No, I don't see Donaldson's name here, and no one is assigned to the infirmary for the night. Where do you think he might be?"

"You got me," I said. Donaldson was one of those guys I barely knew, other than the fact that he was in my platoon. He was a heavyset guy from Minnesota. I never sat with him at chow because he'd been ordered to sit at the "Fat Man's Table" from the first week. Anybody who was overweight according to the Army's weight tables had to sit and eat at the fat-man's table each meal, which meant no extra bread, no dessert, and smaller servings. Each candidate designated a "fat man" had to tell the servers in the line, yelling out "Fat Man's meal, please" to the civilian servers. Donaldson hadn't yet been assigned to any particularly visible leadership roles either, so he was like a number of the others in the company, simply another name and body.

"Shit," said Silva, realizing that as the CQ, he was in charge and if somebody had gone AWOL, he would have to call the MPs and maybe even Captain Lederer.

I was perfectly willing to let him take over. I had done my job. I didn't want to get Donaldson in trouble, but I knew if he turned up missing the next morning, everyone on guard duty for the night would be accountable.

"Let's take a turn around the barracks and see if we can find out anything," Silva suggested. So we went out the front door and around the barracks looking to see if there was any indication of what had happened to Donaldson.

It was a dark, starry Georgia night, crisp and cool out in our T-shirts, but it didn't take us long until we were back to the front door.

"Let's go back in and decide what to do," Silva indicated, motioning me to follow him.

"I hate to call the CO," he said. "What do you think?"

"I don't know. Is there some kind of book of procedures for the CQ?" I asked.

"Yeah. Good idea. Let's take a look."

Silva got the SOP manual for CQ duty and read, "In the event of a serious circumstance, notify the tactical officer in charge of the platoon involved. If an event occurs that affects the entire company, notify the commanding officer or the executive officer."

"Your TAC is Rancek, isn't it?"

"That's right. Are you going to call him?"

"Yeah, I think that's what we should do first. Do you want to do it?"

"No, no, not me," I said quickly. "Besides, you're CQ; it's your job."

"Yeah, I guess you're right," said Silva, looking up Rancek's phone number in the book. He dialed it, and it seemed like it rang for minutes before anyone answered. Silva identified himself and began explaining, then stopped.

"Yes, sir. I'm sure you're sleeping and don't want to be bothered, but I'm just following the CQ SOP book, and Donaldson is from your platoon."

He paused, then went on, "Yes, sir, we've checked the latrine and around the barracks, the obvious places." Another pause.

"No, sir. We haven't looked anywhere else. But we will go look at the dayroom and the mess hall now. Yes, sir, we'll see you shortly."

Silva hung up and looked at me. "Boy, did he sound pissed. He's on his way, but he wants us to look around inside before he gets here."

"All right," I said. "Maybe I should go look at his room again before we look anywhere else."

I went back to the platoon. The latrine was empty and so was Donaldson's bunk.

I hustled back to the CQ. "No luck," I said to Silva.

"Let's go look around," he said, grabbing a big flashlight from the desk.

We went down through the dayroom toward the back entrance to the mess hall. Silva shined the flashlight on the pool table in the dayroom, off limits to candidates, of course, as was the entire dayroom so far. We looked longingly at the TV set for a minute, knowing there probably wasn't anything on this time of night. We moved on through to the mess hall. Silva cut the light and opened the door quietly. We stood and listened. We could hear sounds from the darkened room.

Silva whispered, "Do you know where to turn on the lights?"

"No. Probably on the wall by the door."

We went over by the door, found the switches, and turned them on.

Donaldson sat in the dark at the table where the officers usually sat. In front of him were five or six empty candy bar wrappers and several unopened Butterfingers and Baby Ruths. Looking like a fat rat, Donaldson blinked in the sudden light and tried to hide the empty wrappers. All of the cabinets stood open, where he had obviously searched for something to eat.

"What the hell do you think you're doing?" Silva asked.

"Come on guys, I'm hungry. I haven't gotten anything decent to eat in weeks. I couldn't sleep I was so hungry. These candy bars were the only thing I could find here. Don't turn me in. It's no big deal. Here, I'll clean everything up. You just act like nothing happened, and no one will ever know."

"I'm afraid it's not that simple," I told him.

"Why not? It's no skin off your noses."

"When we couldn't find you, we had to report it."

"Report it? Who to?"

Before we could say anything, Rancek stepped into the mess hall carrying a riding crop that he whacked down on a table so hard it sounded like a gunshot. We all jumped and looked around.

His voice dripping with sarcasm, Rancek spoke directly to Donaldson, "So the fat boy got hungry, did he, and he stole the top sergeant's candy bars."

All three of us jumped to attention. Donaldson's hands were stuffed with the empty wrappers.

"Sir, Candidate Donaldson. I'm sorry, sir. I just got hungry. I promise you it will never happen again."

"Oh, you don't need to promise me that, Former Candidate Donaldson. I know it won't happen again. I'm just not sure what is the appropriate punishment for a gobby fat piece of shit that causes me to have to get up in the middle of the night and leave my warm bed. What do you think I ought to do to you, Former Candidate Donaldson?"

"Sir, Candidate Donaldson. I have not dropped out of the program. I am still a candidate, and I think running some laps around the Airborne track would be an appropriate punishment."

"You just haven't dropped out yet, fat boy, but the night is not over. And I don't feel like going to the track. I want you out in the company area in two minutes, and I want you to start doing pushups until I tell you to quit."

He looked at me and Silva.

"CQ. Get back to your post. Adams, you go out with fat ass here and make sure he does what I've told him. Have him keep count, and if he doesn't do them right, you are to make him. Do you understand?"

"Sir, Candidate Adams. Understood."

I noticed that Rancek was wearing a ragged T-shirt with his name on the front under his fatigue jacket, a leftover from his OCS days, I suspected. Donaldson and I went out the front door, and he started doing his pushups. I felt awful for him, humiliating himself like that, but when he tried to go all the way to the ground and rest between his pushups, I spoke sharply to him, trying to keep from yelling in the night air.

"C'mon, Donaldson. Keep your belly off the ground. Get your butt down. You know what you're supposed to do. You better do them right. Rancek will be out here any minute."

Donaldson kept at it, but it was clear that he was trying to goldbrick until Rancek got out. His count at twenty-five, he was clearly struggling when Rancek came out.

"All right, Adams, back to your post now. I'm going to see that this lardass gets what he deserves. Get that butt down. Speed it up, Donaldson."

Just as I turned to go, Donaldson spoke up. "Sir, I think I'm going to be sick."

But Rancek would have none of that. "Faster you gross gob of flab."

I walked back to the doorway into the second platoon. Behind me I heard Donaldson begin throwing up on the company area. His heaves echoed off the walls of 59th Company and followed me as I walked inside to wake up Lewis, the next scheduled guard.

I sat in my bunk in the dark and took off my boots, torn between disgust and pity for Donaldson. It was an awful, upside-down world, where men could feel compelled to steal candy bars and others could look at them with contempt.

I was sure that Donaldson would be sitting at the drop table and not at the fat man's table tomorrow. And that meant that he, like almost all of the others, would be on their way to Vietnam as soon as they finished the required six weeks of Infantry training and three weeks in Casual Company. They shipped out, that is, unless they went AWOL or to jail.

Ten

The Spirit of the Bayonet

He ain't heavy, he's my brother.
—The Hollies

The next few days dragged by as we all were focused on leaving for Christmas. The TACs seemed almost as distracted as we were. Our training classes were fairly routine—PT, weapons training (M-60 machine gun), a couple of classes on military justice. But then we had bayonet training.

I had had classes on bayonet training in basic and AIT at Fort Polk, but no one there seemed to take it seriously. Here, though, they did. At first, I couldn't quite figure out why. Bayonet fighting seemed unnecessary for the kind of jungle conflict in Vietnam. "Fix Bayonets!" "Charge!" The whole idea of duking it out with a twelve-inch bayonet on some level plain seemed ridiculous for Vietnam, a holdover from the Civil War, San Juan Hill, or Normandy, and far, far away from the Gulf of Tonkin, Tet, Khe Sanh, and Hamburger Hill. Still, bayonet training took a significant period of training time in OCS.

I decided that it wasn't the need to understand the principle of fighting with bayonets. Instead, bayonet training took on a level of symbolism that the Army wanted to stress. It also became another flash point for observing men under physical stress.

The symbolism was central and repeated whenever troops began formal training. After pairing off with an opponent, everyone put on wire mesh face masks and leather crotch protectors fastened over the top of our fatigue pants. But instead of actually using bayonets, we used pugil sticks, which were supposed to teach the basic movements of "parry and thrust" without the actual danger of killing someone. At the beginning of each exercise, in response to the trainer's question, "What is the spirit of the bayonet?" we had to yell, "To kill! To kill!"

On one level, it was absurdly humorous to step back from the training and look at the whole thing from outside. The sight of over 200 men wearing these strange masks and crotch protectors and carrying rifle-length sticks with padded ends was comic, a ridiculous ballet. We looked like one-eyed, magnified ants carrying stingers rather than having them affixed. But if you're inside the ant colony instead of outside the jar, everything that happens is heightened, accentuated, pointed. And we were definitely inside the jar.

I knew from my Fort Polk days that the best way to make it through was to be a good actor and to have a partner who understood that this was a dumb show. Yell loud, thrust vigorously, fall convincingly. It should be like the World Wrestling Federation, Gorgeous George in pantomime. So when it came time to pair up, you ought to get with someone you knew was theatrical enough to carry off the show believably.

To my horror, when I got in the line to get my gear, Hays was behind me in the line. At that moment Candidate Billy Hays from third platoon was the perfect embodiment of the senselessness and absurdity that bayonet training represented. A college dropout from some unaccredited bible school in the Midwest, Hays was supposed to be a minister of some sort, one of those holy roller sects that believes in trances and speaking in tongues. The first week or two, he started trying to convert his roommates and word got out that Hays was a Jesus freak. The TACs started calling him "Sergeant York," after the war hero Gary Cooper portrayed in an old movie, who had to overcome his religious training to be able to kill the enemy. Hays backed off from preaching, but the Sergeant York label stuck.

But another problem for Hays was his voice. It was high-pitched and effeminate, a terrible handicap in the triple macho military world. And to top off the effect, Hays moved in an effete, mincing way that everybody recognized, true or not, as a sure sign of homosexuality. How he had gotten into OCS was anybody's guess, a recruiter's idea of a cruel joke or a month end, last-minute quota filler.

All this package made Hays a sure nominee for scrutiny. He was inspected and observed, analyzed and examined, dissected like a specimen.

For the first few weeks he had made it through without any major problems. The word had gotten around that Hays was married, so he must be "okay." And he had been smart enough to give up the proselytizing. But when the duty roster came out for the sixth week, this our last week before the Christmas break, Candidate Hays was listed as the student company commander for the week. And now here he stood behind me in the line. I had a fifty-fifty chance of ending up with him as my bayonet training partner.

I looked around to see if I could slip out of line, but it was already set. I tried to count to see if I would end up paired with Hays or Toshiro, a Japanese-American from fifth platoon who was ahead of me in the line, but I couldn't tell exactly until we got closer. By then it would be too late. I thought about trying to ask to go to the latrine, but there was nothing close, and even so the protocol was to return to your place in the line if you went out of it for any reason. So I decided I just had to take my chances and hope that if I ended up with Hays, he would be savvy enough to play out the game for both of our benefit.

The closer we got to the equipment handout station, the clearer it was that it would be me and Hays. The TACs were standing near the training NCO in charge, looking for likely matchups for them to focus on. It wasn't unusual for the TACs to break the normal order. If two candidates had clashed in any way, the bayonet training field was one place that the TACs liked to see ill feelings worked out. So they might designate that Fisher take on Spenser in bayonet drills. The TACs would then circle around the two combatants and urge each on: "Fisher, parry and thrust! Get him in the gut! That's it. Again. Again. Again." The pair caught in this spotlight couldn't brother-in-law each other and act out the game. Each one had to go after the other with fury, and it wasn't unusual for someone to get banged up. A good, hard swack against the side of the head with a pugil stick would ring the ears for hours.

Sure enough, when Hays got to the front of the line, the TACs seemed ready to make him the first candidate to fall under their scrutiny.

"Ho, ho. Well, what do we have here?" Satmonelli began. "I do believe that it's the Reverend Candidate Hays, our splendid weekly leader. What's the spirit of the bayonet, Sergeant York?"

"Sir, Candidate Hays. The spirit of the bayonet is to kill."

"Oh, come on, York. You sound like a pussified wimp. You can do better than that."

"Sir, I am Candidate Hays, and the good Lord gave me this voice."

"Louder, York!"

"Sir, I am Candidate Hays, and the good Lord gave me this voice!"

"No, you dip shit. I want you to tell me the spirit of the bayonet louder, not your friggin' name!"

"To kill!" Hays high pitched voice turned into a shriek when he tried to yell, but Satmonelli kept at it.

"Louder!"

"TO KILL!"

"LOUDER!"

"TO KILL!"

"That's better, Sergeant York. Now let's see who you'll be trying to kill today." Satmonelli turned to me.

"So, it's another Texan. Isn't that right?" he asked, looking at me.

"Sir, Candidate Adams. Yes, sir, I am from Texas."

"Well, Mr. Texan. We expect to see some good parry and thrusting between you and Sergeant York. You know, we've often wondered about York's thrusting, and now we get a chance to watch him. Are you boys ready?"

We took that as the signal to get our things together and move to the exercise field. I hoped the TACs would go on to the next men in line, but as I feared, they followed us. We were to be the first to get the treatment for the day. They trailed us while the rest of the men in line got their equipment and spread out over the field in rows of twenty pairs.

I began tying the leather crotch protector around my hips and adjusting the straps on the mask to fit tightly around my face. Hays' thick glasses caused him trouble with his mask. I wanted to tell him how to act out the falls if I had the chance, so I went over to help him with his mask. When I was close, I tried whispering to him.

"Hays, let's just try to act our way through this," I said quietly while I was working on the mask. "Whenever I thrust at you, you just yell like I've hit you, and I'll do the same thing."

Hays looked at me aghast.

"Oh, no, Candidate Adams. That wouldn't be right."

I knew then that we were both in for trouble. I continued to try to help him adjust the mask and finally told him just to take off the glasses and leave them with his cap, but he told me that he could not see without his glasses.

"You mean you can't even see well enough to see my outline?"

"No, you'd just be a big blur."

"My God, man. How'd you ever get in OCS with vision like that."

"My recruiter helped me pass the test. He said they needed men like me."

I could tell that the mask fit askew over his glasses, but that was the best we could do.

The drill worked so that the whole company followed the NCO in charge in unison. He stood on a platform in the middle of the field and explained how we were to stand toe to toe with our partner and that each one would parry and thrust in alternating practice attempts until we began the full-speed workouts. Even in the quarter-speed drills, though, he began with the required yells.

"Now men, we're going to go through it quarter speed, just for you to get the feel for having something in your hand and visualize yourselves responding to your attacker. So when I yell, 'What is the spirit of the bayonet?' I want you to yell in unison, 'To kill!' And then the man on my right will thrust at the man on my left who will parry the blow and then thrust in return. Do you have it?"

"Yes, sergeant!" we yelled in unison.

"All right, now, what is the spirit of the bayonet?"

And with that we began the slow-motion drill, doing it over and over again. The TACs moved away from Hays and me and walked around the field looking the others over, and I began to hope that they would forget us and become distracted by some other likely pairs. But after several minutes of the beginning drill, Sgt. Baker announced that it was now time for us to work on the drill full speed.

"When I give you the signal, you men commence. Your tactical officers and I will move through and watch your parrying and thrusting. So now, "What is the spirit of the bayonet?"

Hays and I were standing almost toe to toe, pugil sticks in hand. "To kill!" I yelled, and as Hays thrust at me with the padded end of his stick, I parried it aside and immediately thumped the side of his mask. As the mask slid around knocking his glasses further askew, I thrust the padded "bayonet" end of the stick into his gut, knocking the wind out of him. Ireland, Martin, and Satmonelli came over and circled around him.

"Hays here has forgotten that he's supposed to be like Sergeant York, feared killer," said Ireland. "Let's see you men line up again."

Hays was trying to adjust the mask over his glasses, but he still had the same problem, and as soon as we started the drill again, I did the same thing. I could tell this was no contest. I had had several sessions with these drills before, enough to know something about the general way to move, but Hays was still trying to get his bearings, and his skewed glasses put him at a distinct disadvantage. Almost every time we started, Hays' mask would work his glasses down or sideways so that he couldn't see. I wanted to tell him again that we should just playact, but I knew it would do no good, and I was going to end up beating Hays silly.

Sure enough, the TACs continued to have us line up and begin again. I decided to try to let Hays have a few chances to take a shot at me, so when he thrust at me, I tried to act like I was working against him so that he could get a touch, but when he realized that I hadn't knocked his stick aside, he whacked me against the side of my head and then stabbed the padded end of the stick into the front of my mask so hard that it knocked me backwards, and I dropped my stick.

"Now, that's it, York," Satmonelli said. "We knew you could do it." And to me, "Little Miss Texas, I think you're dead. You're on your ass without your bayonet."

Standing, I grabbed my stick and decided that I would do Hays no more favors.

Sgt. Baker told us to take a break in place for five minutes. I tightened my mask and tried to look at Hays. He seemed lost somehow. He didn't even try to adjust the mask. When the break was up and we began again, I showed Hays no quarter, battering him across the side of the head and deep into his stomach. Almost without realizing it, whenever Baker called out his beginning question, I screamed out my response and attacked

Hays furiously, hitting him again and again. Beneath his crooked glasses, his nose began to bleed, blood running down his face and under the mask, wiping across his cheeks and chin, giving him an eerie look.

The TACs got more and more interested in our pas de deux, urging me on and screaming at Hays to protect himself and counterattack. But he seemed to lose more and more steam. The blood dripped down on the three silver circles that he wore on his collar, the insignia for the student company commander. He lost energy, and he didn't even raise his stick much higher than his waist.

Lt. Martin seemed disgusted with him.

"Hays," he said, calling him by his name instead of by the nickname, "You are the sorriest specimen of a man that I have seen out here. What made you think you had the stuff to be a leader of men?"

Hays, glassy-eyed, offered no protests. With that, the TACs moved to a different part of the field, while Hays and I went through the final motions. It seemed clear that he was broken. He would have to try to get enough sense of himself together to lead the company back to the barracks after this, but I was sure that Hays would be one of the ones who wouldn't return after Christmas, and I bore some of the responsibility.

Eleven

Leaving on a Jet Plane

Don't know when I'll be home again.
—John Denver

The rest of that week after bayonet drill passed in a fog. Hays was still the student company commander, but it was clear to everyone but him that he was finished, sooner rather than later probably. He tried to keep up a good front, but his weak voice deteriorated as the week wore on. Whenever he tried to call the company to attention, he screeched like a peahen. Floating through the uneasy nights, I began to see him in my dreams, his face bleeding and bloated. I could drive it away only by concentrating on the break.

Throughout that last week, one song played through my head like a stuck record. All I heard was "Leavin' on a Jet Plane." I found myself looking to the sky, thinking about escape. And soon enough it came. The Friday afternoon we got back early so we could square away the barracks. We had to lock away all of the gear that was normally displayed and pack our duffel bags with enough to get us home. As soon as 1700 hours came, the earliest anyone could check out, guys raced to the top sergeant's desk, married guys whose wives had driven in to pick them up, anyone who lived close enough to catch a ride somewhere. Most of us were on a bus to Atlanta to catch a plane, and it didn't leave until 7 P.M., so we let the others sign out first. I slept most of the way there, and as much as I had thought about the moment of liftoff on that flight home, I can barely remember it. We just took off into that dark night, and before long I was back home in Mariposa, almost as if I had never left except when I looked at myself in the mirror and saw my skinned head. Just so we wouldn't forget and so anyone who saw us would know, too, the TACs had run us through the barbershop right before we returned to the barracks on Friday. It was the decade of long-hair, from the Beatles to the Cowsills. "Give me a head with hair, long beautiful hair, shining, gleaming, streaming, flaxen, waxen" and I was buzzed to the skin.

But I was home, and Texas never looked so good. All I wanted to do for the first few days was nothing—to lie around and sleep. Some of my friends from high school were around, the ones like Billy Kennedy who'd gotten lucky and failed his draft physical or Tony Varva who'd gotten married early and had kids. I wasn't sure why, but I didn't want to see them. Others already had their orders and were overseas.

Mother, as usual, wanted to be sure that she talked to me about religion and kept trying to get me to go to church with her, and, as usual, I resisted. She was firm in her religious beliefs, and they had helped her deal with the hardships of living through the Depression and losing my dad. But I was beginning to think that her religion didn't help much in the face of Vietnam. Granddad had moved into town to stay with Mother two years before, and he always took my side when Mother got on me about going to church. Soon Granddad arranged for us to go out to his ranch to ride Chief Bowles and to go fishing in a stock tank at Mr. McIntyre's place, one of his friends.

The day began with a beautiful Texas morning, and just like when I was a kid, I always looked forward to visiting my grandfather out at the ranch. I would help feed the cows, skip rocks on the pond, and chase the wild cats that hung around the barn waiting for the rats to sneak in after the sweetened feed. We weren't going to spend much time at the pasture this time, though. Granddad at eighty-two had decided to get rid of his cattle. He had sold them all, save two.

"I'm jest about out of the cattle business," he said. "All that's left is them two wild steers out at Old Man McIntyre's." Granddad called him "Old Man" even though McIntyre was twenty years younger because Mac had had a series of heart attacks and was very feeble.

"That old man should've never bought them wild steers. He's too old to be messin' with 'em anymore, and he got took on the deal. He was jest about ready to get shed of 'em any way he could, so I give him $50 apiece for 'em. They're nice-looking steers; I'll get $300 for 'em at the auction."

It was for Granddad a typical act. He always seemed torn in two directions at once. On the one hand he was a very generous person, especially toward people in need. Old people, kids, blacks, Mexicans—anyone who Granddad thought needed help—could turn to Granddad, that's what everybody called him. At the same time, though, he was an old horse trader who would rather lose a leg than lose a dollar. I had seen him turn away from buying a pickup he really wanted once because he couldn't get the dealer to come down $5 off the asking price.

"Gol-darn you, you can drive that Ford up yore rear gate!" he blustered, red-faced and slobbering spit down the corners of his mouth. As soon as we were out the door, he winked at me and said, "Hot-damn, you really gotta jew 'em down these days."

He bought that car the next week for $25 less than the first offer.

So when he bought those wild steers, he saw himself doing Old Man McIntyre a favor and making a good deal at the same time. The trouble was that for him to make a decent profit, he had to round up the steers without having to pay too much for the effort.

That's where I came in.

When the December sun rose and beamed down its bright rays, Granddad suggested that we go out and fish in McIntyre's tank before going to his pasture for me to ride.

"That old man seldom gits out there these days, and there's some nice crappie, perch, bass, and catfish in there. We can have a fine time."

I was delighted, of course, and I said sure. OCS seemed far away, and this December day was warm and bright, almost springlike. It wasn't until we had loaded his pickup with the fishing poles (Granddad never fished with rod and reel) and the liver Granddad had salvaged from his table scraps and were climbing into the truck that Granddad mentioned what else he had in mind. I should have recognized the motive right away, but I had gotten rusty being away from home so long.

"You and me can run them cows up after we git through fishin'," he suggested.

* * * *

Old Man McIntyre lived several miles outside of Mariposa near a small town called Pecan Grove off one of Texas' many narrow farm-to-market roads. This one was quite familiar to me because it was the local drag strip when I was a crew-cut adolescent, and it was a nightly macho ritual to pull up to someone at a red light in town and sneer, "You think you're bad, huh? Well, let's take 'em out to Pecan Grove." It had replaced the walk down in the street as the confrontation of choice in the 1950s West. As we drove down the old stretch of road, I could see no lines to indicate the beginning and ending of the quarter mile as it had been five to ten years ago. No screaming V-8's with solid lifters, three deuces, and four-on-the-floor dueled in these Vietnam-laden nights.

We drove past the town, and Granddad waved at a couple of old codgers in overalls sitting chewing the fat and tobacco on the porch of the store. On down the road we bumped over a cattle guard and pulled into McIntyre's drive to be greeted by a pack of mangy hounds near a row of perfectly aligned pear trees.

"Shut up! Git the hell back!" Granddad yelled.

At the end of the row of pear trees stood a twisted old live oak. Its massive trunk split into two branches that curved back down and touched the ground.

The hounds grew quiet as McIntyre shuffled up, "Shut up, easy now, you mangy dogs, damn it. You sound like a buncha politicians. Howdy, Granddad, Jeff."

"Good mornin', Mr. Mac. We appreciate you lettin' us come out here to fish. Young Jeff here ain't been fishin' since he got drafted. I told him he'll for sure catch somethin' out of your tank."

"You betcha he will," responded McIntyre, rubbing one of his blue tick hounds behind the ear. "I ain't been able to get down there much and them bass are hungrier than the fleas on ol' Hank here."

McIntyre's pond had begun as a rectangular, functional stock tank when it was dug as a WPA project in the depression. But now it had expanded at one end so it looked like a boot. The boot tip slipped deep into a brushy area covered with yaupon, mesquite, and skunk bush braided together with briars. Only a few cattle trails broke the density of the brush. Granddad had persuaded McIntyre to join us and the old man led us into the underbrush where the fishing was supposed to be the best. We baited our hooks, settled in, and sat on the bank waiting for the first bite.

"Mac, this is sure peaceful out here. I bet you got folks beatin' your door down tryin' to beat you outta of the place."

"Naw, Granddad. I ain't had too many offers here. I did git a bite from the Northeastern Fruit Company a while back. That was a humdinger of an offer all right, but I jest couldn't see it."

"How much they offer, a bunch?"

"Well, yes they did. I cain't even recollect now the exact figger, but it was nice. The trouble was they wanted me to stay here as the farm manager. You see, this place grows nice pears, and they wanted to extend that little orchard up there and make the whole place into a pear orchard."

"That sounds right nice."

"Oh, I suppose so. But they sent this young college feller down from New York. He come down here and wandered around for a few days, testin' the soil, drawin' little maps of the place, and I don't know what all. Well, as soon as he gits through with his figgerin' he shows me his plan. He wants to tear down the barn, plow up all my cow pastures, cut down that ole live oak and all Mrs. McIntyre's—God rest her soul—rosebushes, and plant pear trees just by God ever'where. I just couldn't see myself watchin' the place cut up like that, you know. It ain't much, but what's here I've taken care of and watched it grow into what it is. It'd be fine if I didn't have to watch it disappear. If I could sell it and git away from it, I would. But I cain't stay and watch it happen."

"Aw, hell, Mac, that wouldn't be much work."

"Naw, naw, it wouldn't, but that's not all. In pear pickin' time, they would bring in a load a wetbacks from the Valley, and I'd a had to put 'em up. I might let 'em cut down Mrs. Mac's rosebushes, but there ain't no way I could put up with them Meskins."

"Now you got a point there," Granddad agreed.

For as helpful and concerned about others as Granddad was, he had a blindness about races in a truly democratic fashion. He disparaged them all equally, with derogatory names like "Polacks," "Bohunks," "Spics," and "niggers." When Sammy Davis, Jr., one of the few black performers seen much on television, appeared, Granddad would turn off the television in a fit of frothy cussing. Before Martin Luther King, Jr., was assassinated, his face on the news also worked up his lather, but he wouldn't turn off the TV. He'd just say, "There's ol' Martin Luther Coon raisin' hell again."

At the same time, Granddad's regular companion for the last fifteen years had been a black man called Pistol, because his name was Pete, I think. Pistol was mildly retarded, and he had to be told everything to do. Granddad took care of him in a grudging, condescending way: "Damn, that boy is stupid," he would cuss. Then he would have Pistol mow his yard, cut the hedge, and work around the ranch. In turn Granddad gave Pistol pocket change and meals. Pistol would come to the back door, and Granddad would give him leftovers on a plastic plate and cup that Granddad kept just for Pistol. When Pistol got old enough to take a full-time job, Granddad used his connections to get Pistol a job on the trash truck, a lousy job to be sure, but one Pistol could never have gotten on his own. Pistol needed someone to take care of him; Granddad needed someone to fulfill his racist stereotypes. As much as Granddad talked about the virtue of segregation, he spent much of his time with a black man.

When McIntyre said something about race, I tried to change the subject: "Mr. McIntyre, I see there are some plans for a new development out here. I saw a sign down the road that says, 'Coming Soon, Pecan Grove Estates.' Anybody contacted you about that?"

"Well, some feller did come by here and talked to me about the high ground up yonder. He didn't seem to be much interested in most of my land, said somethin' about a 'flood plain.' And I said, hell, when it comes one of our spring gully washers around here, it jest plain floods all right." He chuckled and added, "But, hell, I wouldn't want to see that nice pastureland over there turned into one of them boxy-lookin' developments. Who wants a buncha goddamn insurance men and bankers from Dallas movin' in?"

Granddad livened up. "Mac, if I was you, I'd sell this here place in a minute. You oughta sell and git what you can out of it. Ain't no use in you keepin' it now. You're gittin' old, and hell, it's progress. I been workin' hard for progress almost all my life and this is progress."

"Ain't no money for a small rancher these days," McIntyre countered. "Those boogers in the guv'ment got thangs so screwed up that a man damned near got to pay for the privilege of keepin' cows instead of gittin' money for doin' it."

I could see Granddad's face brighten and his eyes glaze a bit, and I knew that he and McIntyre were off on another anti-government routine for a while. Granddad had been a union man with the railroad for twenty years before he quit and went back to ranching, but he sang the praises of rugged individualism with a loud, clear voice.

I tried to head them off again. "Granddad, here you're talking about how you wanted to get back to the green world of nature, but just a few minute ago you were advising Mr. McIntyre to sell his land to developers. How do you square that?"

Granddad bent down and picked up a stick, reached in his pocket, and pulled out a cheap little pocketknife that he got after he gave me his good Case knife and started whittling before he answered. "Lemme make myself clear. There's a heap of difference between dreamin' and doin'. I was born in 1899, served in Dubya Dubya I, then got me a job with the Sufferin' Pacific Railway Company. I got old watchin' John Wayne and Randolph Scott play cowboys. They helped me do some dreamin'. But I worked for the railroad. Back in the old days I helped 'em lay track into some of the most forlorn, God-forsaken spots in West Texas. Now that was progress. People started makin' money who hadn't never had no better shirts than flour-sack makeovers.

"So I ain't gonna advise nobody like Mr. McIntyre to stand in the way of progress. That's what made this country great. I sure done my share of dreamin' about the wide-open spaces, but I also made my money closin' 'em up when I needed to. That's all I'm sayin'."

After a moment, thinking about what he'd just said about progress, he started again. "I've thought the century was headed in an OK direction a good while now, but the war in Vetnam has got me mixed up. I've always supported my country when the chips were down. I always defended our boy Lyndon, despite what he did for the niggers, because he said we had to stop them commies right there in their tracks. But this stuff I'm readin' about our boys goin' in and killin' women and children makes me think that somethin' ain't right. I fought at Belleau Wood and never saw no American boy kill no woman or child on purpose. Somethin's happened that just throws this whole thing awack."

We sat there quietly then, listening to the slap of the water on the weathered roots along the bank, the rhythmic slice of Granddad's knife, the occasional tapping of a woodpecker, and the quiet call of quail ("Listen to 'em," Granddad noted, "'Bob White, Bob White, Bob White.'") The day wore on, and the sun got low.

We fished longer with no success. Finally Granddad said, "Well I guess them fish just turned in early today. I think we should load up."

We agreed, packed our gear, and headed for the pickup. Overhead the sky darkened quickly, as it often does late in Texas some afternoons. I heard the rumble of distant thunder as Granddad said, "Now let's just head down there and turn them steers up to the barn so's I can take 'em to auction tomorrow."

I had hoped he'd forgotten those steers, ready as I was to go ride Chief Bowles, but I should have known better. The clouds got darker, the lightning brighter, and the thunder closer.

Turning to me, he said, "Let's you and me just mosey on down along the fence and run 'em up here. Go over and cut us some cedar switches to wave at 'em. That Hereford down there ain't quite so skitterish as that black 'un, and he's a follower. You concentrate on the black and the Hereford'll follow."

As I got the switches, I heard McIntyre say he was wore out and was going to the house to rest. Then Granddad and I walked down the fence line toward the steers. They got wary as we approached.

"Now, you go over there on the other side and we can start walkin' 'em up. Whoo, Whoo, go on now; here we go," Granddad coaxed, slapping the cedar branch against his leg. "C'mon now, up we go."

The steers began to move toward the barn until they got about halfway up the hill. Suddenly, the black one stopped, turned, nostrils flaring, and galloped off the way we came, his tail up squirting cow shit marking his path.

"Git in front of him!" Granddad yelled. "Don't let him through."

I raised my switch and tried to turn him, but he blazed past me. The Hereford followed.

Granddad tried running but stopped after a couple of steps. "We'll git 'em this time," he said, as he started down the path toward them.

As we walked along the fence line, Granddad repeated stern advice all the way, "Now don't you let 'em git through this time. Jest step right in front of 'em, turn 'em." I noticed that the sky was getting darker and darker.

As we approached, the cattle were warier than before, their eyes swelling with fear. I felt a few drops of rain, and just as we came close to the barn near the old live oak tree, I heard what sounded like a small explosion. The two steers took off racing between us.

"Stop 'em, stop 'em, " Granddad yelled, and I jumped in front of the black steer. "Whoa, whoa, baby, slow baby, easy now," I urged, but the steer whooshed by me, its lips dripping slobber and its tail up farting and crapping its way past. I turned in time to see Granddad grab it by the tail and hold on at a fast pace for about thirty yards, his hat falling off, gray hair blowing. Suddenly he let go and pitched over headlong into a ditch.

I raced over. His face was red, his nose bleeding slightly when I got there. He was stunned but got up and said he was all right.

"I'm just tired, " he said. "Git me up to the house."

As I helped him up, it began to rain hard, soaking us both to the skin. When we got to the barn, I noticed smoke coming from the other side, and soon I saw why. The live oak tree was split in two, and the rain was putting out a small fire in one of the tree's darkened branches.

McIntyre came out and helped me get Granddad into the house. Granddad insisted on taking care of the steers.

"Call Buck Teckrus. He'll send a couple of his cowboys out, and they'll git them steers."

"Now, Granddad," McIntyre replied, "ol' Buck'll charge you damn near as much as them steers are worth to send a trailer and cowboys out here."

"I don't care. You call him. I've gotta git rid of 'em now."

We lay Granddad on a cot on the screened-in porch, called Buck, and waited. Granddad's face began to get its normal color back, but he stayed quiet.

"I don't like it," McIntyre whispered to me in the kitchen. "I know I'm too damned old to be out chasin' cattle anymore. That's why I stayed here when y'all went down. But there's that old man—I seen him from up here on the porch—holdin' on to a steer's tail and runnin' a lickety split in a lightnin' storm. A man his age has gotta take care of hisself."

Soon we heard the truck and trailer pull up. I went out to meet the cowboys. There were two young black men wearing baseball caps that said "Pearl" unloading their horses when I walked up.

"Hi," one of the said. "Where are those steers?"

"Down in the pasture," I said pointing. They mounted their horses and headed down to the pasture. Within ten minutes they were back, dragging the steers by ropes. They opened the trailer and urged the steers in using an electric cattle prod. Then they loaded their horses, and I signed their receipt.

"We'll take our fee out of what they bring at auction," the one in charge said, as they got into the truck and drove away.

On the porch, Granddad sat quietly for a few more minutes. His hands, scratched when he fell, lay motionless on his lap. Finally, he shook his head and said, "I'll be damned. Buck's got nigger cowboys."

* * * *

Two days later my leave ended. Two weeks after that mother wrote me at OCS to tell me of Granddad's stroke. He wasn't dead, but his left side was almost paralyzed, and he couldn't speak.

"He's alert, but he can't say what he wants to," she explained. "He tries, but he may want to say 'hello' and it comes out 'open the door.' He'll shake his head, frustrated and try again. It's real sad to see him like this."

Twelve

CQ

Come on mothers, throughout the land,
Pack your boys off to Viet Nam.
—"I Feel Like I'm Fixin' to Die Rag"
—Country Joe and the Fish

I thought Granddad's health was going before I left Texas. Chasing those cows wore him out. He sat in the back yard in the old metal chair he kept out there, but he didn't whittle or anything, just sat and looked up at the sky. I was worried about him, but the dread of having to return to Benning concentrated my thoughts.

Mother was worried about him too. I could see her standing in the kitchen, looking out at him sitting there staring. Sitting in the den, I could hear her softly singing "Onward Christian Soldiers," one of her favorite hymns. I noticed that she suddenly stopped singing, so I walked into the kitchen, and she told me she was praying for him. Then she turned to me and said, "I'm praying for you too, Jeff. I know you're facing a hard road ahead, and I hope you make the right choices."

"I don't know, Mother. I don't think I'm going to have any choices. I just follow orders, Ma'am."

"You always have choices, Son. It may not always seem like it, but there are always choices. You just have to know how to make the right ones. I've always looked to scripture to help me, and I've hoped you'd look there too. It disappoints me deeply that you don't want to try to listen to the Lord now, but I take some consolation from knowing that I've tried to teach you to do and think right all your life, and I hope that one day you'll look into your heart and find those teachings there."

I knew that she was trying to be helpful, and I knew too that she thought her way could provide me some comfort. But when my father was sick while I was young, I prayed for him to recover. When he died, my eleven-year-old mind held it against my mother's god. My granddad had been there for me through it all, and now he sat out back. As much as I wanted to help, my thoughts had to focus on the return to Benning.

The return trip was like a bad movie run backwards as I retraced my route from Love Field in Dallas to Atlanta and another bus to Columbus. The atmosphere at 58th Company was like the first day quadrupled, because the first week back was the beginning of our seventh week, which meant the first week that all of those who had chosen or been forced to drop out could physically move out of the barracks to Casual Company. The ones with mental or physical ailments had already gone, but most of the others like Ferona, who had moved into a part of the barracks set aside for the dropouts who had to finish Infantry training, now came back from the break just to pack up their gear and move across the street.

It didn't surprise me too much that some guys who had seemed to be making it okay chose to drop out once they came back. Living on the outside made it too hard to think about eighteen more weeks of harassment. I saw Hays getting his things together and was surprised, figuring that he was going to have to be forced to drop instead of choosing to. But he must have realized he'd never make it, and I felt guilty when I saw him hauling his duffel bag down to the lineup for the dropouts in the company area.

Before long, the massacre at My Lai had a direct impact on OCS, but it wasn't clear at first. The monthly training schedules for each company were set in advance. Most recruits didn't have any idea of what was supposed to happen two, three or, four weeks ahead, but each one got a new weekly training schedule on Friday night for the events beginning the next Monday.

The monthly schedule was available in the CO's office, posted behind the first sergeant's door. I discovered it when I pulled CQ duty. It was a quiet time to spend alone sitting in the top sergeant's chair, reading, writing, napping (if you could risk it), and making occasional fire watch checks of the company area. Usually things were quiet, not like the night Silva and I found Donaldson in the mess hall.

I spent the early hours of the night doing routine things such as checking the platoon areas for lights out at 2230 and then doing the midnight fire watch check from outside the barracks. It was a cool night and the moon rose beckoningly in the crisp night sky. As I walked in the brisk night air, I wondered about Mother and Granddad and tried to think of good times out at the ranch, riding horses, fishing, and swimming in the tank, but I kept seeing Granddad pitching over in the ditch.

Back in the company area I sat at Sgt. Dooley's desk and tried to read some from my collection of Hemingway stories, but when I tried to read, I found myself getting sleepy. I thought about trying to take a nap but decided not to risk it, especially since Bednartz, who had the second four-hour shift, would be in at 0200. Standard procedure was to stand up and walk around when we got sleepy in classes, so I decided to walk around the room. I tried walking around in the first sergeant's office, but it was cluttered with boxes and chairs. I decided to go into the CO's office, which was big and open, but I felt uncomfortable as soon I set foot inside Cpt. Lederer's office.

When I stepped back into the first sergeant's office, I closed the door leading into the CO's room, and it was then that I saw the next month's duty roster on a nail behind the door. I wasn't particularly interested, because I knew that most of the next month was supposed to be dedicated to map reading classes, but I decided to look over the calendar. The standard classes on leadership, character guidance, and military tactics were there, but one two-hour class in character guidance had been crossed through, and Sgt. Dooley had written "Gen Con" over it.

I tried to figure out what the new class was. Character guidance classes were taught by chaplains, and they were fluff that required neither thought nor energy. They were in Infantry Hall, so it would be warm and comfortable and wouldn't require much effort to get there. The new class was also supposed to be in Infantry Hall, in the same room as the character guidance class, so I knew that it wasn't a class on one of the ranges, but I couldn't think of what "Gen Con" stood for. I tried "General Conference" and "Generator Control," but neither of those sounded right.

Looking over the duty roster passed the time and kept me from falling asleep. Bednartz dragged himself in about ten minutes late. The hardest thing about pulling CQ duty was the loss of time. Most of us had learned that we had to be in bed with the lights out from 2230 to 2300 because that was when the last inspections happened. But after the first few weeks few TACs showed up at night any more. So at 2300 the platoons would again become active as people sneaked into the latrine to write letters, clean their brass, shine their shoes, smoke, and take care of the details that they hadn't been able to during the day. The four hours out for CQ duty meant not only less time for sleep but less time to get everything ready for the next day's inspections. Bednartz had probably stayed up until about 0030 to get ready, so he'd probably had only an hour and a half of sleep, the same amount that I would get after going back to my platoon and getting ready for the next day.

"Say, Bednartz," I asked, "do you have any idea about this new class here on next month's training schedule?"

Bednartz blearily looked at the schedule and shook his head.

"Naw, man, I ain't got no idea. But I don't worry about it neither. I don't even check the daily schedule. I just get ready for anything that comes and let the Army do the thinkin' for me."

"You sound like a great soldier," I said sarcastically. "Don't do too much thinking the next four hours; it might tire you out."

Thirteen

Gen Con

War sucks.
—message on helmet.

I didn't have much time to think about the new class, concentrating on the map reading classes inside and the exercises outside. We all knew that map reading was one of the most important skills an Infantry officer needed. "If you don't know where you are, you're not lost, man; you're dead," one of the sergeants liked to say.

Even the day of the new class, I didn't know what it was about. I asked a couple of other people in my platoon if they knew, and nobody had any idea. Like Bednartz, many of them just let things happen. But it was important to know the day's training schedule beforehand, because it made a difference what we wore and what equipment we took. If all our classes were in Infantry Hall for the day, we could get by with wearing new boots and we could keep our canteens empty (and make the weight we carried less). But if we were going on a map-reading exercise, we needed to have broken-in boots, a full canteen, and an extra pair of socks.

Since the class on "Gen Con" was in Infantry Hall, as were all of the classes that day, it didn't make much of an impact. We jogged over as usual and spent the morning listening to some final lectures about map reading and orienteering, pretty standard stuff that we had spent days on already both in OCS and basic training. As I sat in that last lecture, I kept remembering an old joke that Granddad liked to tell after one of the many times he got lost wandering the countryside. He had the habit of coming in late and telling how he'd been driving some back roads and lost his way. Then he'd tell the joke about the Yankee driving over the back roads of West Texas until he's hopelessly lost. Finally, he sees a house set back off the road, and he drives up to find an old man sitting on the porch. He leans out the window of his car and yells at the old man, "Say, old man, which way is north?" The old man spits tobacco, looks out, and says, "Can't say." The easterner then calls back, "Well, which way is south?" "Don't know," the old man says. "What about east?" the traveler yells. "You got me," the old man says. "Well, what about west?" the now-frustrated easterner yells. The old man gives his usual reply of "Don't know," at which the Yankee explodes, "Old man, you don't know nothing." And the old man says, "Yup, but I ain't lost."

After lunch we jogged back to Infantry Hall for the new class. As I got to the classroom, I could read the sign for the class: "Geneva Convention" taught by "Captain Fosse." We did our usual march-in routine and took our seats. The instructor, Cpt. Fosse, stood toward the back of the podium leaning against the wall. Fosse looked young for a captain or maybe just inexperienced wearing his officer green uniform with no ribbons except for a marksman badge—the lowest level of qualification. He was tall and round-shouldered and had a sly grin on his face. It puzzled me that he had no medals. Most of the captains who taught our classes had spent a tour in Vietnam and had several ribbons they displayed proudly. The officers with none were usually second lieutenants who hadn't yet gotten their orders to go over.

Military classes had a recognizable sameness. All the instructors at Fort Benning had to take a three-week instructor training course, and they had to keep a written lesson plan in a plastic folder at the back of the room. Classes almost always began with a joke and then a two-pronged statement of purpose. The joke was to get the audience's attention, and the purpose statement told them first what they would learn and second what they would be able to do with what they learned at the end of the class. Some teachers were better joke-tellers than others, and it soon became clear that Captain Fosse was one of the better ones. In fact, he didn't tell one joke but a series of jokes. He took a minute before he sauntered up to the microphone. I had been trying to figure out who he reminded me of, but I couldn't until he began to speak, and I realized that it was Huntz Hall of the Bowery Boys. Fosse had the same long-face and rather empty sound-ing voice, but it made him a better joke-teller.

"Welcome to my happy home," began Fosse. "I'm Cpt. Fosse from the Judge Advocate General's Office, and I'll be holding you boys' hands for the next two hours. Seeing the way some of you came in the door, it looked like you were dazed and out-of-sorts, and it reminded me of a story."

We recognized that this was the beginning of the class lecture, so we settled back to listen to the joke before drifting off when the class started.

"Did you hear about the time that the general got upset about not getting his jeep back from the motor pool, so he decided to call personally and get results.

"Well, when he called, he demanded from whoever answered, 'What's going on down there?' And the voice at the other end of the line drawled, 'Well, we got one truck with a busted fuel pump, one with no brakes, and we got that fat-ass general's jeep for a tune up. Man, it's all fucked up.'

"To which the general replied, 'Soldier, this is that fat-ass general, and I demand that you identify yourself.'

"The voice at the other end answered, 'Well, General, we're all fucked up around here, but we ain't that fucked up.' Click,'" Fosse says, as he hangs up an invisible phone.

Fifty-eighth Company erupted in laughter, and that led Fosse into a couple more jokes. Because he was good at it, he didn't stop with the customary one joke, but he went on and the company responded to his humor.

"Did you hear about the private who saluted a jeep? He knew it was General Motors. He later saluted the fan. It was General Electric.

"Do you know what they call Eskimo pussy? Cold cunt."

It was when he tried to shift to the subject of the lecture that he ran into trouble. He didn't give a signal that he was now ready to lecture; he just went from the last joke to his subject.

"Men, I'm here to tell you about the Geneva Convention, and the first thing I want you to know is that you can't kill prisoners."

At that moment the class again erupted in laughter, people slapped each other on the back, clapped their hands together, and roared. Fosse was perplexed. Face red, he held his hands up to quiet the crowd.

"No, no, men. I'm telling you the truth. This isn't a laughing matter.

My job is to acquaint you with the behavior expected of American military fighting men that reflects the expectations of a civilized world. According to the Geneva Convention, you are not supposed to kill prisoners. Prisoners have rights too."

Sounds of "bullshit" and "he doesn't know what he's talking about" zipped through the air.

I could see that Fosse was beginning to get flustered. He again held both hands up and tried to motion us to quiet down, and then he tried to regroup. I could see his eyes searching the room for the TAC officers, but they were all behind him in the viewing room, and nobody came out to help.

"Listen to me, men. I was just recently commissioned after completing law school, and this class is a special class instituted in your training schedule because of recent events abroad. But you must listen to me, and you must understand that each soldier in the United States Army has a duty and an obligation to understand and obey the international requirements of the Geneva Convention established in 1949. Not only that but if you are captured, you too have rights under the Geneva Convention that protect you. Know your rights and your duty."

Members of 58th Company stirred in their seats, whispering to one another, laughing aloud at Fosse. Now he was not being funny; he was hilarious.

"Listen, men. There are strict requirements your captors must follow. They cannot require you to give anything other than your name, rank, and serial number. They must treat the wounded as they treat their own. They must allow you to select leaders. Likewise, you must treat them according to the rules. The Vietnamese are people, too, and they have human rights just like you do. You must treat them with the same respect that you would anyone else. The Geneva Convention requires it."

We had heard so many stories about torturing and killing prisoners by that time that nobody found Fosse believable. His Huntz Hall face and manner made it even harder for him to be taken seriously. For us it was just another joke, funnier than a sucking chest wound someone up front muttered. For the rest of the class he tried to impress his point upon us, but we had already learned the truth.

Fourteen

Eighth Week Panel

I don't know but I been told
Eskimo pussy is mighty cold.
—Army marching song

The longer OCS went on, the harder it was for some of the men to keep their bearings. By the end of the seventh week the ones who wanted to leave had transferred to Casual Company. When the eighth week began, we were down to 193 men from the original 256. Most of them dropped out on their own, but a few had been dropped for medical reasons. During the eighth week, the Army had its first chance to evaluate us at what was called the eighth week panel. This was the first chance to get rid of people the Army didn't want.

We had been preparing for this, the first full evaluation since the beginning. We didn't know it until later, but one of the key elements in evaluation came from "peer critiques." Starting in the fourth week each company member had to rank the top five and the bottom five candidates in his platoon. We had to write formal Observation Reports (ORs) about the candidates in leadership positions, and we were told that there was a special notebook kept in each TAC officer's outer office where we could go to write private thoughts about other candidates' performance.

"Look, men," Lt. Ireland, the slim, wispy TAC officer for sixth platoon, explained, "if you see something that causes you to question the courage, judgment, or integrity of another candidate, it is your duty to let us know. It is our job to evaluate each of your leadership abilities. We expect you to help. So your ORs—both the formal ones and the private ones—are very important. If you let a dud get through here and he becomes a platoon leader in Vietnam, your life could depend on it. Watch everyone carefully; report everything questionable."

The most important time that people were evaluated was during leadership tasks. Every Friday night a new duty roster was posted listing the leadership positions for the next week from Student Company Commander, Student Executive Officer, on down to Student Platoon and Squad Leaders. The people listed kept their jobs for a week, and we scrutinized their performance and filled out ORs at the end of the week.

But it became cutthroat. I thought they must have adapted some of the techniques from Korean prisoner of war camps where POWs were broken down by a system of rewards and punishments that made it every man for himself. The "book," as we called it, became the most feared device because it was anonymous. Anybody could sneak into the TAC office and write a damning OR. "Candidate Smith of the platoon was seen copying answers on the first-aid exam," or "OC L. D. Burns failed to buff his section of the platoon floor Tuesday night," or "Candidate Guthrie keeps antiwar literature in his footlocker." People got jumpy; they didn't know who to trust, so they trusted almost nobody.

And there was good reason to trust nobody, especially the TACs. The TACs developed favorites—mainly favorite targets. And if they decided they wanted to get rid of somebody, it was pretty easy for them to do it.

On Friday of the seventh week, the duty roster for week eight came out and was posted after the night's chow. Each platoon would send a representative to get the assignments and report to the rest of the platoon. This week Sugarman, a short Georgia boy, went from our platoon, and when he got back, we assembled in the latrine.

"The Deuce will be well-represented next week," Sugarman drawled, prolonging our anxiety, "Second Platoon gets the week's Company Commander."

People yelled at him; someone threw a roll of toilet paper. "Git on with it, you piece a shit, tell us who it is!"

Sugarman paused and looked carefully around the latrine before he read from his list, "OC Tommy Trailer, Student Company Commander." As he went on down the list, I discovered that I was to be a squad leader for the week—a minor job but a job nonetheless. When we got back to the room, Trailer was excited.

"I'm really glad to be selected to be the CO for next week. I think it means they have confidence in me. You know, we're here for only twenty-four weeks, so I'm one of only twenty-four people to get to do this job."

"I wouldn't be so happy," Budwell said. "You saw what happened to McClain last week when he was CO. They raised hell with him for the way he called the company to attention, calling him a sissy with a pussy voice all week long."

"Yes, but I'm not afraid of that. I learned how to call out loud and clear in OCS prep."

"I don't mean they get you for that. But they'll get you for something if you're not careful. Wait and see."

The eighth week was our first full week of training in 1970. It was a new decade, but we didn't have time to reflect. Besides, the Georgia winter had taken hold. It had been in the mid-twenties since New Year's Day, and the sick-call roster had been looking like a full platoon every morning for the past four days. The word came down that a URI alert had been issued for all of Fort Benning, so no physical training could be required. As CO, Trailer got a stack of orders for the next day's training and read that if the temperature at 0430 hours was below thirty-two degrees, no unit would be allowed to engage in strenuous outdoor exercise. "What's a URI alert?" Trailer asked as he read the order.

"That stands for 'Upper Respiratory Infection,'" Budwell explained. "The Army's decided that it's dangerous to force people to run when it's below freezing, raises the chances of infections."

"The Great God URI," I laughed. "As long as URI keeps us from running around the Airborne track every morning, I'll worship his name. URI, URI, URI," I chanted.

"Hold on, Adams," Trailer cautioned, "it might warm up tonight. If it's above thirty-two on the thermometer out front at 0430, I'm authorized to take this company out for a morning run. It's my responsibility as company commander to get the job done."

"Oh, bullshit, Trailer," I said. "Don't be such a tight ass. This gives you a legitimate reason to ease up on things. You know none of the TACs will be here before 7:00, so no one will know what the temperature is at 4:30 but you. Just plan now that it's going to be below freezing in the morning."

"No, Adams, I'll do it by the book."

"Okay, Trailer," I said. "Have it your way. But it would make for a better night's sleep for all of us if we knew tomorrow morning's run had a high chance of cancellation."

The North Vietnamese were huddled in caves throughout the mountainside while B-52s flew overhead and spread their fertile cargo throughout the green hills where they erupted into sprouting clouds and debris. Suddenly the sound of jet engines drew closer, and a B-52 crashed into the mountain.

As the smoke cleared and the fire died out, the Vietnamese villagers ventured from their hiding places and began working on the plane. I was surprised these Vietnamese looked amazingly like Pueblo Indians from New Mexico and their mountain homes like mud dwellings cut in the side of the mountain. They worked quietly and purposefully dismantling the plane. Miraculously, they took it apart and restored the parts to their original condition. Some transformed the rubber from the plane's tires into a liquid, climbed into a tree, and returned the liquid to its trunk.

Others worked hammering the plane's metal body as well as all of its nuts, bolts, and metal parts into individual pieces of ore and minerals which were then taken to mines and returned carefully to the ground. Still others took plastic covering from the wires and returned the copper to the ground. The same feat was being performed on the petroleum-based plastics as well as the engine oil and fuel, as they were unrefined and returned to the earth. The parachutes were unfolded and unwoven until all of the silk was returned to silkworms who spread out into the jungle canopy. Leather from the seats was removed, hair replaced, and then gently placed around freezing skinless cattle who then romped out into the fields, with their tails high in the air.

The next morning Trailer was up at 0400, a hour earlier than the regular wake-up. I vaguely heard his alarm go off and drifted back to sleep as he got his things together. An hour later I heard him out in the halls yelling that it was time to get up. Then he made it back to the room.

"You're in luck, Adams," he said as he walked in. "It's twenty-five degrees out."

"Bullshit, Trailer. We're all in luck. You too. Now we can spend our time getting the platoon together. The whole company will get fewer demerits for the day's inspection, and you can take the credit for it. So don't rag on me about not having to run."

"I hope you're right about that. But I knew how much you hated to have to run, so I wanted you to be the first to know."

"Thanks for being concerned about little ol' me," I said sarcastically as Trailer went to the door yelling to the rest of the platoon that the morning run was cancelled.

"Bless you, URI, bless you. I'd sacrifice a virgin for you if I had one," I said, kneeling toward the window with its exactly twelve inch opening.

"Fuck you," said Budwell as he finally climbed out of his bunk. "I'll run your three miles and take the virgin. Ain't no virgin sacrifices allowed 'round here while I'm here. Hymen sacrifices maybe, but no virgin sacrifices."

"Yeah, well, I doubt if old 58th Company has seen many of either."

"That's where you're wrong," Budwell countered. "From what I hear this place thrives on the sacrifice of innocents. They just happen to be male, and this place is just a stopping off point in the process. Actually, the twelfth week parties provide a few initiations for virgins of either gender persuasion."

"Where'd you hear that?" I asked.

"I talked to a senior candidate from 59th Company. Someone will be assigned to be the 'Date Officer' for the party. Dates are part of the order of the day for parties. Every candidate must have a date, rent or buy—if he's optimistic—dress blues, and demonstrate that he can become an officer and a gentleman by order of Congress some day."

"Where are we gonna get dates for 190 men in this god-forsaken place? Oh, I just had an idea. We can get my grandfather to send a herd of West

Texas sheep. Some of my friends from back home feel mightily romantic towards ewes."

"Yeah," laughed Budwell, "and I bet I know the prime shepherd—J. B. Adams II."

"Not me, man, I'm allergic to wool."

"Aha. Well at least you've tried it to know."

I tossed my pillow at him and said, "NO, NO, NO. I can truthfully say to any herd of sheep, 'I've never had a piece of ewe, or you, or you, or any of you."

Budwell tossed my pillow back, laughing in the deep-throated way he always did. "Well, the dates won't come from West Texas sheep or from wonderful Columbus. I heard that Trotter from fifth platoon is from Atlanta and that he's got contacts at a nurses' school there. Those girls just can't wait to come down here and meet some future officers. And I think you can bet that by the twelfth week, the amount will be sizably reduced from 190. Particularly after this week's panel."

"Did the senior candidate tell you that?"

"Uh, huh. That and my own gut feeling about what's going on around here."

"Well, maybe you're right," I said. "But enough of this happy palaver. Our duties call. I hear a latrine whistling for me, and your buffer waits for the person first on her dance card, Mr. Budwell."

By the third week, we all had specially assigned platoon tasks. Budwell was first on the floor buffing crew. I had been late to the platoon meeting where tasks were assigned and chosen, so I ended up with the latrine detail, shit-and-piss duty it was called. Actually I had learned to like it. The latrine had developed a personality. It was the place where we sneaked off to after lights out to smoke, to read, to write letters home, for some to masturbate. It had the feeling of being a safe haven, and I had gotten the job of shining the brass floor, door, and faucet fixtures, as well as some commode duty. The routine would be extended this morning without the run, so I'd have plenty of time.

The day's classes included morning instruction in Infantry Hall on M-79 grenade launchers and an afternoon demonstration of them at English Range across the post. The morning classes were uneventful, and the afternoon went routinely except for the cold. It was overcast and warmed up to about thirty-five during most of the day. We all had all our winter gear, fatigue jackets with upturned collars, gloves with wool inserts, and most wore the army-issue woolen longjohns. The Georgia air cut through the fatigue pants, especially sitting on the top row of the outdoor bleachers. On breaks we huddled around fire barrels or tried to stay warm with the coffee from the pogey truck concessionaires who followed OCS training like cattle egrets around a herd of Herefords.

Shortly before the afternoon class ended, the temperature dropped a couple of degrees and a fine icy rain began to fall. Trailer told the company to fall into platoons, our normal routine for leaving a range and returning to the company area for evening chow. But instead of having us move out, Trailer called the company to attention and then told us to take the parade rest position.

We stood that way for several minutes. No one said anything but a quiet uneasiness infiltrated. No one liked standing at the uncomfortable position of parade rest for a long time, especially in an icy rain when a warm mess hall beckoned.

We continued to stand at parade rest, Trailer positioned in the front of the company with his back to us. We couldn't see what had happened to the TAC officers who had walked back toward the range behind us. Finally, I could hear Rancek's voice toward the back of the formation.

"Who's in charge here?" he bellowed.

Trailer came to attention, made an about face, and yelled out, "Sir, Student Company Commander Trailer."

By that time Rancek had made his way to the head of the company. He immediately got close to Trailer's head, inches from his ear and began yelling.

"You lousy piece of shit. Whoever told you that you had the balls to command anything? Here you have your men standing out in a freezing rain for twenty minutes, and you've never once told them to take their ponchos off their pistol belts and protect themselves against the elements. What kind of a leader are you, cuntbreath?"

"Sir, Candidate Trailer, but I...."

Rancek cut him off and continued yelling at him. "Shut up, you dud.

No excuses, get this company out of here, immediately!" So we double-timed back, thankful to be getting out of the cold. For once, running felt good.

That night during study hall in our room, Budwell asked Trailer what had happened that afternoon, and Trailer said that Satmonelli had told him to form the company and get ready to leave but not to do anything until he got back. That was why we stood waiting.

"Did he tell you why you weren't supposed to do anything while you waited?"

"No, he just made it explicit that I was not to do anything without his permission. That's why we just stood there."

"Did you think about telling us to get out our ponchos?"

"Sure I did. But Satmonelli was very clear that we shouldn't do anything."

"Why would he do that?" Budwell asked. "What do you think he had in mind?"

"I thought he and the other TACs had something to talk over for a minute before we left. I didn't think anything about it at first. I began to get uncomfortable in the rain after a few minutes too, but I was just doing what I was told."

Budwell sat quietly for a minute, and then he said, "Trailer, I think you were set up. I'd be careful for the rest of the week if I were you. They may have a few mantraps planned for you."

Startled, Trailer then shook his head, "No way, Budwell. I don't question their motives. Something happened that delayed them, that's all. No big deal."

"Maybe so, Trailer. Now Adams and I know what really happened, and so will a few of the others that you can explain it to. But most of the 190 men who stood around there freezing their asses off today won't, and when it comes time for ORs at the end of the week, they'll remember that you didn't take care of your men—first requirement for a good leader."

The rest of the week demonstrated the truth of Budwell's observations. At every chance the TACs took an opportunity to berate Trailer publicly. Like the problem of keeping the men in the rain, some of Trailer's other difficulties seemed manufactured by the TACs: Trailer had us move out late for one of the classes because Ireland kept him in the CO's office and then Martin tongue-lashed him before the company.

But soon Trailer got addled and began to make plenty of his own mistakes. On Thursday afternoon he misread the training schedule and ordered us to double-time to Infantry Hall when we were supposed to go to an attack simulation and blast at each other with blanks. And before the week was out he lost his most prized possession—his command voice—to laryngitis. So by week's end, everybody knew it had been a disaster, and the eighth week panel began early Saturday morning—the morning after the week's OR reports were due.

The morning of the panel felt like what pro football training camps must be like on the days that athletes get cut. Early Saturday morning each platoon sent someone to the CO's office to get the list of candidates scheduled to be interviewed by the panel made up of the TAC officers. Only those people who were borderline were brought before the board. And just being brought before the board was no indication that you'd be paneled out. But about seventy-five percent were.

Sugarman was again the messenger, and again we huddled in the latrine to hear the news. It seemed to take hours for Sugarman to get back, and when he walked in the door, he wasn't laughing and joking the way he was a week earlier.

"I've got some bad news for some of you in the Big Deuce," he began, "but I guess there ain't no way to make it easy, so I'll just read what it says here: 'The following men from the Second Platoon, 58th OC Company, are ordered to report to the CO's office at 1000 hours—Collins, Lewis; Davis, Thornton; Trailer, Thomas.' That's it, guys."

When we got back to the room, Trailer seemed subdued but not resigned. He still thought he'd be okay.

"I know they've got to call me before the panel. It was a shitty week. But they know why certain things happened the way they did. I think they'll take that into account when they make their decision."

The rest of the day crept by. We didn't usually have any training on Saturdays and Sundays, but we were supposed to use the time to polish our shoes and boots, shine our brass, square away our gear, and study for the next week's classes. With special permission we could check out our

M-16 from the armory downstairs and clean it. On Saturday afternoons the guys who had gotten more than 100 demerits during the week had to march tours in full pack and weapon on the battalion parade ground.

Trailer returned to the room, just as Budwell and I were getting ready to go to chow.

"So, how'd it go?" I asked.

"I don't know," Trailer responded. "I thought it went okay, but who knows."

"Did they give you a chance to respond to their concerns?" Budwell wondered.

"Well, yes. No. Kinda. Mainly they just told me what a lousy job I did. They read some of the comments from company members' ORs and asked me what I thought."

"What kind of things did people say?"

"Oh, they were pretty nasty. Things like 'this guy is a dud, get rid of him.' 'No leader would allow his men to stand in freezing rain. Flush him.' Things like that."

"Well, don't let it get to you, Tommy," Budwell said. "Let's go to chow and forget about it."

After chow Trailer checked out his weapon, and Budwell had Saturday afternoon CQ duty for four hours. Rancek had taken it easy on me since the special session he had taken Garrett and me on. He had even assigned me to be the platoon academic officer, which meant I had to post weekly scores and file grades in candidates' files in his office, usually on Saturday afternoons.

The panel continued all afternoon, so Rancek's office was quiet, a nice place to get away to. All of the TACs took pride in their offices, and like the others, Rancek's was fully decorated. On one wall was a poster that read: "The essence of war is violence, and moderation in war is imbecility." On the ceiling was painted a huge scorpion. On one wall was Rancek's tape player/radio. We had not yet gotten music or radio privileges. That would supposedly come in the eighteenth week, so when I noticed that Rancek had left his radio on, I moved my things over close to the speaker to listen. The first song I heard, the Beatles' "Hey Jude," seemed like the food of life. I sat transfixed for a few moments swaying to the music, then went to work.

For the rest of the time I was there I sat close to the radio and heard songs forever associated in my mind with that moment. Peter, Paul, and Mary's "Leavin' on a Jet Plane" was a special favorite of mine. We had even sung it as a marching song because it reminded us of leaving. Then Sly and the Family Stone's "Let Me Take You Higher" came on. Creedence Clearwater Revival's "Who'll Stop the Rain?" seemed to be all about the never-ending war.

At one point the news came on. One of the stories mentioned that Lt. Calley, the leader of the platoon charged with the atrocities at My Lai, had been assigned to quarters at Fort Benning where his court martial would be held. The announcer for the Columbus station spoke with pride about Calley, mentioning that local groups were coming to his aid and planned to demonstrate on his behalf in a downtown rally.

Luckily I finished my work before Rancek returned, and when I got back to the room, I found Trailer still working on his M-16. The parts lay on the floor as he worked to clean the barrel.

"Any news?" I asked when I got back.

"No, not yet. They're supposed to let us know before chow tonight."

Sure enough, just a few minutes later I heard someone in the hall call out that Collins, Davis, and Trailer were to report to the CO's office immediately. I gave Trailer a thumbs up, and he headed out of the room.

It didn't take very long for him to get back. I could tell by the look on his face that it wasn't good news. He was pale and his eyes looked far away.

"They paneled me out," he said as he walked in. "They did it; they paneled me out. Davis and Collins too. We're gone."

I tried to say something to make him feel better, but I knew there was nothing I could say. Trailer was one of the most dedicated candidates there. He really wanted to be an officer. He'd joined the Army for that purpose, had attended OCS prep, and worked hard. Meanwhile he began to put his weapon back together. It was almost time to go to supper, so I began to get my things together.

What happened next seems like a dream or a slow-motion movie. I was stowing my gear in my footlocker. Trailer was standing behind me. I heard him snap the bolt back into his M-16, but then I heard another snap that didn't register at first. Suddenly I realized that I had heard the clear sound of a magazine being locked in. As I jumped up and turned around, Trailer had already turned the weapon around and put it in his mouth. I had just enough time to yell, "No!" when he pulled the trigger.

Fifteen

New Roomie

If I die in a combat zone,
box me up and ship me home.
—marching song

We were always supposed to get rid of any training ammunition, either blanks or live ammo, at the end of each exercise, but somehow Trailer had kept a magazine full of blanks. His M-16 was on automatic, so he got off two rounds before he dropped the weapon. Even though he had been shooting blanks, the fire, wadding, and gas scorched and bloodied his mouth. At first I thought he had killed himself and expected to the see the back of his head fly off like Kennedy's in the Zapruder film. It took me a few minutes to realize that he'd used blanks rather than live ammo. In that instant most of the platoon had poured into our room. We got him out and to the infirmary, put his things together, and sent them to Casual Company while he was gone. I never saw him again, but we heard that he'd been sent for psychiatric evaluation.

With the loss of three members of the platoon came some shifting. Originally some rooms had four people; now we had few enough people that there would be three people to a room, so Budwell and I got a new roomie, Shrode, an older guy with prior service. Even though we had been there for eight weeks, except for talking with our roommates during the required study hall, we hadn't learned much about other candidates yet. Most people were pretty quiet. The structure of OCS forced men to look out for themselves. The guy next to you might write you up if he thought you were a bullshitter, someone not serious about becoming an officer. So, most—at least for the first several weeks—kept to themselves.

I did know that Shrode was older. He was one of those graying heads sitting in front of me in class when I surveyed the first class in Infantry Hall. He was rather jovial, smiled a lot, and the TACs seemed to respect him. They knew that he had been a Green Beret and knew more about Vietnam than they did.

Shortly after he got his gear moved in, we had a study hall period when Budwell and I got to ask him some questions. We learned that he was thirty, married with three kids, and that he had spent two tours in Vietnam, most of the time as a LRRP, or long range reconnaissance patrol. The LRRPs were notoriously on their own. Out there without contact with headquarters, they had to take care of themselves and live the jungle life.

"Why'd you decide to go to OCS?" Budwell asked.

"Actually, my last CO got me interested. He knew that I was in charge of our last operation. I was a buck sergeant at the time, and I made less than $400 a month even with combat and Special Forces pay. He showed me that I could make more money just being in OCS than I could as an NCO, so I told him 'what the hell,' I'd give it a try."

"Do you have any college?" Budwell asked.

"Naw, but I got my GED after I got in. I was one of those kids that the judge told either join the Army or go to reform school, so I took the Army. That was way before Nam heated up. After I got my GED, I was stationed in North Carolina, at Fort Bragg. That's where I met Mary, my wife. We got married and had our first kid while I was there. She was pregnant with the second one when I took my first tour and pregnant with the third one when I left on the second tour. Leave 'em pregnant and you don't have to worry about 'em fuckin' around on you."

"I thought you had to have some college to go to OCS," I said. "Naw," said Shrode, "that's only if you enlist. If you're prior service, all you got to have is your GED and your CO's recommendation. They're dyin' for second lieuy combat platoon leaders over there. Those fuckin' ROTC boys last about three weeks in the bush."

We would get to know Shrode better as the week wore on. Compared to the intensity of the eighth week, the ninth was a long breath. We'd lost twenty-five men to the panel, so 58th Company was down to 167 men—down from the 256 that started out. We started a new area of study for the week—tactics—so that meant we were in Infantry Hall for most of the time. The weather stayed cold in the mornings, so we missed the morning runs too.

At a study hall late in the week, Shrode, Budwell, and I talked about some of the information we had been given in class. Shrode scoffed.

"Most of that crap they tell you is bullshit. Stuff like petal defensive positions. Most people are so scared, fucked up on dope, or just generally out of it that nothing works. That's why I volunteered for LRRPs. I knew that those guys had to have their shit together. And they're only four or five guys that you got to worry about rather than a platoon or a whole fuckin' company. Give me five LRRPs and they can do some damage, man."

We hadn't been able to get much out of Shrode earlier in the week, but he began to loosen up. Many of the prior-service guys didn't much like to talk about their experiences in Vietnam, perhaps because they heard so many war stories from the instructors in the classes, but Shrode got on a roll.

"Yeah, I could tell you some stories, all right. It's a different world over there. Unreal, like being in a movie. It's kinda like it's not happening to you but to someone else."

"Why did you go back for the second tour if it seems so weird to you?" Budwell wanted to know.

"That's a good question. You know, my first tour I kept thinking about gittin' short. Like ever'body else, I counted the days till my year was over. But then when I got back home, it was borin'. The old lady was on my ass to do somethin' all the time. The kids were screamin'. So one day I just up and volunteered to go back.

"But maybe over there is real and here is weird. Maybe this is the movie and that's reality. At least I sure feel wired over there. Now I just seem to be waitin' to git back over. That's why all this just seems like bullshit to me. It ain't real."

"What was your most memorable experience over there?" I asked.

Shrode looked at me carefully, then at Budwell, hesitated, and said, "Let me show you something."

He went to his footlocker and got a plastic bag from the bottom, opened it, and took out three wrinkled, brown objects on a piece of rawhide and tossed them on the desk in front of him.

"That's what it's all about over there."

Budwell picked them up and looked carefully at them.

"These aren't for real, are they?" Budwell asked.

"What do you think they are?"

"I recognize what two of them are. They're ears, aren't they?"

"That's right. Cut 'em off a VC in the highlands myself. The guy killed one of my buddies."

I picked up the string and looked at the wrinkled, leathery objects.

"What's the third thing?" I asked.

"Look at it closely and see if you can figure it out."

I looked carefully but had no idea.

"No, I don't know. It's not an ear. Is it a finger?"

"No, man," said Shrode laughing. "That's a gook prick. That's one boy who'll bring no more of those little bastards into this world."

I quickly tossed his rawhide ring back to him, and Shrode hid his prizes in his footlocker.

Sixteen

Night Bivouac

I don't want to sit and cry!
I don't want to wonder why!
I just want to fight and die!
—*marching song*

Our activities intensified in the tenth week, and we moved back away
from Infantry Hall. The major activity was a night bivouac out in the
pine forests that made up a large part of Fort Benning. We were to spend
three nights in the bush. The second night was a low-crawl exercise
beneath live machine-gun fire, and the other nights were night patrol
exercises.

The TAC officers hyped the machine-gun-range crawl, telling us that
the tracers would be set eighteen inches off the ground.

"If you hike your butt up in the air the way you do in the low-crawl
pit, they'll shoot that sucker off. Have you ever seen an officer candidate
without an ass walkin' around here? Well, if you did, he probably lost it in
the machine-gun pit. We ain't shittin' you guys; this is just like the real
thing, so don't fuck it up."

Garrett had been designated the platoon leader for the week, and it was
a hell of a lot harder trying to maintain any kind of order and discipline
on field exercises than it was marching in and out of Infantry Hall. I wondered if Rancek had thought this might be the time to test Garrett. He'd
generally left us alone in the past few weeks, or at least he hadn't shown us
any special antagonism. In fact, he seemed to have decided that I wasn't
worth his special energies. He'd even displayed some kind of confidence in
me, I thought, by assigning me to be the academic officer of the platoon.
It required some of my free time, but it also got me out of some shit

details. When it came time to get people to do some nasty extra work, I could beg off as academic officer.

They trucked us out into the field on Tuesday afternoon. From there we were to march the six miles to the machine-gun range. As we were boarding the trucks, Martin, the TAC officer from third platoon, told us how to treat the other officer-candidate companies that we would pass in the trucks.

"Men, one of the main elements in OCS is espirit de corps. You must believe in your outfit, and you must let everybody else know that you believe fully that your company is the best around. So when you pass the other OCS companies in trucks, I want you to yell out what you think about them. Give them the proper signal." With that, Martin yelled out at imaginary trucks, "PUSSIES, PUSSIES!" And he raised his middle finger in recognizable salute.

And so, as this group of 167 would-be officers and gentlemen trucked by other companies of would-be officers, we gave them Bronx cheers and the finger.

At the bleachers near the bivouac area we lined up in platoon formations and checked our gear. The plan was for each platoon to fan out and march to designated areas and set up camp, just as if we were in the boonies of Vietnam. A platoon of "aggressors" made up of a ragtag element from Casual Company and others awaiting bad conduct discharges were supposed to be in the area the second night, but the first night we were just to get to the right spot and dig in before we started playing the game.

Garrett knew of Shrode's previous experience, so he put him in charge of the map and compass, and we headed out to our designated spot—a hike of six clicks through what appeared on the map to be pretty difficult terrain. But Shrode knew what he was doing and rather than trying to go straight to the spot and up and down through the thick pines of the valleys, he followed the contours of the land and took us along a ridge line and around a stream rather than through it. We got there in less than four hours, so it was still early afternoon when we began to set up camp.

We set up in a circle and dug in around the perimeter. For the second and third nights we were to put out scouts and set up guards beyond the perimeter, but for the first night we just got our stuff together. It was a typical

Georgia winter day, crisp and clear with the sun warm, and it promised to be a typical night with the thermometer at about thirty-five degrees. This first night was an adventure. I felt like a boy scout back on Lake Tawakoni. The feeling seemed to overtake the others too. When C-rations were passed out for chow, the trading began, and we sounded like kids with baseball cards.

"I'll trade a chicken and dumplings for a spaghetti and meatballs," someone would sing out, to be met with hisses and laughter. Others angled for the cinnamon rolls, while the smokers collected the cigarettes. Being away from the barracks lightened everyone's attitude, making it seem like we were on a weekend campout rather than a military training exercise.

After chow, with the sun down, the cold began to creep in. Since we didn't expect any aggressors tonight, we lit a big fire, and the platoon crowded up and gathered around. Rancek had set up a tent near the center of the area and withdrew inside early in the evening, leaving us to sit around the campfire.

Fires are mesmerizing. I could remember often camping with Granddad or the boy scouts and just sitting for hours looking into the crackling flames. For awhile we sat around quietly, but soon someone asked Spenser to sing a song. At first he refused, but then he said he'd sing if the rest of us sang along. When we agreed, Spenser began with "Where Have All the Flowers Gone?" and then followed with almost every popular folk song he knew: "500 Miles" and "Roving Gambler." I asked him to sing "Goodbye, Old Paint" and "The Cowboy's Lament."

After the last song, most of the guys began moving toward their bedrolls, but Budwell, Garrett, Spenser, and I sat quietly for a few minutes, until Spenser asked,

"What do you guys think we'll be doing at this time next year?"

We sat and looked at each other for a minute. Thinking about the future was something we avoided.

Budwell finally answered, "That's a good question, Spenser. Here we are engaged in an activity that has a very clear chronology. We know we have twenty-four weeks of OCS, each week programmed carefully by the best minds Uncle Sam can scrape up. And we must be committed to the thought of getting through, I guess, or we wouldn't have taken this on. Right?

"And we know too the typical shape of a new second lieutenant's life after OCS. It's usually six months on a stateside assignment, let's say as a training officer at Fort Ord, California, then off to Vietnam. So if that's the typical future, it means that's what we'll be doing this time next year."

Garrett stood up and walked over beyond the fire. "I got to piss, man. It don't do no good to dwell on this shit. You start thinkin' about bein' in the Nam and it might make you keep from doing what's got to be done here. So I don't think about it."

"I know what I hoped would happen when I started," I said. "My recruiting sergeant knew I wasn't too hot for going to Vietnam, so he told me how easy it was to branch transfer out of the Infantry. 'Sure, man, it will be easy for you to get out of the Infantry. All of the other branches get their officers from Infantry OCS, so all you have to do is tell them what your plans are,' he told me, the lying asshole. I had this bright idea that I could get into the Adjutant General Corps and become a personnel officer or a records officer in Fort Carson, Colorado, or Fort Sam Houston, Texas. Fat chance."

"What about you, Spenser, why did you ask?"

"Oh, I don't know. I guess losing all these people started me thinking about things. I had a dream the other night, and I think I saw me dead in it. It just spooked me, some."

Dreams interested Budwell: "Tell us about it, Spenser."

"It wasn't anything exciting. But I was in Vietnam and for some reason I was singing in a bar. It looked like an officers club in a city. Saigon, maybe. I was wearing a flowered Hawaiian shirt, sitting at a piano. Bar girls with slit skirts were all around. I was singing Frank Sinatra songs, 'My Way,' I think, when somebody yelled 'Incoming!' The next thing I see is my own corpse. I'm sitting back in a chair, wearing a dark suit of some kind. I've got my hair back and my mustache. I'm wearing real glasses instead of these GI ones, and there's some kind of foggy haze. It gave me a weird feeling."

We all sat quietly, hypnotized by the fire, trying not to think of our own mortality. It had been an unreal evening, almost innocent in the good-humored singing, but now Spenser's dream changed the atmosphere.

Seventeen

Turning Black

Vietnam, Vietnam,
Every night while you're sleepin'
Charlie Cong comes acreepin'
All around.
—marching song sung to tune of "Poison Ivy" by the Coasters

The twelfth week party began to take on mythic proportions. It meant dates for the single guys and the married ones would get to spend the night with their wives coming from out of town, either at the base guesthouse or in the apartments, rooms, or houses the ones who'd come to live in Columbus had rented. True to rumor, Trotter had been assigned as date officer, mainly because he was from Atlanta and had been a frat boy at the University of Georgia at Athens. Most of the guys would end up with nurses or nursing students from a school in Atlanta. A uniform company came in and sized everyone for dress blues and damn near everyone bought them, even those who were still on the bubble and knew it. I even bought mine, as ambivalent as I was about the thought of ever finishing OCS. Even less understandable, I bought the hat with the light blue Infantry stripe and asked for the Infantry stripes to be sewn on the uniform. We were all Infantry, but I still harbored the secret idea that I might be able to branch transfer into Artillery, Signal, or—hope of hopes—the Adjutant General Corps, the paperworks branch of the Army for the clerks and safe-haven base campers. But when I tried on that dress blue uniform and the Infantry hat, I couldn't keep from drawing on all those years of John Wayne in cavalry blues and even my troubled heart swelled, and I wrote the check for almost $100, most of a month's salary.

Trotter got photographs of the nurses who'd signed up as dates. It must have been like a mail order bride service as we crowded around gawking, judging, and critiquing the girls' pictures that Trotter laid out on the lavatory in the latrine.

"Ooowee! That looks like a hot number. Sign me up for her," Stringer yelled out at one of the first girls he looked at. On the backs someone had written the names and vital statistics of the girls, and someone else turned in over and read, "'5' 10", 195 lbs.' Hell, Stringer she'd bounce you to the ceiling and then you'd get lost in folds." String, who was about 5' 6" and 140 decided to keep looking. We had drawn lots for choices, and String had first shot. The only stipulation was that we had ten minutes each to look over the pictures and make a selection. Someone had a ten minute hourglass that Trotter placed next to his clipboard with the names and numbers of the girls. Out of the twenty-five men who were left in the second platoon, eight were married and the rest of us were peering over the shoulders of the others. I had drawn number seven, so I had to wait a while, but I had already spotted one picture that appealed to me, a dark-haired girl wearing her hair in a flip and a wry expression on her face.

"C'mon, dammit, String! Make your move. Ain't got all day."

"Keep it in your britches. I got three more minutes," said String and looked at my girl, as I began to think of her. He turned her over and read "5' 6", 125 lbs. Too tall," and laid her down again. He finally chose a short blond, and Trotter wrote down "Stringer" by the girl's name on a list he carried on a clipboard and removed the picture from the lavatory.

"Hey, I want that," Stringer shouted as Trotter started to slip the picture under the list on the clipboard. Trotter thought for a minute.

"I guess it's okay. We'd didn't promise to give 'em back. But don't jerk off on 'em in case the girls want 'em back."

Stringer snatched his prize, holding it high over his head and dancing around the latrine.

Sugarman was next. Like Stringer he was short, so he eliminated all of the girls over 5' 4". But he also had some specific requirements—he wanted a red-haired girl with freckles, because he had red hair and light freckles sprinkled over his nose. There was only one photo that met his criteria. He looked her over carefully, turned over the picture and read her name out slowly, "Susan St. Lucas." He turned the photo over and over, closed his eyes and looked up at the latrine ceiling. "That's her. That's the one." Trotter duly recorded Sugarman next to her name on the list and went on to number three, Garrett.

Garrett stepped up to the first picture, a long-haired blond in what looked like one of those canned sorority photos where everyone wears the same black, low-cut dress. A low murmur began in the latrine as Garrett picked up the picture and looked it over carefully, weighing her virtues. Garrett knew exactly what he was doing, pricking the oldliners there who, even though they respected Garrett, couldn't imagine him going out with a white woman. No one said anything directly at first, until Thompson, a tall Georgian with a deep voice, spoke: "Move it, Garrett. You ain't gonna bring no white girl to the party, so stop wasting our time."

Garrett kept looking at the picture, never acknowledging Thompson, and then moved to the next picture, a nondescript girl in a black and white photo. He examined it as carefully as the first one; the murmur rose, but Garrett kept moving slowly down the list, taking all of his allotted ten minutes. Finally Trotter announced that his time was up and that he had to chose. Garrett looked back over the pictures lying there, stopping briefly at each one and then chose one of the three black women who had submitted photos. As Trotter recorded the choice, Garrett turned around and stood looking briefly at everyone, landing his gaze on Thompson, his face expressionless. Without saying anything, he stepped back through the crowd and left the latrine.

Budwell was next, but he waved his hand over the lineup of pictures and said that he'd wait and take his chance at the end, following his philosophy of willing whatever might happen, I guess, or maybe thinking about the last chosen.

I waited for the next two, hoping that my girl would still be there when my time came, thinking how weird it was to have developed this possessiveness over a photo in such a short time. The other two guys, Livingston, a tall, lanky Louisianan, and Garcia, the Chicano from Chicago as he liked to proclaim, seemed to have decided early like me, for they went directly to photos and made their selection. Garcia had already determined that no Latinas were in the group, so he selected the little blond whose picture was at the beginning of the lineup. Although some of the guys might have felt the same about Garcia and a white girl, they didn't react the same as they did with Garrett, mainly because they had accepted the notion that Chicanos were "white." But if there had been a brown-skinned girl in the group, they would have expected Garcia to choose her.

It was my time, but I decided I didn't want to jump too quickly to my chosen one. I looked perfunctorily at the other photos before stopping at the face I had seen over the backs of the others. I turned it over and read "Mary O'Hara, 5' 6" 125 lbs. Millersville, Georgia." I turned it back over and looked into the eyes of Mary O'Hara and into that steady gaze and smile.

"This one's mine," I told Trotter, sliding the picture into the pocket of my fatigue shirt and stepping out through the smoke-filled latrine.

* * * *

From then on everything seemed suspended waiting for the party. I had been assigned to the printing detail, which meant I had to get the program designed and printed. One of the guys in the sixth platoon named Umlauf had been an art major in college, so I sought him out on a break at Infantry Hall, and he agreed to come up with a cover.

"What's the theme?" he asked.

"Well, it's the beginning of a new decade, so I think that should be the theme, new decade, new beginning."

"All right. I'll get to work and have you a couple of ideas in a day or two."

True to his word, Umlauf came up with a couple of designs and showed me his drawings on another break. His ideas were based upon the shape of the 5 and the 8 in the company number. He made the five into a futuristic rocket ship taking off into the 8 leaned over into an infinity symbol.

"I'd recommend using bright colors on these. Get a kind of psychedelic look to this notion of the future. We could have the words 'Into the Future' at the top."

I had all the copy for the program, standard stuff like the list of duties, date officer, printing, food, and so on, and the names of the chain of command for 58th Company. Most of the programs I looked at had a couple of quotations on the inside, so I requested permission from Rancek to go to the post library for an hour to look for some quotes.

"This is bullshit. Just use something like 'Duty, Honor, and Country' like most of them and get on with it," he responded.

"Sir, Candidate Adams. I'd like to see something new to correspond to our theme. You don't want our program to look like all the rest of them, do you, sir?"

"Don't you presume to tell me what I think, you slime," Rancek said getting up into my face. But he seemed to think it over.

"You have an hour after chow tonight, and if you're not back and signed in by then, I'll have your ass on the Airborne track."

"Yessir, an hour it is."

The post library was only about fifty yards from 58th Company, but it was like another world, a haven with books and magazines and a few newspapers. Most of the books were paperbacks donated by one organization or another. I didn't have time to browse, so I went immediately to the reference section and found a book with quotations. Nothing seemed right at first, but then I found two that I thought would work. The first one was from Walt Whitman:

> *Years of the modern! Years of the unperform'd!*
> *Your horizon rises, I see it parting away for more august*
> *drama,*
> *I see not America only, not only Liberty's nation but other*
> *nations preparing,*
> *I see tremendous entrances and exits, new combinations, the*
> *solidarity of races. . .*
> *I see Freedom, completely armed and victorious and very*
> *haughty, with Law on one side and Peace on the other,*
> *A stupendous trio all issuing forth against the idea of caste;*
> *What historic denouements are these we so rapidly approach? . . .*
> *The earth, restive, confronts a new era. . . .*
>
> *Walt Whitman*
> *"Years of the Modern" (1865)*

The second one was probably more subversive, but since it was from John Kennedy, I figured I could get it in:

> *I look forward to a great future for America—a future in which our country will match its military strength with our moral restraint, its wealth with our wisdom, its power with our purpose.*
>
> *I look forward to an America which will not be afraid of grace and beauty, which will protect the beauty of our natural environment. ...*
>
> *I look forward to an America which will reward achievement in the arts as we reward achievement in business or statecraft.*
>
> *I look forward to an America which will steadily raise the standards of artistic accomplishment and which will steadily enlarge cultural opportunities for all of our citizens.*
>
> *And I look forward to an America which commands respect throughout the world, not only for its strength, but for its civilization as well.*
>
> *And I look forward to a world which will be safe not only for democracy and diversity but also for personal distinction.*
> *John F. Kennedy*
> *Amherst College*
> *October 26, 1963*

But I wasn't quite satisfied with just these two. I had one older quotation from a poet whose name most would recognize even in the Army and one from a dead president. But I wanted something else, and I had only ten more minutes. I sat down with the current magazines and started flipping through them, and then suddenly there it was, the last quote:

> *Ok, if you really want to know the truth. All remarks about the future are at best remarks about the present—at worst, about one's own temperament. You can now predict a comparably wide range of futures for an individual, a nation, the planet ... the grand scenario of our collective future revises*

itself according to the disposition of the moment. It undulates,
soars, or plunges.
Jacob Brackman
"The Past as Present: A Non-Linear Probe"
January, 1970

My job was almost done once I got the design, the quotes, and the names with assigned duties to the printer. The work had taken so much of my concentration that I had almost forgotten about Mary O'Hara, but once I sent the material off, my mind turned to the party and the face of Mary O'Hara that stared out from my locker door with a challenging smile. I knew nothing about her except that she was a nursing student from Millersville, Georgia, and that she was coming on the afternoon train on Saturday of our twelfth week, February 14, 1970, Valentine's Day.

We all thought that there was something prophetic about Friday the 13th falling during our twelfth week. I feared that my program would come in with some stupid error or with the cover design backward, or worst of all, wouldn't come in at all. But about three that Friday afternoon, while we were lined up to get our dress blue uniforms and try them on for the last time, the printer delivered the programs, and I was called out of the line to inspect them in the CO's office. I cut through the mess hall, past the day room, and into the first sergeant's office, where the programs sat on the desk, clearly marked, "Intermediate Informal, Class 10-70, 14 February, 1970." I opened the first box, and they stared out with those vivid colors, and they were perfect.

I went back and picked up my blues, knowing that we would labor into the night getting ready for the next day. I had to spit shine my black dress shoes. They normally sat under my bunk, carefully displayed three inches from the footrail. I had learned that after shining them, I could put a coat of liquid floor polish on the toes, and it would seal the shine, allowing me simply to wipe off the toes in the morning, check the placement and take off. But you couldn't wear the shoes after coating them with floor polish, or the shine would crack like a broken windshield. So I had to remove the polish and take the shoes down to the leather and then build up the spit shine. It was a tedious job with shoe polish and lighter fluid and the right combination of heated polish, water, and elbow grease, but I was still enthralled by the thought of Mary O'Hara and "turning black."

The twelfth week marked the halfway point in OCS, and it was signaled by placing the black circles on the baseball caps that we wore, all ready by Monday morning fall-out time. I was trying to get ready for the party the next day, get some of my things done for Monday, and do my usual latrine duty of cleaning the toilets, brassoing the drains, and mopping the floors.

So we were all in bed by lights out, but as soon as the inspection was over, everyone crept into the latrine for the long night of work. Some stayed in their bunks and worked under the covers by flashlights. By this time the TACs rarely came through for the late night bed checks that were routine during the early weeks, but it was just perverse enough for one of them to decide to make a check on the night before a big party. Everyone was vigilant.

I got a couple of hours of interrupted sleep, punctuated by dreams dominated by my mother.

Obsessed with religion, secreted inside her biblical passages, my mother lived in worlds apart from me, worlds I fought to flee as soon as I found voice and freedom. Her spirituality allowed her to escape from the workaday world she inhabited helping my father in his various failed business ventures until he died, but that religion stifled me like a straitjacket. When I entered church with her, it was like being pulled inside a sarcophagus.

Frozen now in the grave of memory, the congregation stands, arms outstretched with open hymnals, all with mouths congealed open, strangely resembling the O-shaped mouth in the famous Edvard Munch painting "The Scream." Either that or the socket mouths of corpses. For me her church was deadly, and I could not wait to leave it. For her it was her greatest blessing.

Maybe it was the excitement of my first date in a while, but I had a weird dream recalling old girlfriends and one specific moment with my mother, an experience with this odd mixture of sexuality and its opposite, those aseptic images of my mother's enervative religious fervor.

I am fifteen, and I am driving the 1954 Ford my brother and I bought with the earnings from our paper route. It's Texas, 1960, and you can get a driver's license at fourteen, the effect of large ranches and long distances between them and the need for young sons to be out in pickups as soon as their boots reach the pedals.

I'm wearing penny loafers, Lee jeans, a white T-shirt with my sleeves rolled up, where I carry my Marlboro pack at the Dairy Queen, but not now, because I'm on my way to visit Mother in the hospital. In a paper sack on the seat beside me are the things she asked me to bring: a can of tomato juice, her hair brush and rollers, her purse, and a bar of Dove soap.

I don't know much about why she is in the hospital. I knew she was supposed to go in, "It's one of those female things," she had told me a few days before. "It's routine, so you don't need to worry about me. But I'll want you to come over and bring me some things while I'm in the hospital. Your brother will be working at the drug store and won't be able to get away. Do you think you'll be able to drive all that way without any trouble?"

"Aw, Mother. Sure I can." It was all of fourteen miles from Mariposa to Waxahachie where the hospital was, and she was probably right to worry about the driving habits of a fifteen-year-old, but at that time I wanted to think of myself as an adult to add to my years as quickly as possible.

It is a quiet fall day, and I'm pleased to have a written excuse to leave class early. Driving to the hospital I head west of Mariposa, drive past what is then called Little Mexico, where the migrant workers live during cotton picking season, but it's fall now and the area of dilapidated shacks is almost empty, except for a few old cars—a '49 black Chevy with fender skirts, an aging Hudson Hornet. Beyond that on the right I pass what my father called "The Ranch" where we lived when I was about two. It was his last attempt to raise his sons to the ranch life, which was his ideal. He should have been a cowboy. That's where his heart and skills were, but a failed early marriage and then the Depression had driven him (and hundreds of others) out of the cattle business and into something else. The something else for Dad was always elusive—truck driving, short order cook, selling cars, the restaurant business, a hamburger joint that catered to the high school lunch crowd, even a parakeet aviary, of all things. But these schemes never really worked, and Dad smoked and worked himself into an early grave at fifty-five.

I'm driving the '54 Ford west to Waxahachie, past the ranch, where we'd lived for only a couple of years before we'd moved back to town. The ranch was another of my father's pipe dreams—failure that matched his life perfectly. Perhaps that's what drove Mother to church; maybe other-worldly pleasures could make up for the sorrows of her life with him in this one.

At any rate, he had been dead for five or six years by the time I had to drive her things over to her at the hospital. I drive by the Waxahachie Square and the Dairy Queen before heading to the hospital, where I park, grab the things from the car, and walk in. Entering the hospital is like walking into church; it must be the scrubbed institutional quality of both. I stop at the nurse's station and find out Mother's room number and take the wide, double-sided elevator up to the second floor.

I knock and get no response, so I open the door quietly and walk inside. Mother is sleeping when I walk in, so I put the things on top of the rolling table that sits by the side of the bed. I call gently to her, then louder before she wakes up slowly. She seems very groggy, but she smiles at me and asks me about the drive.

"It was fine, no problems. I drove past the ranch on the way."

"Your daddy would have been so proud of you," she says for the thou-sandth time. It was her almost automatic comment whenever we talked of him. "Tom was so proud of you boys; you were his life, you know."

"Yes, Mother," I respond automatically, too.

But she sounds different today, not the same as usual, perhaps it's the medicine she's taking, I don't know. She encourages me to sit down, and I pull up an orange vinyl-covered chair.

"How are you feeling?" I ask, but I'm just making small talk, ready to walk back out the door and get out of the uncomfortable and restrictive hospital.

"I have felt better," she says and smiles. "Pull your chair over here closer, so I can hold your hand."

"Aw, Mother," I protest, but I do as she wishes. Her hands are cold and soft, and I notice the veins standing out on the back of them.

"I want to tell you about the operation," she says.

"Everything okay?" I ask.

"Yes, yes, fine," she says. "But I think you ought to know about it.

You're old enough. I had a hysterectomy, you know. It's a major operation, and I'll have to stay here for another few days before I can come home."

"Well, I'm glad everything's okay," I say reassuringly. I don't really know what a hysterectomy is, and I don't really care. Female problems seem something that happens to old women like her, and their experiences and concerns are beyond my level of interest.

"Yes, a hysterectomy. They've removed my uterus," she says gravely.

"Uh-huh," I say looking at her hand.

"You know the uterus is a lady's womb. That's where the sperm enters and fertilizes the egg and the baby begins to grow."

Of course I know about sperm and babies. My friends and I have been exchanging information about the birds and the bees for years, but that talk is reserved for the boys in the car circling the Dairy Queen. My father and I never had discussed anything before he died, and this is the first time in my life that my mother has uttered a word about sex. But she's somehow decided that now is the time, either that or the painkillers have deadened her usual compunctions against talking about such an unsavory subject with her son. She drives on.

"Yes, you know the man inserts his penis in the vagina and deposits his sperm there, and they make their way up to the uterus. But when a woman has passed her childbearing years, she no longer needs or uses all of her organs."

I cannot believe that my mother has mentioned the word *penis* in my presence. For all of my fifteen years, this entire subject has been one of the darkest taboos of my life. She's holding my hand so I cannot escape, but I can feel my face flushing—*penis, vagina, sperm, womb*—I am awash in words reserved for another sphere.

"Sure, Mother, I know all about that," I blurt out, trying to cut off the flow.

"The plumbing just doesn't work any more," she says with a weak laugh.

I sit aflame. Of course I know about women. Or at least I think I know something. After all I am no longer a virgin. That is for five days I am no longer a virgin. Just a few nights before I had picked up Sally Walker, driven out into the country, and finally used the condom I had carried in my billfold so long that a round circle had been imprinted in the leather. So for the last week I have been unable to think about anything except penises, vaginas, and sperm, and now here my mother has intruded into my most secret world.

"Yes, they've removed the uterus. I have a large incision across my abdomen. That's what takes the time to recover. They had to cut through those stomach muscles. But there are some benefits from this."

"Uh-huh. That's good," I murmur. "You'll feel better now," I offer.

"Yes, that's true. And I'll have more energy the doctor says. And of course, I won't have any more periods ever again."

Omigod, I stand suddenly, pulling my hand away from her, and walk to the window where I look out across the parking lot, searching for my car. *Penises, vaginas, sperm, and now periods*—the curse, riding the red river. Another topic for the boys in the car, not now, not here, not with my mother.

"Well, Mother, I think I better be getting on back now," I say, hoping that I can escape this unrelenting agony of having to stay and talk more with her.

"Not quite, yet, honey," she says. "I want to speak with you about another subject."

Oh, no. I blanch and can't imagine what else she might want to discuss, now that the floodgates have opened.

"I really should get back; I don't want to drive in the dark," I try to argue, but it's only a few minutes after three, a good three hours before dark.

"No, sit down. I discussed something with Dr. Kenneally before the operation, and I think now is the time you and I should talk about it. He is a surgeon after all, and I wanted to speak with him about you."

Stunned, I cannot imagine what she might talk with the doctor who removed her womb about me. But I stand still with my back to her, looking out the window.

"I spoke with him about your moles."

Now she'd reached another area that I treated like poison. I was the usual self-conscious teenager, but I was especially self-conscious about the mottled body I was born with. As a child I blithely shucked my shirt and leaped into the pool without ever thinking about it, but once I had gotten to teenage years, the numerous dark moles that dotted my body kept me from going shirtless. My skin whitened in its seclusion and made the dark moles stand out like leeches, or at least as I viewed them in the privacy of my bathroom mirror. The dark of the back of my car the week before allowed me the pleasure of its shadows with Sally.

"I asked him about removing some of those moles," she announces.

"Uh-huh."

"Yes, I am especially concerned about that one."

I know, of course, immediately the one she's talking about, but I still feel as if my head is inside a bell, my ears ringing. I do not want to tread the path she's leading me to.

"Aw, I'm fine, Mama, just leave me alone. C'mon now. I gotta be goin'," I lapse into my best kidspeak to try to stave off the horror of this discussion.

"Of course," she continues, "I think those big ones on your back should be removed, and there is one on the front there beside your nipple" (now, *nipple*, oh god). "But the one that really concerns me is the other one."

I turn and walk toward the door, not believing that this is happening. But as much as I want to run out the door and seclude myself inside the warm naugahyde of my tuck-n-roll seats where Sally lay last week, I know I cannot escape this.

"Yes, Dr. Kenneally thinks that he can and should remove those moles. The one beside your penis might get in the way after you're married and become irritated and cause you great difficulty in your marriage."

I feel as though I have been shot, run over by a truck, caught in a grenade explosion. That she was talking about her own private parts was awful enough, but now that she has dragged my own out into the light of day, I feel as though a tornado has blown through the hospital and left me naked, with some large spotlight shining on the mole with which I had been blessed growing beside my penis.

"Yes," she rushes on, "your wife one day will thank me and thank Dr. Kenneally for this. It will make all the difference in the world for you."

"No, no, no, no, Mama," I finally get my voice, get up, and begin to gather my football sweater. "I'm not talking about this any more, Mother."

"Well, it's all scheduled. Next Tuesday, you will meet Dr. Kenneally in his office in Mariposa at 10:00 A.M. He has a new procedure. It's some kind of electrical device that he will use to remove those moles. It fries them, as I understand it, then they will drop off. You will have to cover them for a while. And of course, if you get an erection" (*erection*, how could she?) "then that might cause some irritation and bleeding, but we'll just have to deal with it as we can."

I am suddenly humiliated by the image of my mother kneeling over my penis, applying some kind of salve to this puny, bleeding organ, but in the instant that I reached that layer of memory, the morning whistle rousted me from my dream.

* * * *

Despite this disconcerting dream memory, I got everything done. I had extra work to do on the latrine after a long night of the platoon smoking and working there. The buffing crew worked extra on the floors too, since the girls would be inspecting the barracks before the party. Swanson, the first platoon TAC, took us on an early morning run, but he didn't push us extra; the one turn around the Airborne track now seemed like a cakewalk. Then it was back to the barracks for the last few hours of readying for our dates' arrival on the train from Atlanta at four that afternoon.

Trotter was going in with a small welcoming committee. The women were staying across from the train station in the Old Rock Hotel near the Chattahoochee in downtown Columbus, where they would check in after the train arrived. Trotter had arranged for a couple of Army olive-drab schoolbuses to pick them up in their formals to bring them out to post at seven for their barracks walkthrough. Then everyone would gather out on the tarmac for the formal date introductions and walk over to the battalion auditorium where the party would take place.

We still had no idea what would come after the party. Some companies got liberty for the night, but we had heard nothing and were planning for nothing more than the party. So we didn't know what to make of it when someone started yelling, "Fall Out!" around mid-morning.

"What the hell is happening?" Sugarman asked. "Are those bastards going to make us go on another run?"

"No, I don't think so," said Budwell. "Just some last minute character guidance points probably."

Sure enough, it was Capt. Lederer himself that we saw standing on the steps leading to his office while Swanson called us to attention. Lederer rarely talked to us these days. We'd see him heading into his office, but he didn't even take chow with us or any of the other TACs. The rumor was that, disgusted as he was with the state of the world, he'd turned in a discharge request and was going to law school as soon as he got out, but no one knew for sure.

As usual, Captain Lederer spoke to us in almost a whisper, and we strained to hear his words, which urged and cajoled us.

"You men are to be congratulated for reaching this point in your training. I shall not dwell on your accomplishments, on the rigorous demands that you have met with enthusiasm and success, on the changes you have seen in yourselves and your comrades, for these things you know far better that I could express them here.

"Instead I point toward the road that you have taken to becoming commissioned officers in the Army of the United States. The road you chose is not an easy one. It demands the requisite knowledge of the tools and techniques of the profession—professional competence. It demands special personal qualities: hard, dedicated work; sacrifice, of yourself, of your men, sometimes of your family; loyalty, to your nation that feeds and clothes you, to your superiors who depend on you, to your men, who have only you as their hope, their protection, their guide and leader; honor, to uphold that code as old as the profession of arms, the code that calls for protection of the innocent, mercy for the weak, and justice, sure and swift, for the wrongdoer."

Rustling fatigues made it hard to hear. Some shushed their neighbors and crowded closer to Lederer, who somehow seemed older and sadder than he had twelve weeks before when he first addressed us.

"The demands of this road are heavy ones, unmarked by apparent rewards. You will not find adequate monetary rewards for that which is asked of you. In this now self-indulgent world devoid too often of discipline, you will frequently be jeered more often than cheered by those whom you defend. The rewards are there for those who see and value them. They are rewards far beyond the powers of others to give or withhold. You will find them in your own self-satisfaction, of responsibility accepted, of duty well discharged, of pride in yourself and your uniform, of respect rendered by those whose opinions you respect, of the deep inner knowledge, perhaps never spoken that there exists between you, the flag, and the nation—a special relationship denied to other men."

I turned and looked around the group, all of whom seemed transfixed by this melancholy man, speaking what seemed like final words to us, for reasons we only understood through a glass darkly. Lederer didn't seem to be looking directly at any one of us down below him. His gaze seemed focused over our heads toward the western horizon beyond the steam rising from the heating tanks. He continued.

"You will always know that your experiences here in OCS have marked you forever and that you are better for having been here. For those of you who move beyond this special time and make it to the end of your time, I will know that I am a better man for having known you. And now God speed and good luck with the rest of your venture down this road."

We began to clap, but now he looked down at us and raised his arms in signal to quiet the group.

"Tonight you pass that special mid-point in your travels, and in recognition of that event I grant you, the members of Class 10-70, 58th Company, liberty from midnight tonight until 0700 tomorrow. Act always with dignity."

With that the company went wild, throwing hats in the air and dancing around, yelling, "God Bless Captain Lederer!" The TACs tried gaining order, yelling attention, and grabbing the most obvious celebrants and pushing them toward the tarmac.

The company was giddy with the thought of liberty, the first since returning from Christmas, but there was something about the captain's words that chastened some others. We fell to attention long enough to be dismissed to continue our preparations.

I walked in with Budwell and asked him what he made of the captain's speech.

"Sounded like he was about to go put a bullet through his head instead of about to go to law school." Then Budwell laughed, "Of course, they might be the same thing."

"Well, at least he gave us an overnight pass. I heard that 51st Company that turned black last week didn't get any liberty. They hit midnight and turned into pumpkins, had to send their dates back to Columbus by themselves on the buses."

"Yeah, so what are you going to do?"

"I guess that depends on one Mary O'Hara," I laughed.

Budwell dug his fist into my ribs, "So, you think you might get lucky?"

"I've been gazing into my date's eyes in that picture on my locker for days, planning what I'll say to her."

"Yeah, well, you better not plan too much. Things often work out differently than you hope."

"And what about you? What are you planning?"

"I'll just let the evening pass. Let it be. Whatever will, will."

"Oh, yes, old Zen master. Is that why you just took whatever was left of the dates? Did you get a dog?"

"I don't know. We'll see what Miss Karen Cook is like tonight. I just thought it didn't make much difference what those pictures looked like."

"I happen to think it's better to try to grab hold of the world instead of it grabbing hold of you."

"Spoken like a draftee," Budwell laughed. "When I think it's right, I'll make a choice. Right now, I choose to take a piss," and he headed for the latrine.

Trotter had asked for a group of three to go meet the train with him and get the girls squared away. We took a taxi in and waited at the train station for the four o'clock, the 1600, arrival. Dickie Swain from first platoon had joined Trotter and me. The train was about fifteen minutes late, and we all hung around, nervously looking down the tracks to the north. Finally, the lights of the engine appeared in the distance, and we straightened our caps, dusted the toes of our boots, and stood waiting. We were wearing our fatigues, newly starched ones for this meeting. We would just walk them all over to the hotel and arrange to be back to meet them when the buses arrived at seven.

God, I thought to myself. Why am I so nervous? You'd think you never had a date. I watched carefully as each of the girls got off the train. I tried to decide if I should try to find Mary O'Hara now or just wait until the girls came out on the buses tonight. As I stood there trying to help some of the girls get their suitcases, a dark haired young woman was standing beside me looking at my nametag.

"Are there several men named Adams?" she asked.

I looked into the eyes of Mary O'Hara from Millersville, Georgia, and found myself almost unable to speak.

"No, I'm the only one."

"Then you must be Jeff Adams from Texas."

"Yes, and you must be Mary O'Hara from Georgia."

She held out her hand, and I felt like I must have looked at it stupidly before I reached out and shook it, "Welcome to Columbus. Do you have a suitcase?"

There were only three of us on the welcoming committee, and there were over 100 women who had come in on the train. Trotter had arranged for some people from the hotel to bring cars over to carry suitcases. I helped Mary get her suitcase. I had somehow expected her to be especially friendly, but she seemed distant and quiet. I tried to make some conversation with her, but she kept her answers short and offered no other information.

I told her goodbye at the hotel and went glumly back to the taxi.

"Why the long face?" asked Trotter.

"I've been dreaming about my date for days, and she didn't seem all that interested in talking to me."

"Well, maybe she's shy. I wouldn't worry about it. You'll get plenty of time to get to know her tonight."

"Yeah, I guess so. It just almost seemed like she didn't want to be here. They all signed up voluntarily, didn't they?"

"Sure, don't worry about it. Let's get back. Once she sees you in those dress blues, she'll be starry-eyed."

"I hope you're right," I said, but I wasn't at all sure now. I had spent long hours rehearsing what I was going to say when I first met her, and chance had blown all those plans away.

As I got dressed, I was puzzled by what had happened that afternoon and tried to think through a few new scenarios about how the evening might go, but where the plans I had run through my head before I met

Mary all seemed possible, now everything I thought about seemed to run into the quiet and distant figure of my date. I took my time and placed my brass carefully on the new dress blue uniform, measuring exactly where it all went. When I finally put the uniform on and looked at myself in the mirror, I had an odd, mixed reaction. On one hand, I was taken with myself, thinking that the Infantry blue stripe banded by yellow piping was terribly smart-looking. But the visual echoes of John Wayne, Henry Fonda, and all those other bluebelly cavalrymen from the westerns I had grown up with crowded up against the reality that I was in OCS training for a disquieting war. But at this moment I was preparing to spend the evening with a woman whose image smiling out at me from the locker had intrigued me for days.

The party was held at battalion auditorium. The preparation committee had worked on it much of the day, carrying through the "Into the Future" theme and the colors I'd selected for the program as well as the Valentine's Day theme with red hearts and bunting. We marched as a company over to battalion HQ, where we stood at parade rest until the buses arrived with the girls after their brief walkthrough of the barracks. The wives and dates who drove onto post had arrived early and stood to the side. It was a cool but not cold Georgia evening.

When the buses pulled into the parking lot, one candidate was assigned to call out each girl's name as she stepped off, and the candidate who was her date was to step up and escort her inside. It was a slow but militarily formal process. A local cover band had been hired to play for the program, and we could hear their music as we stood outside, but they were playing soft music like "Moon River" and nothing from contemporary rock-n-roll. Most of the names meant nothing to me, but when I heard "Karen Cook," I cut my eyes and saw Budwell walk over and offer his arm. About halfway through, the name of Mary O'Hara rang out, and I stepped up and offered my arm. She was wearing a black strapless evening dress with long white gloves. Her hair was down, long and flowing over her shoulders, and she was beautiful. She looked at me for a moment, almost as if she were thinking about taking it, before she slipped her hand inside my elbow.

Once inside, I found the corsage table and got the box I'd ordered. I tried to pin it to her dress, but it was awkward trying to find a place on the strapless dress. Some of the guys had ordered wrist corsages, knowing their dates had strapless dresses, and I began to feel stupid for not checking. But Mary saw my discomfort and pinched some of the fabric near the décolleté and offered it. I fumbled, tried to apologize for not getting the right kind of corsage and pinned it on. She told me not to worry about it and straightened the dress and flower.

So again the evening wasn't going as I had played it out in my head, but most of the rest of the dinner went as expected. The officers and staff sat on a dais and were served, while the candidates and their dates went through a buffet of roast beef, mashed potatoes, and green peas. Even the military parties have a standard operating procedure. There was a bar set up, and we were supposed to limit ourselves to no more than three glasses of wine for the evening. After dinner was a formal period for cigars and port while the speakers from the dais addressed the group.

All of this drifted along. Mary still seemed distant and aloof. She talked some with the girl across the table but asked me almost nothing as we got served and ate dinner, lit the cigars (for the men only, of course), and poured the port. The battalion commander, Lt. Col. Anaya, presided over most of the formal process, which was nice and short, filled with expected clichés. When all of that was over, he announced that the dance was about to begin, and the tables were moved back as the band came back in. Col. Anaya and his wife got the first dance.

I tried to make more conversation with Mary, asking such questions as "Do you like to dance?" and "What kind of music do you like?" But she would just barely answer, "Yes" and "I like most kinds of music." I decided she wasn't really shy but that she just didn't seem to want to talk to me.

We danced to some slow songs from the 50s and to the band's version of "Suspicious Minds," and I thought about being caught in a trap and not getting out, as the song said. I held Mary at arm's length to keep from mashing her corsage and decided that there just must be no chemistry, despite my attraction for the smile in the photograph. She barely smiled all night and seemed ill at ease and uncomfortable. I drank my third glass of wine, which, along with the port and the fact that except for a few beers over Christmas break, I had had almost nothing to drink in months, began to go to my head. I danced with Budwell's date, went for a fourth glass of wine, and began to get loud. I sat across the table from my date, while she sat quietly.

A few minutes before midnight, someone announced that anyone who wasn't sleeping in the barracks tonight had to sign out, causing a rush to the first sergeant's office.

Eighteen

The Silver Slipper

We were waist deep in the Big Muddy and the big fool said to push on.
—*"The Big Muddy"*
—*Pete Seeger*

Budwell and I decided to take a taxi into town instead of waiting to ride the buses, and all four of us sat in the backseat for the ride into Columbus. A light mist was falling and Brook Benton's "Rainy Night in Georgia" was on the radio. None of us knew much about places to go, but I had heard of a place called the Silver Slipper and asked the taxi driver if he knew where it was.

"The Silver Slipper? Sure," he said. "It's over the tracks, if you know what I mean. I don't think you want to take these girls there."

I knew that the Silver Slipper was in the black section of town and that it had a reputation for catering to soldiers on pass. If Mary O'Hara hadn't been so distant and unfriendly and if I hadn't exceeded my drink limit, I probably wouldn't have even thought about taking her there, but I was disturbed by her attitude and emboldened by the evening. I expected Budwell to protest, but he was always open for anything.

"The Silver Slipper it is. What time do they stay open to?" he asked the taxi driver.

"They're supposed to close at two on Saturday night, but that place plays by its own rules. I'll take you, but you better be careful there, especially in those fancy uniforms."

We soon pulled up to a large building set back from the road. Loud soul music floated out of the doorway, where two large black men stood talking to an equally large white man in a sheriff's uniform.

"How are you boys doing tonight?" the sheriff asked.

"Fine," said Budwell. "We're celebrating."

"What're you all celebrating?"

"We just got back from the Nam, and we're here with our wives to hear some good soul music to celebrate that we made it back alive," Budwell lied.

"Well, we're mighty proud of you boys. Step right in. They'll take good care of you in the Silver Slipper."

"Thank you much," said Budwell, and I nodded and we walked in.

As we were going in, it seemed to dawn on the sheriff that we were not wearing regular uniforms. He called out something and gestured toward his coat. Budwell waved at him, and we slipped in the door.

The place was crammed with GIs, mainly enlisted men and a lot of short-haired guys who were probably military. Fifteen or twenty black women in slinky dresses, most of them with large Afros, sat or strolled about the large room. Several large black men stood near the door, and another white sheriff stood at the bar. There was no band. The music blasted out of large speakers attached to the wall at the end of the bar. The bartender, a young black guy, tended the eight track tape player.

We were the only guys in dress blues in the place, and our dates were the only white women there, at least at first. The group looked at us warily; even the white GIs seemed to see us as outsiders with our dates in their evening dresses and corsages. Budwell and I ordered Schlitz for all of us, and we sat back at a table in the corner. Mary O'Hara still maintained her cool distance, and I had just about given up on her. In a few minutes the door opened and in came Candidate Garrett with his date in her evening gown. We called to him, and he came over to sit with us.

We had not met his date earlier, and he introduced us to her, Dinah Jefferson, a nursing student from Waycross, Georgia.

"Hi, I'm Jeff Adams. Actually Jefferson Adams. We may be kinfolks," I laughed, shaking her hand.

She took my hand, looked at me without laughing and said, "Yes, my family is kin to Thomas Jefferson, I've always heard. Yours is too?"

"No, I'm actually named for Jefferson Davis, I think. I don't know about the last name."

"Jefferson Davis? He had something to do with the Civil War?"

"President of the Confederacy, I'm afraid."

She looked at me silently for a moment.

"So your family owned slaves?"

"I guess so. A few. We didn't have a big plantation or anything, just a small ranch in Texas."

"Don't take but one to make you a slave owner."

"Yes, I guess you're right."

"And it only takes one murder to make you a murderer," Mary O'Hara said, surprising me by breaking her silence.

"Hi, Dinah," she said. "I don't think we've met yet."

I was beginning to feel really uncomfortable, so I finished my beer and decided to have another one. While I was standing at the bar, a black woman with a short Afro came up and asked me to dance. I took her out on the floor, and we danced to Sly and the Family Stone. When we were through, she asked me my name, told me that she was named Felicia, and asked me to buy her a drink. At the bar, she leaned into me and began to rub my thigh.

"Say, honey. Do you want a date?"

"No thanks," I said. "I have a date. She's probably getting mad at me for leaving her alone so long."

"No, honey, that's not what I mean," she said, running her hand up between my legs and giving me a squeeze. "I mean do you want some pussy? This here is the Silver Slipper. You white boys come here for a little black stuff. Let's go to my room downstairs out back."

She had caught me by surprise and continued rubbing between my legs with one hand and running the other hand under the back of my dress blue jacket, squeezing my cheeks. I had been away from women so long, had had four glasses of wine and a couple of beers already, and my mind was fogged.

"You got money, doncha?" she asked.

"Uh-huh." I said getting more and more lost, thinking only about her hand between my legs.

"Well, you need to let Felicia fuck or suck you, baby. Come on, now let's go. You got some money. I can git you some good weed, and you git some good pussy."

I felt her take my hand and begin to lead me to a dark hall leading to a stair to the back. As we got to the stairs, she turned and kissed me and continued to rub me, and all I could think about was her musky smell. Just as she turned to the door, Garrett stepped into the hall.

"Adams. What the hell are you doing, man?"

"I'm just talking to this sister here."

Garrett walked up. "Bullshit, man, this here's a hooker. You know that. You better check your wallet."

I reached to my back pocket and sure enough my wallet was gone.

"It's not in my pocket. I musta left it at the bar."

"Uh-huh," said Garrett. "Let's have it, sister." He took her hands and began patting her down and sure enough she had my wallet stuffed down her dress.

Garrett handed it to me, while I tried to say I didn't have any idea how she could have gotten it out of my pocket.

"Who the fuck made you king?" she said.

"Go on back," Garrett told her, "find some other drunk to roll."

"Adams, you got a damn nice-looking date sitting back at that table. I think you better go back and take care of her."

I suddenly remembered Mary and felt guilty and walked with Garrett back to the table where Mary turned away from me when I sat down.

"I'm sorry," I told her. "I misplaced my wallet and Garrett helped me find it. Sorry to leave you alone for so long."

She still seemed to ignore me, while I felt a mixture of anger and guilt. Just then out of the large speakers came the sounds of B.B. King's "The Thrill Is Gone," so I stood up and took Mary's hand, "Let's dance."

She looked up at me as if she were considering it and then stood up and walked with me to the dance floor. It was a slow song, and I tried pulling her close to me. She resisted.

"Don't worry about that corsage. It's about gone anyway," I told her.

"I'm not worried about the corsage."

"Well, I guess it's just me then."

She didn't say anything, and I began to get mad. The song wasn't quite over, but I took her hand and headed back toward the table.

"I don't think you're having any fun. Maybe I should just take you back."

"Yes, maybe you should."

We went back to the table. Budwell and his date were holding hands and laughing, having a good time.

"Say guys. Mary thinks she's ready to go back, so we're going to get a ride into town. Y'all stay here, and I'll catch you later."

We went out to the parking lot and saw a taxi sitting there, and I asked the cabbie to take us to the Old Rock Hotel. Bob Dylan's "Lay, Lady, Lay" was on the radio, and I sat listening to Dylan, wondering what had gone wrong that night. When we got downtown, it was quiet. As we got out, the moon glistened and a brisk breeze blew over the Chattahoochee River. I took off my jacket and put it around Mary's shoulders.

"Let's walk along the boardwalk by the river for a minute and then I'll walk you to the door."

"All right." We walked down past the statue erected to honor the Confederate dead, saying nothing to each other.

I finally turned to her and said, "You know, I kept your picture on the inside of my wall locker door and felt like I knew you by looking into your eyes. Boy was I wrong. I'm sorry I wasn't what you wanted."

She looked at me, and I thought she was going to say something. When she didn't, I asked her, "What are you looking for?"

"I'm not looking for anything," she said. "I just don't want to have anything to do with killers."

I stopped suddenly, not sure that I'd heard her right.

"Killers? I'm not a killer. Who told you such a story?"

"You're all training to be killers. Murderers of babies, old women, children, and old men. I know you're going to go over to Vietnam and wipe out more villages. It's disgusting."

"So that's why you've been mad at me all night. You think I want to go wipe out a village like My Lai? What gave you that idea?"

"I've been reading the paper, and I talked to some of my friends about what happens here at OCS. I've heard how they get rid of those candidates who don't really want to go to Vietnam. And I heard about your company cheer."

"Company cheer?"

"Yes, something about raping and burning. I hate the thought of it. I'm studying to take care of people. Almost every day we see someone in the hospital who was hurt in Vietnam, either physically or mentally, and every night on the television we see more pictures of people killed, of innocent children killed or napalmed, that awful picture of that naked girl running down the road. Or pictures of people shot, like that Vietnamese man shot in the head by the other one holding a pistol.

"I should have never agreed to put my name on the date list, but I didn't know enough about it when I did. I shouldn't have come."

"Look, Mary. I'm here because I got drafted, not because I want to go kill anyone. I came because of an old man whose heart would break if I tried to avoid the draft or go to Canada," I said.

I took her by the hands and sat down on a nearby wooden bench.

"Let me tell you something. I don't know if I'll ever finish OCS, and if I do, I don't know what I'll do when I get orders for Vietnam. But I'll promise you now that I'll never, never, kill a child or any innocent person. This is a solemn oath," I said, crossing my chest.

She turned to look at me, the full moon illuminating her face, and I could see for the first time since I met her, the smile of Mary O'Hara that had filled my imagination with the capacity for wonder.

Nineteen

Driving Rusty

If I had a low IQ
I could be a lifer too.
—marching song

I knew the world was turned upside down a few days later as soon as the first sergeant came in. I could tell he was upset about something as he slammed around the office while I worked recording the platoon's scores for the company academic officer.

"What's up, Top?"

"Bullshit, as usual. Damn Army, you can't tell what's going to happen any more, and you can't depend on nothing. That company clerk was supposed to be here today, and I need him to be a driver. The turd came in moping around and went on sick call, and I still need a driver."

He looked at me as if he'd had an idea and asked me if I could drive.

"Sure, Top. Why do you ask?"

"OK, that'll work. I don't like to take an officer candidate away from his duties, but battalion has been passing this around on the sly, and it's our turn to take care of him today, so I'm just going to have to ask you to do it for me.

"Here's what I want you to do. Here are the keys to that Army limousine out there. Drive over to the PX. You'll find a first lieutenant wearing dress greens sitting out front. Your job is to pick him up and drive him wherever he wants to go."

"That sounds easy enough, Top. What's his name?"

"Name? Why do you want to know his name? Oh, all right. His name is Calley. Little guy with red hair."

"Lt. Calley? Isn't that the guy that's under house arrest here for killing those—"

Top turned on me sharply.

"Shut the fuck up, candidate. Keep you mouth shut and do what the lieutenant tells you to. Don't ask no questions."

"But, Top, what do I do if he wants to go off post. He's not supposed to leave."

The first sergeant shook his head wearily.

"Damn it. You're in OCS, and you're not supposed to be reading no newspapers or watching no TV. All that civilian bullshit don't mean nothing out here. We take care of our own. If the lieutenant wants to go off post, you go off post. He'll let you be back by 1700. Just do what I tell you and keep quiet about it."

Taking the keys and grabbing my baseball cap with a blue OCS patch, I headed out the door, "Yes sir, boss."

"Don't call me 'sir'; I work for a living," he yelled after me as I walked out.

* * * *

I passed the adjutant general's office, pulled up to the PX, and parked the nondescript, olive-drab Chevy out front. I looked around at the various soldiers there. Most were enlisted men wearing standard-issue fatigues. Then I noticed a short, chubby man in officer greens sitting on a bench off to the side. He was so short that his feet didn't even seem to reach the ground, and he sat quietly swinging them back and forth like a child. I walked over and when I got close enough, I confirmed from his nametag that he was Lt. Calley. I walked up, saluted, and presented myself in official OCS fashion.

"Lt. Calley, sir! OC Adams, 58th OC Company, sir! I'm assigned to be your driver, sir! May I assist you, sir!"

Calley looked uncomfortable, his eyes darting from side to side.

"Quiet down," he answered. "Don't yell out my name around here, damn it. You'll have them reporters on us. Hell, Seymour Hersch'll jump out of that garbage can. Just get me to the car, and let's get out of here."

I led him to the car and opened the back door for him.

"Go on, get behind the wheel. Can open my own door," he said sliding over on the seat and taking off his hat. "What you doing driving me? Usually send the company clerk or somebody from the mess hall."

"Sir, OC Adams. The company clerk reported in sick, sir!" I yelled out.

"At ease, at ease, candidate. Shit, just about forgotten all this OCS bull-shit. You just take it easy, buddy. Your first name?"

"Jeff, sir."

"Ease up, Jeff. Call me Rusty. Just about had enough of the military routine. Let's just head into town. Need to stop by Millers Discount Store for some personal items and then want to go get a beer at the Foxhole. Do you know where they are?"

"No sir, I've never driven off post."

"That's all right. Both are easy to find just down Victory Drive. Just head off post and I'll show you."

As I drove off, I looked into the rearview mirror and examined my pas-senger. I had noticed how short he was when I first picked him up. No more than five-three, I guessed. As I looked at his freckled face with his red hair thinning at the temples and curling in a curious pompadour on top, I thought he looked like Howdy Doody in uniform, and I tried to remember what I'd read about him in the paper I'd found in the garbage behind the mess hall.

As I remembered the story, Calley was in charge of an Infantry pla-toon on a search and destroy mission in a little village complex called My Lai 4 a couple of years earlier in 1968. They had rounded up a group of old men, women, and children, herded them into a ditch, and massacred them, according to the story. Then they went on about their business, and Calley eventually came back to the states. Just before he was about to be discharged, a chopper pilot who had landed at the vil-lage while the civilians were being killed broke the story to a *New York Times* reporter. Calley had been charged with murder. His court martial trial was being held at Fort Benning, and Calley was supposed to be under house arrest.

Up ahead I saw the MP station, and I began to get uncomfortable. It would be strange enough for them to see someone from Officer Candidate School driving off post, but I was afraid that I'd have to smuggle my pas-senger off.

"Sir?"

"Yeah? Rusty, remember."

"Right. Rusty. Can you tell me what's going to happen up here at the guard station? Aren't you supposed to be under house arrest or something?"

He laughed with a strange, high-pitched sound in two repeated bursts. "Hee-hee, hee-hee."

"Not to worry. Not to worry. Be okay, you'll see."

I pulled up to the guard house, stopped, and waited as the MP came over. The MP held his M-16 in the present arms position, his white gloves in sharp contrast to the dark metal, and walked cautiously to the car. Antiwar protestors continued to threaten to disrupt military bases, so the guards were always wary. They had much less to worry about from cars leaving, I thought. Still, they were obligated to check every vehicle.

The guard came over and looked at me quizzically. Bending down, he looked in the back seat and smiled.

"Good afternoon, lieutenant. It's good to see you again. You headed to the Foxhole?"

"That's right, soldier. Gonna down a few after sittin' in that courtroom. Can we pass?"

"Absolutely, sir. And have a couple for me. We're all behind you here, sir. Good luck."

"We'll be back before 1700," Calley answered, waving me on.

My passenger was quiet as we drove past the tall pines that lined the road. As we reached Victory Drive, Columbus' main road, my passenger told me to take a left and pointed out a large discount store just beyond Vick's Jewelry across the road.

After I parked, I jumped out to get his door, but he already had it open.

"Forget that crap. C'mon, let's go in."

I followed him into the store, and as we walked in it was clear that this was a regular stop of his. All sorts of people came over to speak to him, all telling him how much they supported him.

As Calley picked up some toothpaste, an old women pushing a grocery cart came up.

"I just wanted to tell you, lieutenant, that we love you here in

Columbus. We just think you're wonderful and that it's terrible what they're doing to you."

Calley flashed a boyish smile, bent slightly at the waist, and said, "Why, thank you, ma'am, 'preciate your support."

"You shoulda killed 'em all. Wipe out the gooks," the grandmotherly lady replied. "We were talking about you at the Ladies Auxiliary just this morning. We want you to win, and you take care, now," she said as she pushed her basket off down the aisle with toilet paper and paper towels.

As Rusty picked up some razor blades and then Cokes, the scene was repeated. It seemed like everyone there knew him and all made an effort to speak words of encouragement. After he paid at the register, he bowed again to a group of people standing there looking at him, and we got back into the car.

"One of my favorite places. Could probably save money at the PX but couldn't get to see real folks like these here. A great town, gonna settle here some day, open a store, have a family. If I make it outta this jam."

It seemed odd to me that this man who'd been charged with a massacre was treated so well, but I didn't say anything, and Calley went on.

"That's what I like about a military town. Know the score, these people do. Know what happens over there. Know I was just doing what they wanted me to, that's all. Pull in over there. That's the place."

I turned into a parking lot with a blinking neon sign that read, "The Foxhole."

"Let's go get a beer," he said. "I'm buying."

As we walked in, the scene from the discount store was repeated. All the people seemed to know Rusty, calling out to him and wishing him luck.

He selected a booth in the back, sat down, and ordered us both a Schlitz.

"So, you're in OCS. That's where it all began for me. You know, I ain't no rocket scientist. Hell, just barely got a year of junior college. Never much thought about nothin'. I mean there was a war going on. Never even thought I could get into OCS, I'm only five-three. And I was a good clerk. Got outta clerk's school and somebody saw I'd gone to a military school as a kid, so they sent me off to OCS. Weren't too particular about who they might send over to be in the Infantry."

He laughed his funny high-pitched laugh. "You know why I went to that military school? Failed seventh grade. Got caught cheating on an exam. Let another guy copy from me."

I wondered for a moment about the other guy, the one who'd copy from Rusty, and then I just sat quietly and let him go on. My being in OCS seemed to have caused him to reflect on his own experiences.

"You know, they never did tell us much about not killing prisoners when I was going through OCS. Just didn't seem necessary, I guess. I mean, they told us all them stories about how if you wanted to get a prisoner to talk, you'd just take his buddy up into a chopper and push him out. Then the other'd talk. They tell you that story, Adams?"

"Yes, sir, I've heard it."

"I mean, we didn't talk about communism, either. Just bad, that's all. Like southerners and niggers. Grow up knowin' what they're supposed to feel about them. Same thing with communists. Grew up knowing they were bad, enemies. Never talked about it in OCS. Go over and kill 'em, body counts. That's what it was all about."

He sat back in the booth, looking like a child playing dress up, and continued to nod and acknowledge the people who came by and spoke to him. He suddenly asked me what I knew about him.

"Not much, sir. We're not allowed paper privileges. But I've picked up a few papers. I know you're being court martialed here for something that happened in Vietnam."

"Just doing my job. Medina. Captain Medina. You know what they called him. 'Mad Dog.' Nickname. 'Mad Dog.'" He sat shaking his head from side to side like it was controlled by an invisible string.

"Told me to take care of those people. Search and destroy. Body count. Scorched earth. Elephant walk. Take care of them. You know who Medina got to defend him? Bailey. F. Fuckin' Lee Bailey. Ain't that something? Goddamn spic's got a big dick lawyer. You know, he's got to put it off on me. Hell, he told me to take care of 'em, and that's what we did.

"So I told Meadlo to waste 'em. Meadlo. Was the best damn soldier in the whole platoon. Do anything I told him. Crippled now, lost his foot. Not like some of those other bastards. They hated me. Thought I was too short to be worth shit. But Meadlo, he'd do what I said. He was crying and spraying that ditch with his M-16. On automatic. Me too; I opened up."

He sat there quietly for a few minutes, reflecting.

"Can I ask you a question, sir?"

"Rusty, remember. Sure."

"Rusty. Did you think they were VC?"

"VC? Sure, how do you know? Man, they all look alike."

"But weren't there some kids, too? Babies?"

He sat quietly for a moment. "Sure some babies. Grow up, don't they? Get bigger, carry weapons and information. Wasn't prudent to let them grow up, but wasn't my job to think about any of that. Just doing my job. Trying to TCB, take care of business.

"Didn't let anybody get away with something wrong. Caught one grunt trying to get a blow job. Walked up on him while he had his bayonet out cutting off this gook girl's black pajamas and told him right off that we weren't there to get our rocks off and to get to work."

He turned to me suddenly and asked, "What would you do, Jeff? We thought we were going into enemy territory. Had lost friends to booby traps and grenades thrown by kids. What have they taught you in OCS about it?"

He caught me off guard, and I felt like I'd just been jerked by some invisible rope tied around my chest. I looked at him and blinked. "I don't know, Rusty. Don't know. I guess they haven't taught us much about it yet."

"Well, you better get ready, Jeff. Gonna have to make some decisions, too, when you get over there. Not gonna be like you expect. Not John Wayne and the Indians. A lot more confused."

A drunk came over to our booth and slid in next to Calley.

"You the fuckin' hero, ain't you?" he asked.

"Naw, " Calley replied, "Just a goddamn grunt. No hero. Just like every other man."

"Well, man," the drunk replied, "let me play you some music. I got a dime here. What's your favorite song?"

"In-A-Gadda-Da-Vida."

"Okay, lootenant," the drunk said. "You fought for my freedom, goddamnit. If we don't stop them commies over there, the next damn thing you know they'll be landing on Myrtle Beach and heading down here to Columbus."

Stumbling to his feet, he stood and spoke to the rest of the bar.

"Three cheers for the lootenant," he yelled out, holding his beer into the air and leading the yells. Calley looked embarrassed and waved to the other patrons in the bar. The drunk got up and wobbled to the juke box.

"Want me to be their martyr. Christ. Don't want to be no Christ but shit, it'd be a better view from the cross. I've always been looking up at things. You know what they called me in OCS? 'Surfside 5 1/2.' A joke. Not big enough to be 'Surfside 6.'"

The pounding sounds of "In-A-Gadda-Da-Vida" filled the bar and Calley sat.

"You were just following orders then," I said to him.

"That's right. You know we thought Pinkville was bad shit. That's what we called it, Pinkville. We'd been there before, couldn't get any information from those bastards. Medina said take care of 'em, and I did."

He turned to me. "Let me ask you something. How many times you heard somebody say to you, 'You ain't paid to think'?"

"Every day," I said.

"There you are. Ain't paid to think. Ain't paid to think." He looked at his watch.

"Gonna stay another few minutes. Waiting for somebody."

The door opened at just that moment, and I looked up to see a nondescript man in a dark blue suit step in and wait for his eyes to adjust to the dark of the bar. Calley waved to the guy, who came over to our booth and stood there. Rusty told him to sit down.

"No sir. Thank you anyhow. I just wanted to tell you I was sorry about what I had to say on the stand today. You know, nothing personal, sir. I just had to tell the truth."

"That's all right, Dursi, and you don't have to call me sir anymore. You're a free man. Why don't you sit down and have a beer with us."

"No sir, that's all I wanted to say." With that he turned and left.

Calley sat for a moment. "Funny. Sent me a message to meet him here after his testimony. Thought he wanted to chew the fat."

He downed his beer. "Well, Candidate Adams, that's about it."

He stopped for a moment before he slid out of the booth, looking up into the smoke swirling over the bar. "You know what my middle name is?" he asked.

"No," I said.

"Laws. William Laws Calley, Jr."

As he stood, his combat infantry badge glinted under the neon light over the booth. "Back to jail," he said as we drove down Victory Drive toward Fort Benning.

Twenty

Losing Rancek

Yea though I walk through the valley of death, I will fear no
evil, for I am the meanest motherfucker in the valley.
—Infantry school joke

After turning black, we found that OCS relaxed some. The philosophy for the first twelve weeks was "Total Control-Lockdown," meaning
that every hour was controlled, no passes, no phone, no radio, or newspaper privileges. After the eighth- and twelfth-week panels had bounced
out the weakest candidates, we began to get a few privileges, but they
might be granted for one platoon for one night and not for the next.
We might get coffee privileges on breaks one day and have them denied
the next.

Rancek seemed to be especially erratic. One morning he told us we
could have paper privileges before we marched over to Infantry Hall for
day-long instruction on night patrols. I bought a paper in the hall at the
first break and was standing there reading it and smoking a cigarette when
he came by and ripped into me.

"Adams, what the hell do you think you're doing reading that paper?
Just who told you you had paper privileges?"

"Sir, Candidate Adams. You did, sir. This morning."

He looked at me blankly for a moment and then said, "As you were,
Adams. I was just checking to make sure you were alert."

As the academic officer I ended up down in the TAC office entering
grades almost every night for awhile. Rancek had grown more tolerant
over the weeks, but now he seemed more and more distracted. The next
night after he'd given us paper privileges, I was in his office working.
Usually these nights he would be gone after chow, and I could work

alone during the regular study hall hours, another benefit of being academic officer.

Muttering to himself that there was nothing left to lose, Rancek came in quickly and acted like I wasn't there. I was sitting on the floor sorting the test results on tactics from the week before. He turned on the stereo he kept behind his desk, the one I'd sneaked a listen to over the weeks when I was sure he wasn't going to come in on me. He put on a Rolling Stones album and turned it up loud, and the sounds of "Sympathy for the Devil" reverberated off the walls. I started to say something to him, but I figured he'd speak to me when and if he was ready.

He leaned back in the chair with his arms behind his head, closed his eyes for a few minutes, then took a key from his pocket and unlocked his desk drawer. I watched quietly as he brought out a small leather pouch and a packet of rolling papers. He took out a paper, tapped some of the contents of the pouch into the paper, rolled it into a cigarette, and licked the edge.

I had never seen Rancek smoke, and even though we had been allowed to smoke in our rooms during study hall, he was adamant that no one could smoke in the TAC office. He reached into the back of the desk drawer and pulled out an ashtray and some matches. He looked over the smoke he'd rolled, licked the edges again, and lit it up. The smoke began to fill the room, and I recognized the sweet smell of marijuana.

I couldn't believe that Rancek was actually smoking dope in the TAC office. It wasn't particularly dangerous to smoke there, because the second platoon TAC office was at the far end of the building, isolated from the CO's office, the other platoons, and from our rooms upstairs. And since it was late in our training cycle, most of the other officers were gone by this time of the evening, and one TAC officer rarely went into another platoon anyway. Still, something odd must have happened for Rancek to take such a chance. It was incredible that he would risk lighting up there, especially in front of me. I thought that he must not have seen me on the floor when he came in, and I began to wonder how I should handle this strange turn of events. I thought for a minute that I would just sit silently and maybe he wouldn't realize I was there, but the longer I sat watching him, the more uncomfortable I became. I decided that maybe I should just leave the test results lying there, get up quietly, and slip out. I noticed that he would take a toke and lean back with his eyes closed listening to the music. That seemed to be a good time for me to try to get to the door and leave. I waited until the next toke, and as soon as he closed his eyes, I stood up, sorry I was wearing fatigues with heavy starch, because they rustled loudly.

Stepping over the papers, trying to keep my legs apart so the starched pant legs wouldn't touch, I eased across the room watching Rancek as he leaned back listening to the Stones. I had just about made it to the door when Rancek spoke quietly.

"Take your seat, Adams."

"Sir, Candidate Adams, I thought you didn't see me here."

"I saw you, and cut the 'sir' shit. My name is Timothy."

I'm sure I must have known his first name, but I don't think I had ever thought of him as anything but Rancek.

"Yes sir."

"Timothy, remember. Take a seat."

I sat in the chair beside the desk, the one we usually had to sit on the edge of at a kind of sitting attention, but this time I sat back normally. Rancek looked at his joint as if he were going to offer it to me and then thought better of it.

"I'm going."

"Sir?"

"I got my orders. Leave in two weeks."

"To Nam?"

"That's right. First Cav platoon leader. I got fourteen more days stateside, and then it's across the waters."

I didn't quite know what to say. "Well, congratulations, sir."

"Congratulations? What the hell do you mean, man? Why do you want to congratulate me for going over to get my ass shot off?"

"I thought you were just waiting to get to go. I've heard you say you couldn't wait to get your orders."

"Jesus, man. Not because I want to get killed. I'm just tired of living in limbo. I can't stand this waiting for something to happen. I'd rather take my chances with Charlie."

He stood up, walked to the small closet near his desk, and opened the door. On the wall was a small light fixture that he bent over and plugged in. The deep purple haze of a black light tinged the room. Then Rancek turned off the light in the office and moved over to the picture of Richard Nixon that hung on the wall. As he took the picture off the wall and sat it on the floor, the clear outline of a peace symbol glowed on the wall beneath the picture.

Dumbfounded, I stood looking at the peace symbol.

"I hate this fucking war," said Rancek. "I have this dream almost every night. I'm on a night patrol in the jungle. Can't see shit. I'm working through the doleful darkness with my patrol, passing the night vision viewer back and forth and then suddenly something blows up in back of me and in that flash I wake up. I always heard if you awake from a dream, you'll be all right, but I inevitably get this eerie feeling that I'm seeing myself dead in that jungle, in the dusky mist of Vietnam, far from home.

"This dream has been with me since I first got in the Army. It started in basic, lasted through AIT, and then began to be with me almost every night in OCS. I graduated last year about this time, and that dream has stayed with me, haunting me.

"That's why I'm tough on people like you and Garrett and that little dud we got rid of earlier, whatever his name was."

"Trailer."

"That's him. I only want people there I can depend on."

The Stones LP ended, and Rancek put on Blood, Sweat, and Tears.

He took another drag, closed his eyes for a moment, and looked at the peace sign glowing there.

"Goddamn, I hoped it'd be done with over there before I got these orders, but it won't be in two weeks. It might be by the time you might have to go. They'll run that shithead Nixon off, assassinate his goofy ass. But it's too late for me."

"I don't know what to say," I told him. "I thought you were committed to the war. You work us so hard and seem intent on getting only the best officers you can."

"Hell, man, that ain't because I'm full of patriotic bullshit. I just want to be as sure as I can that the sonofabitch leadin' the platoon on my left can take care of his end of the deal. I think that dream is one of the reasons I work you guys so hard. If I try to be sure that all of the men around me are good, have their shit together like I do, then maybe I can get back. This is about survival, not duty, honor, and country. All that crap went out the window with the Gulf of Tonkin and Tet. We're livin' in a different world now. God, Nixon's got some kind of secret shit in Cambodia. It's got to be in the streets or this thing will never end."

He relit the roach, took a deep drag and listened to BS and T sing "And When I Die."

"Make your plans, man. Revolution. In the streets. You better be ready."

I could hear someone walking down the hallway. Rancek calmly sat up and looked at me.

"Candidate Adams. What is the OCS Code of Honor?"

It took me a minute to realize that we were back into military bearing. I stood up quickly and yelled, "Sir Candidate Adams, an officer candidate will not lie, cheat, or steal, nor tolerate those who do."

"Good. Now, let's hear your General Orders."

"Sir, Candidate Adams, my General Orders are, first, I will guard everything within the limits of my post and quit my post only when properly relieved. Second, I will obey my special orders and perform all my duties in a military manner. Third, I will report violations of my special orders, emergencies, and anything not covered in my instructions to the Commander of the Relief."

"Good, Now I want you to sing the Alma Mater."

As I had done hundreds of times since I'd been there, I sang out,

Far across the Chattahoochee, to the Upatoi. OCS our Alma Mater, Benning's pride and joy. Forward ever, backward never, faithfully we strive. To the ports of embarkation, follow me with pride. When it's time and we are called to guard our country's might, we'll be there, with heads held high in peacetime and in fight. Yearning ever, failing never, to guard the memory. The call is clear we must meet the task for FREEDOM'S NEVER FREE!

While I was singing, Rancek calmly replaced Nixon's picture, turned off the black light, locked up his desk with the pouch and fixings, and resumed being the TAC officer I hated. I felt a little like I'd just seen the tooth fairy take a crap on the living-room floor. Rancek was the hardest TAC we had. Everything he'd done seemed absolutely dedicated to getting us ready to go to Vietnam. He'd convinced me that he believed completely in everything he'd been drilling into us for almost four months, and now here he was saying that it was all an act. It wasn't because of any latent idealism; I wasn't sorry that he didn't believe in the war. By that time I didn't know many who really did believe in it. It was just that I'd completely misjudged him. He had become the complete embodiment of everything I didn't like about OCS, its rigidity and inhumanity. I thought briefly about turning him in and getting him busted to get back at him, but I realized that he was showing me that he was just as scared and confused as I was. And in two weeks he was on his way to Nam.

* * * *

During mail call the next day, I got a big envelope from Mary O'Hara, even though I wasn't expecting anything. I dropped it on my bunk and sat down without thinking much about it. When I opened it, I was surprised to find a packet of anti-war materials—clippings from the Atlanta newspapers, an issue of *Ramparts* magazine with several articles dissecting our involvement in the war, a book about Vietnam by David Halberstam titled *The Making of a Quagmire*, and a large peace symbol decal superimposed over a circular American flag.

As I looked over the clippings, Budwell walked in and sat down at his study desk in the middle of the room. My initial instinct was to try to hide the material Mary had sent, since anything anti-war was looked upon as subversive and traitorous at OCS. One of the worst charges that could be made in those anonymous ORs was that you were secretly anti-war.

But Budwell quietly and conspiratorially set my mind at ease as he saw me trying to slide the envelope over the peace symbol.

"So our friend Mary must be trying to work her will on you," he said. I had told him about my conversation with Mary the night of the party.

"Yeah, she's sent me some light reading," I laughed, tossing the book on the desk.

"You better put that stuff away before Shrode gets here. You know how he raves on about those long-haired hippie weirdos. If he thinks you're a closet commie, he's liable to slice you up."

I decided to tell Budwell about my odd experience with Rancek the night before, but Budwell wasn't surprised.

"It's a strange, old world," he said, "and this war is one of the stranger parts of it right now. Your friend Mary may be on the right track."

I was surprised to hear Budwell say that. "If she is," I said, "we aren't."

He looked at me for a moment and said, "I've been thinking about that."

Twenty-one

Getting Kochs

If I die on the gooks' front
Bury me with a gook cunt.
—marching song

After that night in his office it was hard to see Rancek in the same way, but it was clear that he was a short timer, with only two more weeks with us. He had to process out, so we didn't see much of him in the time he had left. A couple of days later we were called out of the barracks a few minutes early. Rancek was standing there with another second lieutenant, a young, compactly built man, with blond hair and a goofy, crooked smile. Actually, I don't think his smile was crooked, but his two front teeth were chipped off at an odd angle, leaving him with a snaggle-toothed smirk that made it look like his head was cocked whenever he grinned.

I knew that Rancek was about to announce that he was leaving, but I had stolen his thunder by passing around the word in the platoon that he had gotten his orders. But this meeting would be the first time that he had spoken to us since he got his orders. He stood up on the porch.

"At ease, men, gather round. I have been your TAC officer since you began your program back in November. I have watched you grow and mature, and we've gotten rid of over a hundred duds in this company. We're getting lean and mean, a real fightin' machine.

"And now I'm proud to say that I'm about to get to use some of that fine Fort Benning training. I've got my orders to join the 1st Cavalry in Quang Tri Province in the Republic of Vietnam on 21 March 1970, and I'll be leaving you."

A groan went around the platoon. Even though they knew what was going on before he announced it, they also knew that they were supposed to act out their apparent surprise and loss of their beloved TAC. It was a game. Almost everybody was happy to see Rancek go. No one in the platoon had avoided his wrath, and everyone had decided that it had to be better with the devil we didn't know instead of the devil we did. I hadn't told anyone but Budwell of the odd, joint-smoking Rancek with the black light peace symbol, mainly because I thought they wouldn't believe me but also because the odd competitive system there made everyone secretive and isolated. We'd gotten too used to the guy next to us sneaking into the office to write up a critical OR.

"I'm here to introduce you to my replacement, who will square you guys away and take up exactly where I leave you."

With that, he gestured to the other lieutenant to join him. The guy with the goofy smile stood next to him awkwardly and crossed his hands in front of his crotch.

"This is your new tactical officer, Lt. Bernard Kochs from West Virginia."

We clapped and yelled, not too much because we knew Rancek was still in charge.

"Take a look at his nametag. That's Lt. Kochs, pronounced 'COCKS.' As of tomorrow morning at 0500, Lt. Kochs takes over the second platoon, and I expect you to treat him with the same respect you've shown for me, and I expect you to perform. I've molded you men into the best damn platoon at the United States Infantry School, and you damn well better not let me down."

We again yelled out things like "Go, Deuce," "You damn betcha," "Hell yes!" and other such expressions until Rancek motioned for silence.

"And now I give you Lt. Kochs."

Kochs had taken off his cunt cap after he stepped up beside Rancek, revealing a slicked down, blond flattop. He now carefully replaced his cap as we clapped. When he stepped forward on the porch, I noticed he wore an Airborne patch. He reminded me something of Jimmy Cagney as the commander in *Mister Roberts*. Kochs was taller than Cagney, but he was similarly square and pugnacious and seemed to stand there jutting his chin.

"Good morning, men. I am pleased as punch to be taking over from an officer like Lt. Rancek. I know his reputation. He's hard as nails, and you'll find out the same for me. Hard but fair as the day is long. His word is his bond. If he tells you something, you can take it to the bank. And you can count on me just like him. I'll be hard on you when you need it, but I'll let you cut loose when I think you need a break. So know that my door is always open, but you better be strac when you darken that door. If you're not, you better give your heart to God, 'cause your ass is mine. And I want you to remember my personal motto—duty, honor, and country. And don't you ever forget it."

There was something almost childlike about Lt. Kochs. I knew he was an OCS graduate, had finished jump school too, but despite his truculent, defiant manner, he seemed like a belligerent child, play-acting like a real TAC officer, full of somebody else's ideas.

Rancek was a hard-ass for sure, but he wasn't a dumb-ass. I'd sat there often enough in the office working and looking at his diploma from Rutgers University, BS in Political Science, 1967. Kochs, on the other hand, struck me as rough-edged and unformed. I didn't know yet about his background, but then I didn't care too much about any of it. I just wanted to know if he was going to be as consistently mean as Rancek.

It would be a few days before we had a chance to see him in action. We were spending most of the days in classes in Infantry Hall studying "The Five Paragraph Operation Order," spending hours on each one: 1. Situation, 2. Mission, 3. Execution, 4. Service Support, and 5. Command and Signal. Our heads were filled with words like "maneuver," "counter air operations," "intelligence," and "combat support." Meanwhile, Kochs was getting moved in to Rancek's office.

That was when I began to learn a little more about him. I went down to do my mid-week posting of grades. Rancek's diploma was gone, but the picture of Nixon was still there, still with its invisible peace symbol underneath, I suspected, but the black light was gone. Rancek had cleaned out his desk too.

Kochs came in with some of his things that night. After I went through the usual jumping to attention, he had me continue and began to chat while I worked.

"So you're the academic officer. Hard at it. Nose to the grindstone.

Damn, I never thought I was gonna make it through OCS, them tests give me hell. Never was any good on tests, but you put me in the field, and I was hell on wheels. Top shot in my company. Fastest in the mile. I could tear them monkey bars up."

I didn't say anything, while he went about putting some of his things away. He told me to continue with my work while he was going to take care of some of his business. I kept recording the grades, trying to get through quickly so I wouldn't have to be any more visible than I had to.

Kochs was working on something, writing on a tablet with a pencil, when he turned to me suddenly and asked, "How do you spell Louisiana? L-A what?"

I was caught off guard and didn't quite understand what he was asking me. "Sir, Candidate Adams, I'm sorry, sir, but I did not understand your question."

"I'm writing this here letter and I'm trying to address it, but I can't remember how to spell Louisiana. I just got the first two letters, L-A- and don't quite remember how to finish it."

"Sir, Louisiana is spelled L-O-U-I-S-I-A-N-A."

"Oh, yeah," he laughed. "Told you I wasn't too good with the academics."

I finished my work and headed to the room. I wanted to turn in early because I knew that the next day we were to have one of the several forced marches scheduled during the intermediate phase. I also needed to be sure I had extra socks and plenty of Band-Aids.

The day turned out to be a typical March day in Georgia, starting out cool and clear and warming as the day wore on. We marched in full gear, which included pack and pistol belt, and we checked out our M-16s early. We marched often in OCS, starting out with five miles at a fairly gentle, twenty minute a mile pace and working up to a fifteen minutes a mile as the weeks wore on. The march this day was to be out past Garnsey Range and back, a distance of about twelve miles, and it was to be our first major experience with Lt. Kochs.

Kochs was clearly excited about being in charge. He was pumped, yelling even before we left the company area.

"All right, men. Up and at 'em. Let's get it ON. We gonna leave a long olive-drab streak in our wake today. Be streamlined and ready to rock-n-roll."

Forced marches usually began with the company double-timing out of the company area all the way to the end of the black-topped road, about a mile. Then the actual march would begin as we slowed down and got into marching formation.

Kochs wanted to show us how much he was in shape, so while we double-timed with our weapons, he either jogged backward or ran all the way around the platoon, slowing down to shout out on one side and then running around to the other.

Forced marches were in some ways harder than the runs because of the extra equipment we carried and because of the requirement to stay in formation. When you got tired, you tried to slow down, but that meant the guy behind you would have to slow down too. That would unstagger his line, and everyone behind him would have to slow down. So if you tried to slow down, the guys behind would begin yelling, "Pick it up! Get in formation!" And often the guy behind, trying to keep in line with the men to his left, would start stepping on the backs of your combat boots. One of the worst things about a long march was blisters. If you had a couple of pairs of socks and some well-broken-in and good-fitting boots, you could avoid blisters. But all it takes to turn a good fit into a bad one is a single hard step on the back of the heel, which would twist the socks and begin the rub leading to a good blister.

I'd learned the hard way on one of the first forced marches, had slowed down and gotten stepped on, and then tried to pick it up and keep on. It wasn't until the blister on the heel was already blowing up to the size of small bubble gum bubble, that I began to feel it and pulled out of the formation to take off the boot, apply a Band-Aid, straighten the socks, and return to the formation. That last requirement was easier said than done, because by the time you'd finished, the platoon was three quarters of a mile ahead, and you had to double-time to catch up, meaning that by the time you got back you were winded, tired, needing to slow down, and the whole round would begin again.

The best place to be was on the last row, so you had some more space behind you to lag, but we lined up by squad, with the squad leader on the end of the row to the right, and I was designated the leader of the second squad for the week. That meant I was close to the front and on the outside, an uncomfortably visible spot. I knew I had to conserve my energy to keep ahead of the guy's boots behind me. Just as Kochs was trying to make a good early impression on us by demonstrating his physical ability, we were trying to make a decent impression on him or at least trying to keep from making a bad one.

We had finished the run out to the end of the blacktop and were about three miles into the march. I was paying attention to what I was doing, trying to calculate how long before getting to the range, where we would stop for a few minutes and have lunch, and not very aware of anyone else except Kochs. But I began to notice that the guy in front of me was beginning to lag. I stepped on his right heel and yelled out for him to pick it up. It was Bigham, a slim, dark-haired guy from Pennsylvania. He was always getting in trouble for having a too heavy beard. Often he would be sent back into the platoon after the morning inspection to shave, and he would still get demerits. I liked Bigham. He was something of an intellectual. I think maybe he'd even been a philosophy major in college, had a degree. But none of that mattered at that point. He was just a body in front of me, someone whose boots I stepped on, someone who jolted my rhythm, someone who might cause me trouble.

I stepped on him at least two more times before lunch and yelled at him both times. I could tell he was trying. What I could see of the back of his fatigue jacket under his pack was soaking wet; even his pants were wet. But I was afraid the guy behind me would step on me if I slowed down and damn sure didn't want to have to fight the blisters all afternoon.

We made it to the range and stopped for lunch. After we broke out the C-rations and our canteens, everyone took off his boots to change to clean socks. I sought out Bigham to tell him to keep up the pace. I found him sitting by himself with his boots off and both heels bleeding. He was bent over blowing at his bloody heels when I walked up.

"C'mon, Bigham. You got to keep up the pace. I'm stepping all over you."

He looked up at me with that sad face gazing out of that dark beard. He'd taken off his cap and his face was white, his clothes soaking wet. The sun had come up, and the day was warm. It looked like the afternoon would be even warmer.

"So it's you, Adams. I wasn't sure who was behind me, but I can assure you that I know you're there," nodding to his feet.

"Well, hell, man. You know I didn't do it on purpose. I'm just trying to keep from getting stepped on."

I bent over and looked at his feet, the skin ripped from the blisters and the flesh laid bare.

"You're going to have a hell of a time this afternoon going back," I said. "Do you have some clean socks and Band-Aids?"

"I just have one pair of socks. I was going to put them on and use the other pair too, but they're soaked with blood and sweat, and they won't be much good. Do you have an extra pair?" he asked.

I had put on my two clean pair already, but one pair I'd taken off wasn't too sweaty, so I offered them to him just as we heard the call to formation to head back. As we began getting lined up, Kochs came back looking as fresh as he had when we started and was still yelling. He stopped at Bigham.

"What's your name again, candidate?"

"Sir, Candidate Bigham!"

"You're laggin', Bigham. You better pick it up on the way back. I don't want no slackards in my platoon."

"Sir, Candidate Bigham. I have badly blistered feet and request permission to visit the first-aid truck."

"Permission denied. You're an infantryman, Bigham, and you have to learn to live with pain."

On these long marches a first-aid truck always followed along behind, but you had to be damn near dying to use it. It was a mark against any platoon whose men had to get on the truck during any march, so the competition to keep anyone away from it was high.

Bigham didn't protest, and on the way back we started out pretty well. I often tried to keep the rhythm of a song running through my head to try to keep my mind clear. I was focused on "Traveling Band" by Creedence Clearwater Revival—"Playin' on the left, tryin' to get ahead, Baby, I'm a traveling band." I had no idea what the real words were, but those were the ones that kept playing a drumbeat through my head, crowding out any other thoughts. I just wanted to keep marching, hold my weapon over my shoulder, and stay in line. For the first couple of miles back, everything went fine. We were marching quickly, but nothing was upsetting the rhythm until I suddenly bumped into Bigham's heel again.

That brought me back into the present, and I looked up and barked out at Bigham, "C'mon, Bigham, be careful."

Suddenly aware of him again after my rock-n-roll reverie, I noticed that the back of his shirt was drying out, leaving a salt stain at the edges, and I knew that was not a good sign.

We kept walking, but he kept slowing down, so I would yell at him to keep up. Suddenly he almost stopped dead in front of me, and I reached up and shoved him forward, yelling at him to get moving. When I pushed him, Bigham pitched over forward landing on top of his M-16 while I stumbled over the top of him. The platoon behind us moved around and kept marching. As I stood up and got my weapon that I'd pitched as I fell, Kochs came over and started yelling at Bigham to get up, but Bigham didn't move.

"Godddam your ass! Get up, on your feet, back in formation!" shouted Kochs.

I went over and felt Bigham's forehead. He was burning up, but as I'd noticed, he wasn't sweating.

"Sir, I think we better get him to the first-aid truck."

"Oh, bullshit. Get him up."

"Excuse me, sir, but I saw this happen at Fort Polk. I think he's overheated. If we don't cool him off, he might be in bad shape."

Kochs ignored me and kept yelling at Bigham, who was just lying there, unmoving. I got up to flag down the truck and saw Kochs kick Bigham in the side, still thinking that he was malingering. Kochs had to know about heat exhaustion, but he just wasn't going to accept that one of his men wouldn't complete the first task Kochs was responsible for.

The medic stopped the truck, got out, and felt of Bigham's head, and said we had to get him cooled off immediately. The medic took off Bigham's pack and shirt and poured the end of the canteen over his head and T-shirt and asked me to help load him in the truck. Bigham seemed about half conscious as we lifted him into the back of the truck. He kept mumbling something about "Philadelphia, City of Brotherly Love," something that didn't make any sense, maybe his marching mantra. The medic put a couple of bags of ice under each of Bigham's arms and then sprang into the cab and began driving. Kochs jumped on one running board and I on the other and rode along until we caught up with the platoon, where we both dropped off and watched the truck kick up the red Georgia dust as it raced toward the Fort Benning hospital.

Twenty-two

Turning Blue

Kill them all. Let God sort them out.
—*t-shirt slogan*

It was late that night, well after we'd gotten back, before we learned what happened to Bigham. Durham from first platoon was CQ for the night and someone called in a report. Bigham had suffered a heat stroke. His temperature was 106 degrees when he got to the hospital. They'd packed him in ice to lower his temperature and thought they were going to lose him. But after a couple of hours, his temperature went down, and they believed they had everything under control by the time they called the company. As it turned out, this was the second time that Bigham had passed out from the heat. It had happened once before when Bigham was in AIT. The second one disqualified Bigham from any further strenuous exercise. It wasn't going to get him out of the Army, but it would get him dropped from OCS, and it would mean that he would be transferred out of a combat outfit, probably into a clerking unit.

I had an odd mixed reaction to Bigham's good misfortune. I was sorry that he had made it as far as he had through OCS with only about six more weeks before graduation, then to be dropped. But I thought that it was good that he would get out of the Infantry. As much as I wanted to get it out of my mind, I couldn't help but think that I was partly responsible for what had happened, since I was the one who'd stepped on his heels. His shadowed face began to enter my recurring dreams, repeating his phrase about Philadelphia.

As usual, though, I didn't have much time to think about it, because we were about to turn blue and graduate to the senior phase of OCS. We were down to 110 men from our original 256, had lost two TACs, Rancek and Swanson, and would probably lose at least one more before graduation. The TACs had slacked off, thinking I guess that they'd identified and gotten rid of most of the unqualified candidates. So we were marking time, going to classes, trying not to think too far ahead.

The eighteenth week party didn't have the same atmosphere as the twelfth did. There was none of the tension of a big panel that would bounce out another large bunch of us. We anticipated the benefits of turning blue. We'd get to paint our black helmets infantry blue, wear the distinctive white scarves with the blue OCS patches, get weekend passes, and we could walk through the battalion area raising hell with the beginning OCS companies, just as we had been harassed when we arrived.

Even before the official party acknowledging our passage, Kochs gave us full music privileges. We could have radios or tape players, anything small enough to fit in our wall or footlockers. Like most of my generation, I'd grown up with music everywhere. I'd come to consciousness in the middle of the fifties just as rock'n'roll began to dominate the air waves and juke boxes, had listened to Elvis sing "Blue Suede Shoes" before I was a teenager, had watched the Beatles on Ed Sullivan, and had heard the Doors through a psychedelic haze. Music just seemed part of the air, as natural as breathing. Even in Basic and AIT we got to have portable radios and could listen at nights and on weekends. But in OCS with music declared contraband, the silence seemed frightening, foreboding, ominous. Sitting at night in silent study hall, I would spin records in my head. Maybe that was why I remember that time with music so fully, since I was always trying to recall lyrics and melodies.

So getting full music privileges seemed like grace. The song that March that will forever be wedded in my memory with that moment was Simon and Garfunkle's "Bridge Over Troubled Water." I sat transfixed listening to the lines about growing weary and feeling small, hoping for someone to be on your side when times get rough and no friends to be found. I longed to be like a bridge over troubled water, so I could just lay me down.

I had felt like I was drowning in troubled waters, just barely keeping my head above the choppy breakers. Turning blue meant a lull in the storm, at least for the time being in this small cove of the world. But radio privileges also meant hearing more about the world out there, and the troubled waters of the world seemed to be roiling.

The Paris Peace Talks had begun a couple of years earlier and then stalled into a farcical show with arguments on the shape of the table while men were dying. Nixon, Kissinger, and Laird talked about the "Vietnamization" of the war, which must have been the secret plan that had gotten Nixon elected. And he'd gained good will by announcing withdrawals of American forces before 1969 was over. But with the great moratorium in fall '69 and with the beginning of 1970 and no end in sight, people had begun to lose faith in the thought that the war might ever end. And now the rest of the region seemed in an uproar. There'd been rumblings about secret activity in Laos and Cambodia. We'd replaced the Cambodian Prince Sihanouk with Lon Nol when the prince had gone to France for his annual obesity treatment. And through it all Nixon talked about "peace with honor."

I listened to the news with great interest and usually responded with greater despair. Calley's trial on the other side of the post was beginning to gear up, and I thought about him sitting there with his feet dangling from his chair.

My job for the senior party was pretty insignificant, mainly helping with getting the battalion headquarters ready for the dinner. We weren't even going to have a band, just the sit-down formal dinner with the cigars and port and some speechifying afterward. I'd called Mary O'Hara and asked her to come down again, and she'd agreed. Once we'd finally gotten to the point where we could talk to one another, we'd discovered we had a lot to say. And I still found that her smile spoke to me from the photo in my wall locker.

About mid-afternoon on the Saturday of the dinner, I was working on getting my uniform ready for the party when we had mail call. Every week someone was designated as the mail officer, who would go down to the CO's office and pick up the platoon mail. For the first few weeks we gathered in the hall while the mail officer called out the names on the letters. Now that everyone knew everyone else's name well, the mail officer would simply walk through the barracks and leave mail on our desks, calling our names as he walked through the hall. Spenser was mail officer this week, and he liked to sing out the names. My fingers were blackened with shoe polish when he came by my room, so he left the letter sitting propped against the study lamp on my desk. I could see that it was from my mother, but I had to wipe my hands before I opened it.

Dear Jeff,

I am sorry to be writing you this letter, but I could not get through to you by phone. Your Granddad passed this morning. He was sick and weak ever since the stroke. I'm sending you a picture of him, but you should remember him the way he was as a strong and cranky man.

They'll have services at the church, but the Red Cross told me that you could only get out of OCS for services for your immediate family, not grandparents or uncles and cousins and such. I tried to tell them that he was like a Daddy to you, but they said that it did not matter.

Well dear it is close to time for the postman to come by so I will stop now.

God the Father wants to help you to bear your burdens, please draw near to him. Nothing can be lost. Man is not Supreme, no matter how much it is taught, or by whom.

"Ye shall know the Truth and the truth will make you free." Never be afraid to investigate for the truth of the Bible.

Love,
Mother

Granddad had gone home from the hospital and lingered, crippled and almost mute for several weeks, long enough for Mother to take the photograph she'd sent. He's sitting in the backyard under the pecan tree in that rusty outdoor chair where he used to sit to clean quail. Now, though, things are different. Instead of his usual robust grin, the right side of his face is slack, giving him a wry half-smile. Instead of its healthy tan, his skin looks pale and wan. I turn the picture over. On the back Mother has written: "Granddad, two weeks after the stroke."

I turn it back over because something else about the photograph bothers me. When I look again, I realize that it's his hands. I had always been awed by Granddad's hands because they were huge; he wore a size thirteen ring although he was only medium build. Besides that, his hands were scratched and scabbed all the time. Nearly every time he started doing something, he would skin his hands and complain, "Hell, with this onion skin of mine, it's a wonder I got any blood left." But the thing I remember most is that he couldn't ever get his fingernails clean. He had worked for the railroad for forty years before he retired to raise cattle, and those nails carried rail grease that probably went back to 1920. In this picture, the grease is still there, but the hands, like dying birds, lie limply in his lap.

Above and in the distance two cattle egrets seem to be circling in the picture. They feed on insects around cattle, I know, but they look like sea birds 300 miles from home.

I had hoped to talk to him on the phone, but I knew he just couldn't say what he meant. I wanted to tell him about Bill Pickett, Bose Ikard, and George McJunkin, black cowboys who went up the old Western and the Goodnight-Loving trails back in the golden days of cowboying, but I didn't get the chance, and I knew he wouldn't want to listen.

Just before he died that spring, he spoke to Mother and said, "Take me across the river and into the trees." Then he shook his head as if that weren't really what he meant to say, and I wondered if his recalling Stonewall Jackson's last words meant he was thinking of me and war.

I remember sitting in the yard at the ranch after we got back that day of the fishing trip. At my feet were mounds of feisty fire ants imported from South Africa in copra ships in 1918 and moving west at twenty-five to thirty miles a year. In the distance I could hear a Southern Pacific freight train. They were supposed to close the yard there soon. John Wayne had lung cancer. I checked the sky: not a single cattle egret to be seen.

I sat in my room at Fort Benning after reading the letter and noticed that my fingernails, blackened from the shoe polish, looked nothing like Granddad's. My hands were small and slight. Even the months in the Army had not hardened my hands so they were anything like the lifetime of work that showed in his, and it seemed like I'd never have the hands that indicated the kind of life Granddad had lived.

The letter made the evening seem even odder than the circumstances might have warranted. Even though turning blue marked passage to greater freedoms, it also meant that we were closer to graduation and therefore closer to facing orders to Vietnam. For most of the candidates who were left, those orders were what they wanted, but for me, it meant moving deeper into the murky waters I'd been paddling in since I arrived.

The party that night was almost a fog. I wasn't on the welcoming committee for the train this time, so I met Mary when she came out from Columbus on the bus. She again looked beautiful, and I remember her smile and blue dress. But the party dragged along through the toasts and speeches, the cigars and port.

We took a taxi into town and got out near the river rather aimlessly. The last time we were together we had spent the first part of the evening in different worlds before I learned why Mary was mad at me. Tonight Mary sensed the same of me as we walked along the boardwalk in the crisp March air.

"So, where are you tonight?" she asked. "You've seemed in some never-never land since I got here. You've barely said a word that wasn't required for civility."

"I'm sorry, but I've been distracted ever since I got this letter in mail call this afternoon."

I handed her the letter, and we sat on one of the benches under a lamp while she read it.

"I'm sorry to learn about your Granddad. It's too bad you can't go home for the funeral," she said. "I can tell from your mother's letter that the ceremony will be important."

"It will be important to her, but it wouldn't mean anything to Granddad. He hasn't darkened the door of the church for forty years. My mother is something of a fanatic, as you can see by the way she ends her letters, always a mini-sermon. I can hear the preacher saying something about Granddad that's probably false. I'd probably just get mad hearing him say something about how he was a God-fearing man and how he was now in heaven or something, and if Granddad were alive, he'd be blustering 'bullshit!'

"I don't mean that he had no religion. It was just that he couldn't stand organized religion. It had almost estranged him from his daughter-in-law, my mother, who had her religion in her head like a stinger. He thought that a lot of the town's staunchest religious leaders were some of the biggest hypocrites and didn't want to have anything to do with them."

"Still, it's too bad you won't be there. I know you were close to him."

"Yes, in many ways he's why I'm here. When I got drafted, I felt almost as ambivalent about this war as I do now, but I knew I couldn't dodge military service or it would kill him. He was so proud when I told him I'd signed up for OCS. He was an enlisted man during World War I, and when he would talk about Lt. Bierce, his CO for most of his time, there was a reverence in his voice. Being an 'officer' meant something to him."

"Did he want you to go to Vietnam?"

"Maybe at first. But the stories about massacres and killing of innocents bothered him. He mentioned it in the only letter he wrote me, and we talked about it over Christmas. He knew that wasn't the army he served in."

Mary stood up and took my hand, "Come on. Let's go to my room. I brought a flask of whiskey on a whim, and it sounds like you need a stiff drink. It won't be the Silver Slipper, but let's drink a toast to the memory of your Granddad."

We walked down the boardwalk and crossed the street to the Old Rock. In the lobby was a small statue of a bearded man on horseback. A small plaque there identified him as " 'Old Rock' Benning":

> *Henry Lewis Benning, for whom Fort Benning was named, saw careers as a soldier, attorney, politician, and Justice of the Georgia Supreme Court. A native Georgian, Benning's career began in Columbus in 1835 when he set up residence and began practicing law. At the age of 39, two years after his unsuccessful campaign for Congress, he was elected associate justice of the Georgia Supreme Court. He was the youngest man to hold that office.*

> *Benning was a staunch advocate of States Rights and took a prominent part in the conventions concerning secession prior to the War Between the States.*

With the start of the War Between the States, Benning recruited men to form the 17th Regiment of Georgia Volunteers. During the first year and a half of the war, he fought with General Robert E. Lee, and attained the rank of major general. Because of his coolness in battle, he became known to his troops as "Old Rock."

After the war, Benning returned to his law practice in Columbus. He died in 1875 at the age of 61.

As I bent over reading the plaque, Mary came up after getting her key. "You can't get away from it around here, can you? Let it be. Let's go up, and we'll try to escape."

Up in her room, she took a silver flask out of her purse. "There, Candidate Adams, would you do the honors?"

"Let me get the ice. Do you want me to get a Coke from the machine?"

"Oh, no. This is in honor of your granddad, and you told me he drank bourbon and branch. I hope he would have liked J.T.S. Brown."

"I think Old Forester was his brand of choice, but Mr. Brown will be a fine substitute. I'll go get the ice and be right back."

When I got back to the room, Mary was in the bathroom, so I got the glasses and fixed us both drinks. Just as I got through, I heard her open the door and walk in. Turning, I saw her standing in the doorway. She had changed into a transparent nightgown and looked like a sexy madonna, as she stood there with that smile on her face.

"You've turned blue, but I don't want you to be blue. This is in memory of your granddad," and she undid the nightgown to reveal large breasts completely covered by her large brown nipples.

"When you think back on OCS, I want you to remember me," she said, "not this," sweeping her arm around toward Fort Benning.

I sat my drink aside and lay my head in the soft safety between those brown aureoles.

Twenty-Three

Ranger Week

Only we can prevent forests.
—Ranch Hands, Agent Orange Operation Motto

After turning blue, everything was relaxed, and we took advantage of the new freedom. We could walk through the company area, strutting with our new white scarves just as we had seen the other senior candidates do all along. We could walk to the companies still in the basic phase and try to terrify the candidates there.

Our last few weeks in the classroom were fairly standard, mainly review of material all leading to the last major event, the culminating OCS assignment called Ranger Week, which was a week in the field simulating actual conditions. That meant a week sleeping outside and eating C-rations, long marches through the Georgia countryside to test map-reading skills, night patrols, chopper rides to LZs marked with smoke grenades, calling in air and mortar support, all with "aggressors" made up of enlisted men assigned to Fort Benning. It wasn't really like the real thing, because we were all playacting and knew it, but no one wanted to screw up and make a fool of himself.

We were out in the field for seven nights and eight days and each assignment lasted two days before a rotation. I started out as a squad leader, was in charge of the platoon for two days, then had two days as a simple grunt, and spent the last two days as a squad leader. It was a fairly simple schedule, no company-wide tasks. Budwell and I were to be sharing a tent for Ranger Week.

We trucked out to the southeastern corner of the post to start our first day's activities, a six-mile hike through the boonies. A six-mile hike on a road was a fairly easy task, but six miles through pine forests and heavy understory, up and down riparian gullies, was a job, and it was going to take all day. We were also on full alert, marching as a company in single file with a man on point and another on drag and everyone on the lookout for the aggressors. We were also supposed to be aware of tripwires and camouflaged pits layered with simulated punji sticks. We had been led to believe that all of this would be real-world, and maybe it was, because we didn't find anything that first day. But we moved at a snail's pace with whoever was on point checking every inch carefully before moving. By noon I think we had only gotten about a mile, and we still had five more miles to go to make base camp.

At lunch we had to set out perimeter guards, and Budwell, Garrett, and I ended up on the west side of the company in a heavily wooded area. We selected a spot near a large loblolly pine and sat with our backs to the company, looking out through the trunks of the pines toward the Chattahoochee. The rust-colored pine needles made a natural table cloth for our C-rations. I had a small container of Sterno that I used to warm up a can of beef stew.

For the first time I could appreciate the Chattahoochee Valley. The pine forest was varied with longleaf, loblolly, and slash covering the landscape. The dogwoods, redbuds, and trout lilies were beginning to bloom in this early spring.

Budwell seemed distracted as we sat, which was strange for him, because he usually was one of the most easygoing men I'd ever met.

"What's up, Hugh? You thinking about the Easter egg hunt you missed?"

Budwell sat quietly for a moment before responding.

"I'd almost forgotten that it was Easter, but it's an appropriate time for what I'm thinking about—change and new beginnings, the death of the innocents."

"Heavy stuff, man," said Garrett. "Don't get ahead of yourself. We got two weeks before graduation."

"I wasn't thinking much about that, only wondering what we're getting ourselves into. I was reading newspapers over the weekend, and there's all this shit floating around about something secret going on in Cambodia and Laos. It's frightening. We're getting in deeper and deeper into this tarbaby. I've been trying to think through it."

"Many times you've told me just to let whatever happens, happen," I said. "Since when did you decide to take an active part in thinking about what happens?"

"Oh, you've misunderstood me. I have never preached quiescent acquiescence. I've just thought that it was better to let things happen as long as you got your mind around it and were ready to flow in its direction."

"Yeah, that sounds simple enough. But what if your mind is flowing in several directions at once?" I asked.

"Good question. I've always thought that many currents flowed in different directions at once, kind of like those arrows in wind direction on weather maps. But there's usually a prevailing current in those synapses, and that's what I've always tried to get in touch with. When I left that law firm, I thought I had gotten the ambient swell. But I tell you I'm beginning to feel strong counter undulations."

"Well, it's a little late for that, isn't it?"

"Oh, no, it's never too late. I'm just looking for the dominant, and then I'll try to go with it. It just seems to me that a lot of counterforces are at work now."

"Yeah," said Garrett, " I got a cousin in school over at Jackson State who keeps writin' me. He says there're a lot of black folks there who don't think it's right for us to be fightin' against other colored folks when our people aren't treated right here. He puts one of those rubber stamp black power salutes on all his letters to me," Garrett said, raising his fist over his head.

I looked down toward the break in the brush where the Chattahoochee ran south and thought about being taken along by the flow of a powerful river when a dark shadow moving through the trees caught my attention.

"Hey, guys, on the double!" I whispered loudly. "We've got company."

Budwell and Garrett jumped up and came over.

"What's up? Do we have aggressors?"

"I don't know. I saw something moving through the trees. Down there," I said, pointing to where I saw the movement, and as we stood looking, I could again see a large, dark shadow moving through the trees.

"You're right," Budwell whispered. "I see something too. Let me get my binoculars."

"Yeah, and we better get our weapons ready, too," Garrett said.

We grabbed our equipment and spread out along the line of the perimeter, while Budwell got out his binoculars. It was only midday, so the sun shone brightly high above the density of the pine forest, but the trees cut out much of the light. Budwell looked carefully with the binoculars and suddenly exclaimed.

"Well, I'll be damned. Don't worry about aggressors. Our friend is four-footed. It's a bear."

"Are your kiddin' me, man?" Garrett asked. "There ain't no bears here."

"If there aren't any bears, then we're looking at a phantom," Budwell said. "Here, take a look," handing Garrett the binoculars.

Garrett took the binoculars and took a look. "Well, I'll be damned. It's a bear, and I'm a buttered Little Black Sambo."

"I think that was a tiger," I said. "Let me see." I reached over and got the binoculars and tried to focus on the dark figure through the dappled trees. Sure enough, the image of the bear clearly showed. It was indifferently moving along down toward the river, stopping occasionally to scratch in the undergrowth, just about a hundred feet from us, moving slowly through the gray-green underbrush in the windless noon. Above and in the tops of the trees I heard squirrels jumping from limb to limb, frightened by the dark mass below. I watched as the bear slowly gutted a log and felt my heart hammer as I watched this ancient creature of the wilderness. It turned and looked at me over its shoulder, crossing the glade without haste.

"Let me see again," Budwell said, taking the binoculars from me. He looked again toward the dark figure. "It's a sign," he said quietly.

"Oh, bullshit," said Garrett. "It's a fuckin' bear. It ain't no fuckin' sign."

"It's a fuckin' bear, and it's a fuckin' sign," Budwell replied. "I just don't know what it's a sign of."

"It's a sign that it's a fuckin' bear," Garrett said. "Hey, I don't think that we can do much damage even with the hundreds of rounds of M-16 blanks we have. Best we could hope would be to scare her."

"Oh, I don't think we have much to worry about," Budwell said, "unless it's a she-bear with cubs around here."

"That's comforting," I said.

The bear continued moving slowly down toward the river as we all sat quietly listening to the squirrels in the trees. It suddenly dawned on me that it was time to rejoin the company from our perimeter position, and I had to return to the reality that the bear's presence had disrupted. I looked at my watch, checked my compass, and grabbed my weapon and pack.

"Come on, guys, let's let mama bear take care of her business; we have to take care of our own. It's almost 1300. Let's head back to the company. That's the way back, " I said, pointing to the northeast.

"TCB," said Garrett.

Budwell continued looking at the bear until Garrett went over and shook him by the shoulder.

"Wake up, Hugh. Let's hit it."

"Look at her," Budwell said. "She's just moving along like bears have done for hundreds of years, oblivious to the political winds. That would be the way to live."

"You're pipe dreaming," I said. "Everything is politics. There's no way to get away from politics, unless you're a bear or a rock. So, let's get it together. It's time."

"Adiós, Urso," said Budwell, waving toward the bear. "Now, let's go."

When we rejoined the company, Silva from first platoon, who was the acting company commander for the first two days, had convinced the TACs that we could not make our objective by the assigned time at our rate of march. He was arranging for the company to be transported by helicopter to a landing zone near the objective. It wasn't such a great conclusion for Silva to reach, since we'd been prepped during the previous week on the need to find alternative plans during Ranger Week. Still, it made the company happy to hear that we didn't face an afternoon of marching through the Georgia countryside.

We moved to a nearby meadow, the LZ for the Huey helicopters that would move us. We were now down to 110 men, plus the five TACs who were still left. Each chopper could carry eight men and there were three choppers assigned to Ranger Week. Since we were only about five miles from our objective, it only took about ten minutes for a chopper to land, pick up a load of men, and ferry them to the objective, but it took most of the afternoon to get everyone over. Still, it was one of those real-world experiences that was to prepare us for what grunts in Nam were doing every day, and it was one of the most dangerous assignments there, since running to or from a chopper in open territory was a vulnerable position for anyone.

Budwell, Garrett, and I had stayed together when we got back, and so we were in a group waiting to be taken. As we waited, I reached into my pocket to get my knife, but it wasn't there.

"Budwell, did you see my knife?" I asked.

"No, didn't you have it when we were on the perimeter?"

"Yeah, I opened my Sterno can with it. Garrett, you didn't pick it up, did you?"

"No, man, I ain't got it. It's just a knife; you can get another one."

"It's not just a knife. It was my Granddad's, one he'd had for years. He gave it to me when I left."

I searched through my pockets, opened up my pack, with no luck. I was heartsick. Granddad had kept that knife for over thirty years, but I had been able to hold onto it for only about six months. Much as I wanted to try to go back and find it, I was in no position to do anything.

We popped yellow smoke to mark the LZ and then piled into the chopper when it sat down, but I was lost in the anguish of losing the last thing my grandfather had given me.

The next few days of Ranger Week went as expected. We were lucky that the weather held, comfortable and sunny during the day, cool but not cold at night. We only had to break out our ponchos once during the eight days for an afternoon shower. Unlike our expectations, we rarely saw the aggressors, but almost every night, there was an alert of some kind. The word would be passed that our perimeter was being tested, and we would blast away for five to ten minutes and then climb back into our sleeping bags for another night of unsettled sleep. On two nights we played out the whole attack charade and blasted away at the Georgia night with our blanks and then threw our mock grenades that blasted like M-80s and lit up the sky momentarily.

At one point I was out in a forward position and heard something out in the bush. I lay quietly with my M-16 at ready. The worst thing that could happen to anyone during Ranger Week was to be captured, so I knew I was vulnerable out there by myself. As soon as I could make out a figure, I blasted away, calling out "You're dead, aggressor!" in a kind of child's game. I turned my flashlight on the guy and realized with a start that the face behind the camouflage paint was the birthday boy Ferona.

"Ferona, is that you?"

"Adams? Is this my old company? Damn, I thought you guys were long gone."

"Yes, sure is. What are you doing?"

"After I washed out, I got transferred first to Casual Company and then to this Aggressor Unit. We come out here every week and play cowboy with OCS companies, but I'm off to Nam in a month."

We heard some other noises in the night, and Ferona waved goodbye and, like a ghost, disappeared into the dark.

The rest of the time was quiet. On one of the last nights someone passed the word that we should blow off all of the rest of our blank ammo when we had the chance, since we weren't supposed to haul it back with us. We climbed into our sleeping bags and waited until the nightly perimeter probe, jumped out, and then blasted away for over a half hour. The night was filled with acrid smoke left by the grenades and thousands of rounds of blanks, and every time we moved we could hear the clink of empty shell casings.

The last day was the reverse of the first one, after we spent an hour picking up the empty shells. We began by being choppered a few miles to a landing zone for our final march back. Over the last few days we had gone around and around in the Georgia forest, and since I had never been in a major leadership position, I had no idea where we were. One place looked pretty much like another, but the last LZ looked familiar. When the last chopper load of men landed, we formed up and started marching back, stopping in early afternoon to have lunch.

Like the first day, Budwell, Garrett, and I took the perimeter. As we began moving out to take our position, I noticed that we headed downhill toward the river, and it dawned on me that this looked exactly like the place we'd been the first day.

"Budwell, does this look familiar?" I asked.

"Sure, it looks like every Georgia pine forest we've been in for the last six months."

As I looked around at the lay of the land with the angle down to the river, I was sure this was close to where we spent the first lunch of Ranger Week.

"Come on, you guys, follow me. I think we're close to where I lost my knife."

We angled down to the river, and sure enough I found the big tree we'd sat under. I bent down and ran my hands through the pine needles, fearful at first of snakes, but then I touched the cool steel of my grandfather's Case knife. At about the same instant, Budwell pointed down toward the river, and I could see the dark image of a bear moving slowly west.

Twenty-Four

Kent State

We were exhausted when we got back to the barracks that Friday night, but we had been eight days without showers, so our stinking bodies got priority over rest at first. It was a race to get both to the showers and to the laundry. Most guys had bought laundry service for the duration of OCS and just deposited their olive-drab laundry bags in a designated area near the day room.

I missed the first wave into the shower, so I pulled on a pair of shorts, gathered up my dirty laundry, and headed down to leave it with the growing stacks of dirty fatigues and filthy socks and underwear. Ever since we'd hit senior status, we'd had television privileges so the TV was usually on. I'd lost track of time while we were gone and realized suddenly when I heard a newsman say that it was May Day that we'd ended the month of April in the Georgia forest. I stopped for a moment to listen to the news. Most of the news that night recounted an address to the nation that Nixon had made the night before, and a segment from his speech was being broadcast. I stepped into the day room and looked into the eyes of Richard Nixon as he gripped his papers and looked over his always darkened upper lip:

> *The action that I have announced tonight puts the leaders of North Vietnam on notice that we will be patient in working for peace; we will be conciliatory at the conference table, but we will not be humiliated. We will not be defeated. We will not allow American men by the thousands to be killed by an enemy from privileged sanctuaries.*

My fellow Americans, we live in an age of anarchy, both
abroad and at home. We see mindless attacks on all the great
institutions which have been created by free civilizations in the
last 500 years. Even here in the United States, great universi-
ties are being systematically destroyed. If, when the chips are
down, the world's most powerful nation, the United States of
America, acts like a pitiful, helpless giant, the forces of totali-
tarianism and anarchy will threaten free nations and free
institutions throughout the world. It is not our power but our
will and character that is being tested tonight.

I have rejected all political considerations in making this deci-
sion. Whether my party gains in November is nothing com-
pared to the lives of 400,000 brave Americans fighting for our
country and for the cause of peace and freedom in Vietnam.
Whether I may be a one-term President is insignificant com-
pared to whether by our failure to act in this crisis the United
States proves itself to be unworthy to lead the forces of freedom
in this critical period in world history. I would rather be a
one-term President and do what I believe is right than to be a
two-term President at the cost of seeing America become a sec-
ond rate power and to see this Nation accept the first defeat in
its proud 190-year history.

The newscaster talked about the "incursion" into Cambodia and
noted that Nixon said it wasn't an invasion because we were attacking
the Vietnamese operating out of the Cambodian sanctuaries immediately above Parrot's Beak and not Cambodia itself. This was what we'd
been hearing about, I thought, the secret operations in Laos and
Cambodia.

I went back to the platoon and found Budwell as he got out of the
shower.

"I just dropped off my laundry and caught a few minutes of the news.
Guess what happened while we were enjoying the countryside."

"I don't know. They declared peace at the talks in Paris?"

"You wish. Nixon announced last night a new operation in Cambodia."

"Oh bullshit. That bastard has been lying to us all along, this crap about Vietnamization and pulling troops out of Vietnam. So he's going to pull them out of Vietnam and send them into Cambodia, a goddamn shell game. What's happening in the country?"

"I don't know, didn't hear the rest of the news. He did say a few things about anarchy and unrest, but I guess he'll leave that for his hatchetman, Agnew."

"You know, we've been hearing things about something secret going on. That's what we were talking about out in the bush."

He stood quietly for a moment and then said, "This changes things. Thanks for telling me. I'm going to see what else I can find out."

Then he looked at me and wrinkled his nose. "And you better get a goddamn shower before you walk in front of a stove and explode with all those gases seeping from your filthy body."

I got cleaned up, and the rest of the evening before lights out was filled with the little details of returning from the field. We had to turn in our field gear, clean and check in our weapons, square away our rooms, and I had to return to my regular latrine duty.

I fell into bed that night expecting to sleep the sleep of the dead but instead had uneasy dreams. Nixon's shadowed face filled the screen of my imagination and then morphed into Rusty Calley's. I dreamed I was leading platoons in high country filled with parrots attacking like those flying monsters in *The Wizard of Oz*. They had the faces of people I'd known throughout the last six months—Trailer, Ferona, Hays, Donaldson, Shrode, Rancek, Lederer—flying and shrieking like harpies with the face of Mary O'Hara superimposed behind all of them.

The next day was Saturday with no official OCS activities planned, but because we were supposed to graduate the next Friday morning, we were to spend this weekend getting all of our equipment ready for the event. We had to buy new officer uniforms—dress greens, hats, new fatigues with second lieutenant bars sewn on. We didn't even have orders yet and wouldn't know until Monday afternoon what our first assignments after graduation were supposed to be. Some of us might get branch transfers, which would mean different insignia, different patches sewn on the fatigues.

In between making plans and getting materials, we listened to the radio, and in between Joe South's "Walk a Mile in My Shoes" and Crosby, Stills, Nash, and Young's "Woodstock," the news came on and recounted stories about responses to Nixon's announcement about Cambodia. There were organized student protests around the country; students at the University of Colorado marched through tear-gassed streets, and at the University of Texas, they gathered at the Armadillo World Headquarters and sang protest songs and planned strategy. At Kent State they took over and set fire to the ROTC building.

Sunday was pretty much the same for us—rushing around and getting ready for the end with just a little time for relaxing. In the afternoon to get some idea of what was happening in the country, I walked down to the newspaper rack outside the back sidewalk and discovered that a copy of the day's *New York Times* was already available, brought in by train, I suppose. There were stories about the student unrest and comments from various political leaders about Nixon's secret war, but the world seemed void of heroes. Robert Kennedy and Martin Luther King had been dead for two years. There were some voices of protest. Ted Kennedy called it "crazy," but he'd lost credibility after a woman died in his car in an accident the summer before. Mike Mansfield, the senate majority leader from Montana, cautiously questioned Nixon's decision, and William Fulbright from Arkansas spoke out, but the war had been going on for a long time, and now it looked like it might keep on going forever and ever.

Monday began the last week, which was to be a combination of processing out interspersed with some final field work. At some point in the morning, I caught the news on the radio that the Pulitzer Prizes were awarded that day and that Seymour Hersh had won for his reporting of My Lai, and I wondered how Rusty's trial was going. Charles Gordone, a black playwright, had won for *No Place to Be Somebody*, a great title, I thought. That afternoon we gathered in the company area to get our orders. The TACs made it a ritual, calling out each man's name alphabetically and handing him a packet of orders. We were to get back into formation and wait until everyone had his packet before we opened ours. My name came early, of course, but I had to stand at parade rest with the packet in my right hand through the other 109 names.

The first sergeant had handled the event. Before he would let us read our orders, he told us to take our packets and strip off the back sheet.

"Take that page, men; it's a summary of your orders. Fold it in quarters and put it in your pocket and keep it with you until you get to your first assignment. That's your ticket to move around the country. Don't lose it. "After you've done that. You may examine your orders."

In a single motion, we all turned our packets over and began to read. As each one got to the place of assignment, he'd yell it out. "Fort Sam Houston!" "Fort Ord!" "Fort Ben Harrison!" "Fort Riley!" "Fort Dix!" I scanned the front page of mine quickly and yelled out, "Fort Carson!" Silva was next to me, and I heard him sing out "Signal Corps, Fort Gordon!" That meant he was branch transferred from the Infantry and would be trained first as a signal officer before his assignment. It was exhilarating knowing where we were headed next, even if it were only for the next ten or twelve months.

Top dismissed us into the barracks and instructed us that we could begin calling our families to tell them what would happen next. I sought out Budwell to find out where his orders would send him.

"Where're you headed, Budwell?"

"My orders say Fort Lewis, Washington, jumping off point for Vietnam. I'm assigned to the processing center there. What about you?"

"I'm headed to Fort Carson, Colorado, supposed to be a training officer."

Just as we got back into the platoon, we were walking by Garcia's room, where the radio was playing, and we heard a newscaster break in.

"We've just received this news bulletin. Four students were killed and several others wounded in Kent, Ohio, today when Ohio National Guardsmen called out by Governor Rhodes opened fire on a group of protesters at Kent State University. No immediate explanation for the actions has been provided. We'll have more news as it becomes available."

Budwell and I just stood there silently with our heads down, just as Garcia came chanting "Fort Belvoir, Fort Belvoir, Fort Belvoir."

When he saw us, he sensed something. "What's wrong?" he asked.

We told him about the newscast.

"Good god," he said. "What's happening to the country? Why'd they shoot those students?"

"Who knows?" said Budwell. "They were probably scared and pissed off that they were having to do that shit. Panicked maybe. It's all coming apart."

"Well, fuck 'em," said Garcia. "That's four fewer to spit on me when I get back from Nam." He walked on down the hall yelling, "I'm headed for Belvoir!"

Budwell and I went to our room, where Hugh seemed lost in thought. After a while, he said to me, "We have our last field exercise tomorrow, don't we?"

"Yes, we have to qualify for the last time on .45s."

Now that we were about to graduate, one of the last things to do was to qualify on the pistol that officers were required to carry, the .45 caliber. We were to spend the day Tuesday at the range for the last time.

"Pack your field stuff when you go tomorrow."

"What do you have in mind?" I asked.

"I'm not sure," Budwell said. "Just pack some socks, underwear, a change of civvies, and your shaving gear. I'm going to go tell Garrett about Kent State and tell him to do the same."

I could tell that the Kent State news had hit Budwell especially hard, and it had shaken me too. I didn't know what Budwell was planning, but I also had the sense that we should do something.

The rest of the afternoon is a blur. We filed out by platoon to the phones to call home about our orders. Mother was happy that I'd be closer to Texas with my assignment to Colorado, but she was in one of her special religious moods and wanted to give me another mini-sermon. I told her I had to hang up and not to worry if she didn't hear from me for awhile because I would be getting ready for the new assignment. She told me she was sorry she couldn't come for the graduation ceremony that Friday, and I told her that only those candidates with family nearby would have guests.

That night Budwell and I had little to say, as we both packed our field gear for the next day. The next morning we went through our usual routine, a quick run around the Airborne track, back to the mess hall for chow and then the usual morning cleaning and preparing for inspection. When we fell out in the company area, I could see that Budwell's, Garrett's, and my packs were fatter than the others.

We were trucked out to a range in the southwestern corner of the base, where we went through our first round of qualifications. In the first round, we each got twelve shots at a stationary target, one of those human-shaped figures with a bullseye on the chest. The second round in the afternoon would be twelve shots each at popup targets.

It was on the break after the first round that Budwell, Garrett, and I had a chance to talk. We got our things and moved off behind the latrine in a stand of tall pines.

We sat on the ground and Budwell reached into his pack and pulled out a copy of the morning *Atlanta Constitution*. On the cover was a head-line that read "4 Kent State Students Killed by Troops," and beneath it was a picture of an anguished, dark-haired woman on one knee over the body of a dead student. Her right arm was bent with the palm up, the left arm was outstretched, and her mouth was slightly open as if in a scream.

"This is what we're part of now," Budwell said as he tossed the paper down. "This is obscene."

Garrett looked at the paper. "Says here the troops thought a sniper was shooting at them."

"So they shoot into a group of a thousand? Look at Nixon's statement." Budwell read from the statement Nixon had issued: " 'This should remind us all once again that when dissent turns to violence it invites tragedy.' What bullshit."

"It's a crazy, upside down world we're in," I said. "All of our usual notions of right and wrong seem to have been tossed aside. But it's been that way for a long time now. I don't see what we or anyone can do about it."

"I think we can do something," Budwell said. "Somebody has to do something sometime to stop the cycle of inhumanity."

"So what do you think we can do?" asked Garrett.

Budwell looked and him and then at me, "We can refuse to go along with it any more."

"A lot of good that will do," Garrett said. "Here we are at the end of our time. We'd be crazy to give it up."

"Well, it might not have much impact outside of here, but it has to start somewhere."

Garrett stood there for a moment, turned, and looked up at the sky.

After a pause he raised his fist over his head briefly, then turned back to Budwell, and said, "All right then, I'm in."

I looked at Budwell and Garrett and at the picture of the stricken young woman in the paper, and I thought about my grandfather, my mother's righteousness, and about my promise to Mary, and I said, "Okay, I am, too."

We three stood there for a moment, realizing, I guess, that we'd stepped across a line and passed a point that would change our lives.

"What's next?" I asked.

"Let's leave," said Budwell, "Go AWOL. Adiós, au revoir OCS."

"We need to tell someone why we're leaving, don't we?" I asked.

"Let's just leave them a signal," Budwell suggested. He took his .45 off his pistol belt. "Let's leave these pistols right here."

I took out Granddad's knife and began digging a small hole. "Let's leave them like this." After I started a hole with the knife, I plunged the barrel of the pistol down into it so the handle stuck out in the air. Budwell took the knife and dug another hole and took out his orders and his ID card.

"Here, drop your orders and ID cards in here." He then set fire to the pile in front of him and dug another small hole where he stuffed his .45, and then Garrett did the same. Budwell then tore the picture and the headline off the paper and put it down in front of the circle of .45s. He gathered some rocks and placed them on the edges of the picture and looked at us.

"Let's go."

We headed west toward the river. Moving through the pines, I thought to look around for some sign of the bear, then slipped into the darkness of the Georgia forest, on into the fading afternoon and into the American night.

Epilogue

I didn't go everywhere I hoped, but I traveled around a great deal, blowing about the country like dead leaves. I'd stop at a place for awhile, long enough to make a few friends, and then roll on like a suddenly dislodged tumbleweed. Budwell, Garrett, and I lost track of one another; it was hard to keep up with men on the run who changed their names like they changed their underwear. But I thought of them constantly. Every time an old song like "Bridge Over Troubled Water" or "Let It Be" came on the radio, I'd stop, and their faces would fill up my imagination like gods. Or I'd be walking along a street at night in a strange city. I'd see someone shambling along in front of me, and I'd be sure it was one of them. I'd run up, tap him on the shoulder, then make my quiet apologies to a stranger.

Then a few months after the Vietnam Memorial opened, I got a letter written to my new name and new address in the Midwest. I recognized the handwriting. We'd agreed on a code before we split up so that when we moved, we could send our new addresses to a P.O. box in Budwell's mother's name in Los Angeles. Other than that I hadn't communicated with either of them. The letter had no return address, and the postmark was unreadable. I opened it warily and read:

> *Say Buddy,*
> *I think it's time for us to get together again, for old times' sake.*
> *I'll meet you on May 4th—the anniversary of our liberation*
> *from 58th OC Company—and Kent State—at the Vietnam*
> *Memorial at high noon (Washington time). Be there or be*
> *square.*
> *Peace,*
> *Hugh*

I decided it was time to move on anyway, still a little paranoid about getting mail from Budwell and afraid that the FBI could be close behind, although by that time deserters were pretty low priority. Still, it seemed right to kill the old self and burst anew like those seventeen-year locusts.

I got to Washington a couple days early, long enough to take some tours, visit the Capitol, and see the Washington Monument. It was early for the tourist season, almost time for the tour buses of high school graduating seniors from around the country. The cherry blossoms had bloomed late that year; Washington was a riot of flowers and homeless people.

I couldn't face the Wall at first; just thinking about it was more than I could bear. I wanted to see the Lincoln Memorial, though, remembering another double-feature night at the drive-in with Granddad. Jimmy Stewart was just after Randolph Scott and John Wayne on Granddad's list of favorite actors, and I recalled the night we went to see *Mr. Deeds Goes to Town* with Gary Cooper and *Mr. Smith Goes to Washington* with Stewart playing an idealistic congressman who visits the Memorial.

I walked slowly up the long stairway at the Lincoln Memorial and moved into the calm coolness of the interior, stepping gently on the fluted shadows on the stony floor. Towering above was the figure of the sad president, brooding in a great stone chair. You had your war and contradictions, I thought, struggled with a divided land, and stood for principles that hold. When I moved back outside, I looked over toward the Vietnam Memorial, but I knew I wasn't ready to see it yet; tomorrow would be soon enough.

The next day, May 4th, I headed toward the Wall early and sat for a while on one of the metal benches near the Lincoln. Finally, I walked toward the Vietnam Memorial. On the right was the statue of soldiers added to the design to satisfy the war mongers who opposed the Wall. I walked past it and looked down the memorial, straining to see Budwell's form. The Wall begins low, because there's not any need for a high structure early in the war when there were few casualties. It's late in the '60s— after TET of '68—that the Wall grows. I stood looking along the dark, v-shaped monument from the end, reluctant to walk any closer. I was convinced that every name would be someone I knew. Finally I began to move slowly down the walkway.

Along the Wall people had left things—pictures, miniature American flags, flowers, packs of cigarettes, messages of all sorts, even some leftover medals. I stopped at the end of 1969 and began to search for familiar names. As I looked at the Wall, I saw Budwell's face reflected next to mine.

"You've gained a little weight, Jeff," he said.

"Well, it happens," I said, turning to him. "You look good, Hugh. Your mustache barely shows in the reflection in the Wall, so I recognized you easily."

We stood quietly for a moment, and then we turned and embraced one another, clasping arms and hugging for several minutes. At that time a black man with long, graying Rastafarian dreadlocks and a full beard stepped up to us. Budwell and I looked at each other and at the figure in the dashiki.

"Well," he said in a Jamaican dialect, "don't you honkies recognize an old friend or do we all look alike to you?"

"Garrett," we said simultaneously, "is that you?"

"Right, mon," he said.

Then he slipped back into his old recognizably Southern voice, "It's me, you all," and the three of us clasped arms and stood rocking together back and forth.

I didn't feel right talking in the reflection of the Wall, so I said we ought to walk back and sit on a bench to catch up on each other's lives.

"How have you guys been?" I asked.

"It could have been easier," Budwell said. "But you know I never wanted to be cursed with an uninteresting life. I've drifted around a good deal. I've been able to get jobs associated with the law over the years. Law clerk or court reporter. You'd be surprised how shitty the background checks are on jobs associated with the law. You?"

"Same here. After we three split, I went to Canada for awhile, but I didn't like the cold. Next I went West—Colorado, New Mexico, and Arizona—and did some ranch work and day labor, but that took it out of me. I've made some good money editing for the last few years. You go into a city and put your name on the board near a college campus, and you can get lots of calls, cash money. What about you, Garrett?"

"You ought to be able to guess where I've been."

"Jamaica?"

"That's right. I got out of the country shortly after we went AWOL; I've been there ever since. I'm an executive in a small reggae recording company." He fumbled with his wallet. "I'm the proud father of two daughters and one son. The girls are named LaTonya and Riwanda. Their mother picked those names. My son is named Jeffhu. I named him."

We looked at the face of a miniature Garrett, peering expectantly and intensely out of a school picture.

"Yeah," Budwell kidded, "you probably call him 'Jeff' for short." Then he handed the pictures back and said, "Well, we've all had to make our way through this world however we could manage it."

"Did you keep up with your anti-war friend, Mary?" Budwell asked.

"Not much. I tried calling a couple of times but didn't get her. I heard after finishing nursing school that she'd volunteered to go to Vietnam, but I never found out for sure."

He turned and looked back down toward the Wall, "Did you see any names you recognize?"

"Not yet," I said. "I'd just started looking when I saw you. I think now I'm ready to look."

We walked back down along the Wall, touching the names, and all of them seemed somehow familiar. Then in 1970 we found one we knew. Thomas H. Trailer.

"There he is," Budwell said. "Dear Tommy, you tried hard. You wanted to be an officer as bad as anyone I ever knew. And at least you died doing what you wanted to do. Rest in peace."

We walked farther, looking at the things left there. By one name, a letter was taped. "Dear Dad," it began, "I never knew you, but I love you." The Wall was overwhelming, a place where flesh became names. Near September 1970 we found what we thought we would find.

"There it is," said Budwell. "Timothy J. Rancek."

We stood looking at it for some time, unable to speak.

"Did you know?" I asked.

"No. But I somehow expected to find him here," Budwell said. "Rancek was a hard man, just the kind of officer who would get fragged. Maybe he pushed them over there the same way he did us. I'm just guessing, but I thought we'd meet him here."

We made our way slowly, looking quietly at each panel without speaking or finding any other names we knew. Finally we walked toward the reflecting pool as the sun dipped back in the west over the Lincoln Memorial. We stopped there, and I asked Budwell what he was going to do next.

"I think I'm going to turn myself in," he said.

"Really, why?"

"It's been a long time. I've been living with a woman for some time now. She knows all about what happened. But the biological clock ticks. She wants kids, and I don't expect to get much punishment anymore, probably a general discharge at the worst. Even Calley got pardoned. You ought to think about it, too. It's time for all of us to put the Army behind us and move on with our lives. The war's over."

"It may be time to move on, but the war's not really over. It'll never be over for us, for any of our generation, for the country," I said.

"Perhaps you're right. But I'm going to try to move beyond it and start a new life for myself. My lady friend is waiting back at the hotel. As soon as I get back, I'm going in. I wanted to see you guys first and see if you wanted to go with me."

"Not me," Garrett said immediately. "I'm headed down south to see the folks, then I'm going back to Jamaica, to my family and my new home. My life has taken a sharp turn, but it's not one that I regret. When my cousin's friends were shot at Jackson State a few days after we took off, I knew then and think now that we did the right thing."

"I do, too," I said. "I kept in touch with Mother, calling occasionally to tell her I was okay and not to worry about me. Sometimes over the years I'd make it home for a little while. I stopped by home shortly after she sold Chief Bowles and the ranch, but my mother and her friends could never understand why I went AWOL just as we were about to finish OCS. They thought we were afraid of going to Vietnam. I would try to tell them that we three had decided after My Lai and Kent State—and everything else— that we just couldn't be a part of the machine any more, but they never seemed to understand."

I turned to Budwell, "But I'm not ready to go in yet. Maybe soon, but not now."

We embraced again, and then Budwell disappeared into a crowd of old people getting off a tour bus, Garrett in the opposite direction. I looked over toward the Wall briefly and then turned down to the river as night descended and a plane flew low overhead. A small boat beat against the current in the river, fragmenting the shadowy glow of the streetlights reflecting off the water. I thought about all our buddies, about Ferona and Trailer, Shrode and Garcia, Bigham and Hays, Rancek and Kochs, about Rusty Calley and the Kent State Four, about Granddad and Mother, and about Mary O'Hara, long lost in a dim past and about all of the people affected by Vietnam, about the country. When we went to OCS, we'd all been looking for something, but then I guess we're all on the trail of something that makes our lives meaningful.

For many people, the thought of America itself had given their lives direction. Like the earliest settlers who headed west searching for the whispering wealth of the virgin land before them, we reach out hoping that when we get to the end of our time, we don't learn that we haven't lived. But many of my generation were stopped in mid-search—either that or they gave it up long ago. Those who went to Vietnam or Canada, those who manufactured medical deferments, those with lucky draft numbers, even those Americans yet to be born—all have been touched by those times. I thought about the promise of American history and wondered if it had passed us back in the American night, or perhaps it's there like a hibernating bear or some long dormant seed, waiting to be reborn.

Acknowledgements

To recognize all who affected a book that took almost thirty years is an impossible task, but I'd first like to thank Tim O'Brien for being the kind of writer and human being that he is. After a chance discussion with Tim in 1998, I went home and started back on this story that I'd worked on for years, and it poured out. I want to thank Tim for reading and commenting on the manuscript too. I also need to acknowledge Cheryl Clements of Blinn College, my friend and former student who kept challenging me over the years not to give up on fiction; Jim Lee, Judy Alter, and Tracy Row of TCU Press for their encouragement and suggestions; Sharon Pogue, my administrative assistant at the Center for the Study of the Southwest, for her help; my friends and confederates in Texas literature, Dick Holland and Tom Zigal, for their suggestions; and my wife, Linda, and son, Josh, for reading the manuscript after I was finally ready to risk letting them see it and for Linda's careful editing along the way.

Finally, I'd like to offer a tip of the cap, a fond salute, to all of the cadre and members of OC Company 10-70, wherever they may be.

Mark Busby
Wimberley, Texas